BEFRIEN

by

Ruth O'Neill

RB

Rossendale Books

Published by Lulu Enterprises Inc.
3101 Hillsborough Street
Suite 210
Raleigh, NC 27607-5436
United States of America

Published in paperback 2018
Category: Fiction
Copyright© 2018 Ruth O'Neill

ISBN: 978-0-244-66655-2

Other works by the author:

Sunshine & Tears, a novel, published 2015

To my mother, Susan

Contents

Chapter 1
December 2015

Gemma Peacock's heart skipped a beat when she saw the dark shadow of the hearse. How long she had stood there, waiting at the window, she didn't know. Since her husband's death, time had stood still for her, for days, so it seemed.

Gemma said a silent prayer, hoping her beloved Ritchie could hear her. She pictured his face, and a tear welled in the corner of her eye. She retrieved a white handkerchief, bought especially for this day, from her handbag and dabbed at her eyes.

"All ready, Gemma?" Maria's voice interrupted her private moment of grief.

"As ready as I'll ever be," she responded. Before following Maria, Gemma took one last look in the wardrobe mirror. The smart black trouser suit she wore made her size six frame look skeletal. Or maybe it was the fact that she'd forgotten to eat anything substantial for ten days; she still didn't feel like eating now, or ever.

How am I going to do this? How am I supposed to live without you, Ritchie?

She paused beside the photograph of the two of them, taken in those heady days in the early part of their relationship. Gemma touched the edge of the frame with a finger, cold despite the warmth of the house.

I remember the weekend we spent in Paris, she thought. *You declared your love for me under the Eiffel Tower. After that sweet, loving kiss we shared, I knew then I wanted to be with you forever. That's not going to happen now. I will never share another kiss with you or anyone else. We had such plans – now those plans are over. Today is going to be such an ordeal for me; it's going to be so tough. I have to say a final farewell to you my love, and I intend to do it with dignity and grace – I owe you that, at least.*

"We need to go, Gemma."

Maria's words gave her the mental shake she needed to leave the bedroom. "I'm ready." Walking towards Maria, Gemma embraced her, thankful she was here.

No one else was here to comfort her in her time of need, only Maria. Maria was tall and athletic, her high cheekbones and full lips an immediate attraction for the opposite sex. Her eyes were a glossy hazel and her skin pale, with freckles slightly reducing her beauty.

Gemma had been in foster homes until the age of eighteen, so she had no parents to support her today – just her friend. As she locked the door behind her, she felt her whole body tremble. Her jagged nerves started to take over her whole body, though she tried her hardest to keep them under control. Today of all days, she had to stay strong, wanting nothing more than to be able to say goodbye to Ritchie without falling to bits. She'd done enough of that lately. Surely, after this, there would be no more tears left.

Maria took Gemma's hand and led the way. The funeral attendant, a stout man with a friendly face, politely gave a reassuring nod as he opened the car door. Gemma climbed in, determined not to let tears flow down her already damp cheeks. The black leather seat felt cold against her hands. Unforced, her eyes locked onto the wood of the pine coffin in the hearse in front of their car. The chrome handles glistened like a star in the night sky. None of it, not the flowers, or the rich warmth of the wood, disguised the knowledge of what lay within that casket; a grim reminder of the life she would never lead.

Maria gave her hand a gentle squeeze to let her know everything would be okay. The heart-breaking journey she was about to make would be painful – there was no doubt. Ritchie would be finally laid to rest and be at peace – Gemma desperately wanted that for him – but peace for herself would be harder to find.

They set off – now Gemma was hardly able to look at the hearse in front carrying her deceased husband. Instead, she forced herself to gaze out of the windows. People turned to stare at the sad procession, their heads bowed out of respect, she supposed. She remembered whenever she had seen a funeral pass before she had always said a silent amen for the people closest to the deceased. She suspected people were doing the same now, but this time it was for her and her husband.

It was the beginning of a long day; a funeral with full mass – a cremation and a burial. Her emotions were already in tatters. How much more would she be able to take?

The church looked gloomy as they approached it; stone bricks stuck out in an abstract pattern, making the brickwork look more organic from a distance. This was the place where she had enjoyed the best day of her life, where she'd married her sweetheart, Ritchie, at the innocent age of eighteen. That day seemed like a lifetime ago now. In fact, it was. Twenty-two years ago she had become Mrs Peacock. But now she was a widow, a woman without a husband. Husbandless at forty years old. She shook her head. Life was supposed to begin at forty, not end.

"You are holding up well, darling, I'm so proud of you." Maria gave Gemma's hand another tight squeeze.

"I'm okay Maria, really." Gemma was glad for Maria's interruption to the silence – at least she didn't have to think then. It wasn't good for her to keep rehashing the euphoria of past memories, especially today, of all days.

`Ave Maria`, which Gemma had numbly selected the week before, started playing as they took their seats in the front pews. She settled on the cold wood, oblivious to the rest of the congregation. They were simply a mass of anonymous faces. Only one person struck her: a beautiful young woman, looking almost too perfect for a funeral, half-hidden behind a wooden beam in an attempt to mask her identity, but unable to, having unwisely chosen to wear an elaborate hat.

Gemma put her from her mind as the noise receded and the celebrant took his place beside her husband's coffin. Her gaze became transfixed on the casket. What she really wanted to do was go up and touch the lacquered pine wood, to stroke it, to let Ritchie know she was near. She knew he would have liked that. But this was a funeral, and you weren't supposed to do things like that. She would have to endure this public part of the process and contain the depth of her grief until she could let it out in private.

The service passed in a blur. Gemma felt numb. Nothing could have prepared her for having to live through this. She was in shock. The hands that grasped hers as she and Maria stood by the entrance to the church with the vicar as her fellow mourners filed out, felt rough and distant. Their voices sounded like they were coming from a long way away, or as if she was underwater.

The first part of the funeral completed, now they had to make the journey to the crematorium, which was twenty minutes away, on the other side of town. Back in the impersonal car, this journey felt a lot longer, somehow, though in reality it was no longer than the first. She supposed it was because each metre they travelled took her closer to having to say goodbye to her beloved Ritchie for good.

The crematorium struck her as unusually grim, in the way only a 1970s municipal concrete structure could. Someone had made an effort to brighten it up a little with flowering plants, but it did little to dispel the overwhelming sense of greyness it exuded.

Entering the cold sombre building, a sudden chill ran through her exhausted body. The building had a kind of grisly grandeur that made her feel edgy. What had she expected of a crematorium? She didn't know, never having been to one before, but it wasn't this. Surely a place where you said your final farewells to your loved ones should have at least a cordial atmosphere? Unsettled, Gemma made her way to the front of the church, passing a bank of half-concealed chairs as she did so. Once again, she spied the woman she'd seen in the church, keeping herself separate from the rest of the congregation, always half in shadow. Did she want Gemma to see her? She frowned and glanced back as she took her seat beside Maria; the anonymous woman caught Gemma's eye for a second before withdrawing completely from view.

Who was she? What was she doing here?

Gemma felt oddly grateful to the woman, and the questions she raised, because it meant she had something else to think about as the celebrant told the stories about Ritchie's life that she had thought appropriate at the interview they had had in the small undertaker's shop in town. It kept her steady, for a short while, at least.

The effect lasted precisely until the curtains at the side of the podium drew, signalling the committal of the body. Her husband's body. Her Ritchie. Gemma gasped in sorrow. A sharp pain clenched in her stomach, making her want to vomit. She steadied herself, holding onto the chair for grim life. She couldn't be sick here. There were too many people – and this was for them, as much as it was for her and Ritchie. She swallowed hard, the taste of bile rising in her throat.

"You okay, Gemma? You've gone white as a sheet," Maria whispered, taking her arm, concerned.

"I need to get out of here, now." People turned to look at her and she realised her voice must have been louder than she had expected.

Maria half-dragged her outside, her legs barely lifting off the ground. They exited the crematorium just in time for Gemma to heave a watery like substance in the bushes beside the pristine green lawn. Tears pricked at her eyes as Maria handed her a tissue.

"Oh love, how you feeling now, any better?" Maria rubbed her hand up and down her back.

"Slightly, I think. Oh God, Maria, I can't take much more. This is so hard!"

"I know – you've been amazing, Ritchie would be proud." Maria assured her.

"Would he?"

"Of course he would! The way you've handled today with such dignity, Gemma. Ritchie is probably up there looking down with that big cheeky grin on his face watching you, giving you strength. You know he loved you so much. He used to tell you every day."

"Yes, I know," Gemma said, with a touch of bitterness. "I wish he was here just to say it one more time."

Feeling more composed, Gemma was ready to stand upright again, or so she thought – Maria grabbed her again just as she was about to fall. "Come on, sit down on the step for a while."

Gemma lowered herself down onto the cool concrete step, her head resting on her knees.

"What am I going to do Maria, without him?"

"Just take it one day at a time," her friend said gently. "I will be there for you. You're a strong, capable woman, and you will get through this. I know you will."

As she looked up into Maria's reassuring face, she noticed the perfectly presented woman with the large hat walk swiftly past, her head down as if trying to masquerade her identity again. But if that was so, why would she walk past her, knowing she would be seen? Did she want to be seen?

"Maria, who is that?"

"Who?"

"That woman who just walked past."

Maria frowned, looking perplexed. "I didn't see any woman."

"She had a big black hat on and was very attractive." Gemma got up and hurried around the corner of the crematorium, hoping she would catch sight of her, but she was already gone. Maria followed her.

"Gemma, what's wrong?"

"I keep seeing this woman," she explained, and described the mysterious lady. "I saw her in the church this morning, and here at the crematorium she was hid behind a pillar during the service, and she just walked past us."

"Gemma, I didn't see any woman walk past us," said Maria slowly, a note of concern in her voice.

"Well, perhaps you weren't looking," said Gemma, gazing out across the car park.

"Are you sure you feel okay?" Maria asked, pressing a cool hand to Gemma's forehead. "Perhaps you just imagined her."

"No I did not," Gemma insisted. "I may be upset, but I'm not hallucinating."

"Okay, okay," Maria said, raising her hands in defeat. "I didn't mean – never mind."

"Sorry, but I know what I saw."

Maria nodded kindly. "Come on, it's time to go anyway. People are leaving, heading to Ritchie's parents' house."

Gemma didn't feel like going – having to be sociable was not high on her list of priorities at this moment – but knew it was something she had to do. Ritchie couldn't be buried for another couple of hours, when his ashes would be ready for collection. She'd just have to put on a brave face and do her duty until then. She would be polite to his family, listen to their nonsense – they'd ask her if there was anything they could do for her again, and she wasn't sure if she'd be able to keep her mouth shut this time. What hypocrites they were! Ritchie's overbearing mother Joan had always hated her. She was demanding and controlling, only happy when she was alone with Ritchie. She made him feel guilty if he neglected her – which was hardly ever – and ensured that Gemma was kept at arm's length. Money was Ritchie's parents' manipulative tool of choice. They were always giving hand-outs to make themselves feel good and make others feel like they owed them something. David wasn't quite as bad as his wife, Gemma reminded herself, it was just that Joan was such a powerful presence that he tended to be swept along with whatever she wanted.

In all the years she'd been married to Ritchie, Gemma could

count on one hand the number of times Joan had invited her to the house. She just didn't want Gemma there, so in the end Gemma had obliged and given up going. To be forced to go now seemed like insult on top of injury, but she would do her best for Ritchie.

As Maria and Gemma arrived at the house, Joan was ready to greet the mourners in all her slightly theatrical glory, looking immaculate in a Versace, royal blue two-piece suit. Aware that she was a part of this show, Gemma kissed her on the cheek as Joan hugged her.

Ritchie had looked nothing like his mother. Joan had a wide, rounded face with high cheekbones. Her narrow, deep-set eyes were a dreary brown with a snub nose above a small narrow mouth, which exuded unfriendliness, even when she was smiling. Her prominent chin could have been likened to that of a despicable witch. She had long, thinning hair, damaged through years of dying her blonde roots. Gemma supposed she might have been beautiful when she was younger, but since she had spent so little time at Joan and David Peacocks' house she couldn't remember seeing a photograph of her younger years.

In contrast to his mother, Ritchie's eyes had been a magnetic blue, accentuated with thick, black lashes that had been the envy of all the women in his life. He'd had a long, angular face that displayed distinguished cheekbones, giving him an almost elfin quality. His nose had had a slight upturn to it that Gemma had always felt was desperately cute. His blond, short hair with a quiff at the front had made him look young for his years. Gemma was forever teasing him about it, telling him to shave it off, since it was hideously old-fashioned, but he wouldn't hear of it. `It adds to *my charisma*` he would say, with a grin.

She forced a painful smile, remembering that she would never see that grin again.

"How are you doing, sweetie?" Joan held Gemma's hands out in front of her and looked Gemma up and down in an exaggerated fashion.

Gemma played along. Until Ritchie had died, it had been months since she'd last seen his mother. It seemed so insincere to be pretending that they cared for one another like this.

"I'm holding it together, Joan – just about," she managed. "How are you coping with today?"

"Well, it's hard, but I can't let Ritchie down," said Joan, and for a moment Gemma felt a fleeting connection with the woman who had made it her mission to make her daughter-in-law's life a misery. "Come on in and have a cup of tea – you're freezing."

A cup of tea? Gemma wanted something stronger; needed something stronger. To sit in this house for two hours would be as uncomfortable as it was possible to get. She didn't want to be there, and Joan didn't want her to be there, either. She sensed it, with every fibre of their being.

Fortunately, more mourners arrived, and Joan immediately detached herself in order to play the grieving-mother-holding-it-together-for-her-angelic-son, giving Gemma a much-needed moment of peace.

Inside Joan's little palace, a light rebounding off the elaborate chandelier caught Gemma's attention, its soft glow outlining pictures hanging in strict formation around the room. Pictures of Ritchie: Ritchie laughing with Joan – Ritchie fishing with his father, David – Ritchie when he was a baby. No pictures of her and Ritchie together, despite twenty years of marriage – not a one.

A mother and son lamp that looked like it might have been attempting to copy an African design stood erect on the plush champagne Persian carpet. All the paintwork was pure white, making the room seem cold and impersonal. It had always made Gemma feel out of place, like she was somehow littering the place with her presence, making it unforgivably untidy.

"Wow, what a place!" Maria exclaimed, scanning the room, intrigued. "It's like tribal Africa meets *Alice in Wonderland*... crazy!"

"Don't think for a minute the outrageous possessions in this house indicate a happy home," Gemma warned in an undertone, "because believe me, they do not."

Her friend tutted. "Don't be so cynical, Gemma."

"Ritchie told me that Joan needed to have such palatial materialistic commodities to prove to everyone how successful she was," Gemma whispered, mindful of Joan greeting people nearby. She was so engrossed in being the party host she probably wasn't listening anyway.

"It's quite sad if that is the case."

"Very sad, yet I have no sympathy for her," Gemma murmured.

"Having a claustrophobic mother was hard for Ritchie. He felt guilty at not seeing his mother enough after we'd married, yet at the same time he didn't want to. It was like he couldn't escape."

She broke off as Joan swept back in, presenting them both with a cup of tea in her finest china cups. The room was now beginning to become occupied with friends and relatives who had attended the service, most of them people Gemma and Ritchie had lost contact with, as they were both always content just to be in their own company. Looking back, Gemma reflected that they had begun to neglect family and friends over the years.

People were offering their condolences to her now they had left the domain of Ritchie's mother, each of them apparently embarrassed about what to say, or not to say. Gemma made sure everyone felt at ease, she didn't want them to feel as uncomfortable as her.

Before long, the photographs emerged from the sideboard cupboard; embossed, annotated photo albums in chronological order.

Did Joan really want to do this now? Gemma wondered, feeling a little ill.

The last thing she wanted to do right now was to look at photographs of parts of her husband's life that she'd had no part in. She sat a little way outside the circle of people cooing over the pictures, and weathered the puzzled, embarrassed looks they sent her when it became clear that Joan had not allowed a single photograph of Gemma – even of her and Ritchie's wedding day – in the house.

Finally, the phone rang, and it was time to move on to the last service of the day – the burial. Despite the nature of the event, it was an immense relief just to get away from the stifling house.

This was to be a private affair, with just Gemma, Maria, Joan and David in attendance. Gemma waited tiredly on the drive beside Joan and David's car. She hadn't seen David all day, except distantly; he hadn't exchanged two words with her, nor offered his condolences, until now. As he left the house she realised with a shock how much Ritchie resembled his father. They had the same quiff of hair, the same opaque blue eyes and bushy eyebrows adding to their distinguished angular faces – even the same dimple on their cheeks. The hint of once a handsome young man was etched across David's face.

He looks sad, she thought. *I never saw Ritchie look like that.*

As David made his way over, a hard lump rose in her throat. Oh, he looked so like Ritchie. She hadn't realised just how much before her husband had left her forever, but now…

"Hello Gem," he said, coming over. "How are you doing? Sorry I haven't had a chance to speak to you yet. I've been doing the rounds. You know how it is." David planted a kiss on the top of her head that felt insincere and out of place.

"That's okay," said Gemma, surprised to find herself speaking. "I presume you have to do what you have to do. Prioritize who you need to see at a time like this."

She turned away, a little shocked at her own courage. Maria scowled at her, but Gemma was tired of playing the part of the darling daughter-in-law, and her friend's consternation made her want to laugh. She stifled it quickly, though David's indignant look did little to suppress her humour as Maria directed her into the car.

"What are you finding so funny?" she hissed.

"Oh, I don't know," said Gemma. "Maybe knowing Ritchie would be laughing at what I just said." Tears pricked at her eyes again, overwhelming sadness flooding her heart. Remembering Ritchie's contagious laugh, the way his forehead wrinkled whenever he found something funny was acutely painful. The smile the thought had brought to her face faded abruptly as the car pulled out.

They were on their way to lay her best friend and lover to rest, to say goodbye for the very last time. The car was silent as they turned into the gravel drive at the churchyard. Gemma's eyes slid from tombstone to tombstone, the different shapes and styles favoured by different ages of mourners holding her gaze as they drove slowly through the cemetery. Some of the older graves had been neglected and brown weeds had been allowed to grow up and cover the inscriptions, obscuring the dates and names. Others were immaculately kept. It was a peaceful, but sad place, that seemed to have been unaffected by the rest of the world, like a space outside of time.

She barely noticed stepping out of the car, or the walk to the grave. Things came to her in flashes. The sound of the gravel underfoot. Fresh earth mounded by the side of the small cremation grave. A bunch of lilies laid precisely on the ground.

Gemma felt oddly disconnected, like she was operating on autopilot.

Standing beside Maria, Joan and David, an eerie silence fell. The celebrant carried Ritchie's cremated remains in a dark oak solid box and placed them respectfully on the ground. Finally, they were ready for the final committal. The personalised words reflecting Ritchie's qualities were spoken, though Gemma barely heard the vicar's voice. As the box lowered into the ground, Gemma's tears flowed freely down her face, dimly aware that nobody else was showing signs of emotion. Maria sniffed into her tissue, but she didn't really count; although she and Ritchie had been friends, she wasn't family. Joan and David remained impassive.

When Ritchie had made his last journey, Gemma took a deep breath. He was finally laid to rest. Now, she felt lonely and scared as she treasured her last moments with her precious husband.

Maria clasped her hand. "Come on love, let's go."

"One more minute," she snivelled.

She realised Joan and David had already left, saying their goodbyes as quickly as they could. Gemma knew she wouldn't be seeing them again for a while.

Walking slowly away from the burial site she turned her head and blew a kiss Ritchie's way, a gesture she had done a thousand times, but this time would be the very last. It was then her eyes fell on the beautiful woman she'd seen at the church and the crematorium. She was standing a fair way away, but close enough to be seen. She was still immaculately dressed all in black, but she had discarded her hat this time, and her flamboyant red hair flowed and snatched around her face.

Who was she?

Chapter 2

She spread the broadsheet out in front of her, smoothing out the upturned corners. Obituaries were on page six. She flicked to it, feeling a thrill of excitement and fear. Part of her knew what to expect, but even so, seeing it in black and white was a very different thing. Page six screamed out at her, adrenalin pumping through her veins. It was time for her to become acquainted with a grieving widow. It hadn't exactly been a part of her future plans, but she was nothing if not flexible. A slow smile grew across her face as she thought about what she was about to do. It wouldn't be easy, but it might be fun.

She stared down at the name, feeling oddly conflicted:

Ritchie Peacock.

Ritchie Peacock had passed away suddenly in tragic circumstances. She gazed for a moment at the photograph included with the obit'. Peacock was a handsome, alpha-male who'd had a kind heart, and some of that came through in his picture. It was sad, really, that he was only forty-two when his life ended, but she could make that work for her. He had a young widow: she read her name: Gemma. She could befriend his widow, she thought. Someone who was the same age, might have the same interests, was probably a beauty and would be more than willing to accept her friendship after such an emotional trauma. She would be devastated by her loss yet compelled to acknowledge a stranger who apparently knew her beloved Ritchie. This was going to be easy – a walk in the park.

A quick Google search about the man and his life only added to her euphoria. He'd had quite an internet presence. There were pages and pages of information on the handsome chap. Peacock had worked in recruitment, had been a keen squash player on the weekends and a Chelsea supporter. One night of research and she would be almost ready to go – there would only be one or two details still to iron out, but those could come later. People were so careless with their social media, posting their entire lives across Facebook, Twitter, Instagram and all the rest, for all the world to see. Altogether, it gave her great insight into how this unfortunate man had lived his life. And if she could find all this out, anyone could.

Indiana was always meticulous about her research. Without good research, the whole thing could fall apart so easily.

Ever since she had been four years old, Indiana had loved funerals. It was nothing morbid, nothing about the absence of a person from the world, but the emotion – the emotion was fuel to her fire. She remembered the feeling of excitement as her mother prepared her for the funeral of her older sister. Indiana had been four and Freya had been six when Freya had lost her battle with leukaemia. Indiana had hated Freya. Her sickly sibling had never been well enough to be a proper elder sister to her. Indiana couldn't remember a time when Freya hadn't been sick. Dressing for the funeral, Indiana had felt her sister got exactly what she deserved. She had lived her whole life in her sister's shadow, never getting any of the attention she craved. Indiana had felt neglected, so seeing people cry over the small coffin her father was carrying and having everyone fawn over her as the surviving sister made her heart jump for joy. She couldn't understand why everyone was so unhappy when she was feeling so animated by people's sorrow.

"Oh, poor little Freya."

She'd heard those four words spoken so often, and they made her blood boil with rage. Poor Freya? What about poor Indiana? What sort of life had she had? Being ignored by her parents in favour of her precious sister. Freya had lorded her deathly illness over Indiana's pre-school years, and Indiana loathed her for it. Her parents were deluded by her sister, and a little frightened by their younger daughter's psychological episodes. Yes, at four years old she already knew she had a darkness within her, and she embraced it. There were always negative thoughts scurrying around her head, waiting to be acted out, and she quickly learned that other people didn't understand how satisfying they were. She learned to conceal her actions and revelled in the pain she could cause.

It could be something as simple as placing a spider near Freya's pillow just to watch her squirm, unable to get away from it, or grabbing the hammer from her daddy's tool box so she could hammer all the ants on the driveway, squashing them into the ground. Seeing the stain of the orangey red liquid on the garden patio felt like Christmas morning to her. Death was her medium – she didn't see why she shouldn't embrace it.

Indiana knew she wasn't like other girls her age. In secondary school she was a loner, which suited her just fine. Her parents thought it was the unbearable loss of Freya that had made her become insecure and unsociable, but honestly, Indiana preferred it that way. They would tell each of her worried teachers that one day she would come to terms with it, but they were fools. Indiana had never had any thoughts or feelings about Freya. Why should she? What was so bad about having no emotional attachment? She liked it that way. There was no one to interfere with the way she wanted to live her life, no positive or negative influences.

Of course, she could be the perfect daughter and idyllic student – when she wanted to be. There were times when she had to be. Creating a false identity came easily to her. It was fun – a game to be played. And while she might not have had many friends, she was seldom truly alone. Vonny made sure of that.

Vonny was a constant presence in her life: her ally, her confidante, her best friend. She had started out as a constant voice in her head, talking to her, comforting her, suggesting what she could do to keep from being bored or lonely. When she'd first named her, Indiana had had the idea in her head that Vonny was a short form of Veronica, and when she was older, she found out that meant 'truthful'. It suited her friend; she had never given Indiana any reason to doubt her. Vonny never judged or failed to listen to her, the way other people did. She never made unreasonable demands, or forgot about her, or told her she was strange, or unpleasant.

Indiana grew to love her.

With Vonny's support, she excelled. She was a top scholar, achieving high marks in everything she did, earning her praise from her parents and teachers. This masked her real personality: when everyone thought you were gifted and talented, they didn't mind when you wanted some time alone – they simply assumed you were studying. Traits that had once had her branded 'antisocial' instead became 'eccentricities'. Indiana learned how to present herself, quickly realising that the way someone dressed or walked could give people a false impression of their wealth and personality. Soon, she had employers thinking she was a high-powered socialite, all of them clamouring to have her on their staff.

Now she was in her late thirties she liked nothing more than portraying herself as an eccentric, highly intelligent, sensual, successful woman. Men fell for her in droves. Women envied her, or tried to enter into her territory in the hope that some of her 'good fortune' might rub off on them. When either became too close she would drop them as quickly as she'd found them.

She reread the obituary: the funeral service was to be held at All Saint's Church, Stourmouth, Kent. All welcome – a phrase that was music to her ears. This was to be followed by cremation, then private burial.

Indiana considered her options.

She needed to make an impression straight away, a statement. To get his widow to notice her and not forget her. She took her time choosing the perfect outfit, running her hands over everything in her wardrobe, weighing the pros and cons of each one. Her black, bodycon midi-dress with matching jacket was ideal. It said 'grieving, but elegant'. The lavish black fur coat with flamboyant organza hat that she paired with it were all too extravagant, but eye-catching. And Indiana wanted to be seen. Ritchie Peacock would have approved, she felt.

The moment she embarked upon one of her schemes, she became alive again. The *real* her, not Indiana Manors. Not the boring girl whose parents ignored her in favour of her ailing, unfortunate sister. New relationships invigorated her. She fed on sorrow – it made her feel alive, not cocooned in a small, lonely world that enveloped her with sadness and despair. She'd lived through that all her young life. She ran her fingers over the smooth black material.

Yes. She would get what she needed from the recently widowed Mrs Peacock.

The widow was walking arm in arm with a pale-skinned, freckled woman who would have been quite pretty if she'd bothered to make herself up. They sat in the front pew, ignoring the nodding heads of the congregation. Indiana watched them, carefully keeping herself concealed until the time was right.

The widow Peacock was naturally beautiful. She had olive skin with dark brown eyebrows, long black lashes and piercing green eyes that Indiana imagined would sparkle and light up in happier times. Her hair was short and brown, cut into a suave, stylish bob. The lost look on her face betrayed her agony. As the widow turned around, Indiana poked her head out from behind the pillar before retreating into the shadows once more. She knew the woman had seen her, it had registered in the dull ache of her expressionless face before her gaze became transfixed on the coffin before her. Careful not to be seen, Indiana sneaked out of the church. That would be enough for now – enough to pique her interest. She could afford to relax now, until the crematorium, where a second glimpse would reinforce the memory of the first.

Lying in wait at the crematorium was easier than expected, given the severely trimmed hedges. It was simply a matter of staying out of sight until she could join the trail of mourners unobserved and follow them into the second service.

From behind, Indiana watched the widow carefully; her body language made the suffering she was going through acutely obvious, and it made Indiana's blood begin dancing in her veins. Vonny told her to calm down, that now was not the time to become too enraptured, but Indiana couldn't help it – soon the widow would be within her grasp.

Once again, Indiana hid herself behind a pillar, ready to act. She caught the widow's eye for a split-second, knowing that by now she must be intrigued by the stranger amongst the throng. Indiana left the crematorium to sit and wait. The service wasn't what she was here for, after all. It didn't take long, the widow came rushing out – pale, unhealthy liquid oozing out of her mouth. Indiana smiled. This was her chance to make a move. As the woman's pale, freckled friend turned her back to her, laying a hand on the widow's shoulder, Indiana took the opportunity to walk past the widow with her head down, then scurried away as soon as she was out of sight. She made it to the back of the crematorium before the widow could catch another glimpse, and from her hiding place, she could hear every word.

"Maria, who is that?"

"Who?"

"That woman who just walked past."

"I didn't see any woman."

"She had a big black hat on and was very attractive."

"Gemma, what's wrong?"

"I keep seeing this woman," the widow explained, and described Indiana precisely. "I saw her in the church this morning, and here at the crematorium she was hid behind a pillar during the service, and she just walked past us."

"Gemma, I didn't see any woman walk past us," said the freckled friend slowly, a note of concern in her voice.

Indiana smiled to herself.

"Well, perhaps you weren't looking."

"Are you sure you feel okay? Perhaps you just imagined her."

"No I did not," the widow insisted. "I may be upset, but I'm not hallucinating."

"Okay, okay. I didn't mean – never mind."

"Sorry, but I know what I saw."

"Come on, it's time to go anyway. People are leaving, heading to Ritchie's parents' house."

Indiana leaned back against the cool concrete wall and grinned. Everything was coming together beautifully.

A little bit of research and some secret tailing in a taxi had brought Indiana to the final destination of the day: the cemetery where Ritchie Peacock would finally be laid to rest. She lurked at the back of the church, counting on the members of this more private, intimate part of the day to be too absorbed in their own grief to notice her – at least until the time was right.

As the vicar went through the usual motions, Indiana removed her hat, running her fingers through her long, red hair. A token mark of respect, but this wasn't the time for her to grieve. She wasn't even sure that she could grieve. The whole process felt alien to her. Silence fell as the box was lowered into the ground. An elderly couple – the deceased's parents, – left, leaving the widow alone with her friend, weeping. The friend walked a short distance away, giving the widow the space she needed to say goodbye.

I'll have to watch that one, Indiana thought. *She really is a good friend.*

The widow blew a kiss to her departed husband and began to turn. Indiana seized her moment. She stood out in the open space, close enough to be seen. The widow spotted her at once, a look of bewilderment on her sorrow-lined face. Indiana walked towards her as the woman stood rigidly, rooted to the spot. She touched her arm.

"I'm sorry for your loss," Indiana said, with studied sympathy.

Gemma Peacock flinched away from the touch. "Thank you, but… who are you?"

"Oh, my name is Indiana Manors, I knew Ritchie well. We met a few years ago, when we worked together for Abacus Recruitment. He was a lovely guy. When I heard about – well… when I found out that he'd passed, I felt a strong compulsion to come here today, to say goodbye to him."

"Ritchie never mentioned you before, but thank you for coming, I appreciate it," said the widow, managing a small smile.

"I didn't work there long, had to move on," Indiana lied comfortably.

It wasn't going to be as easy as Indiana had first thought. Looks were obviously deceiving, and this woman was of stronger, cleverer stuff than she had surmised. Truly, Gemma and Ritchie had been made for each other.

"Would you like my card?" Indiana offered. "I would like nothing more than to meet up with you and talk about Ritchie."

"I – I don't think so," the widow replied. "I should be going, my friend is waiting."

Indiana had to think fast. She was going to lose her if she wasn't careful, and she couldn't – not now, when she was so close!

"Ah, that must be your friend Maria. Ritchie did tell me how close you two were."

Gemma paused, surprised. "Really, he was that open with you?"

"Yes. We shared many an evening talking – enjoying a meal and a few glasses of wine."

She had got her. Her body language said it all. Indiana had spotted the flinch, though the widow remained uptight and stoical. She took the card, studying it for a while, then said a hurried goodbye.

Indiana let her go, pretending to pay her respects at the grave.

As Gemma Peacock left she took one more glance at Indiana through the car window – and it was then Indiana knew her plan had worked.

*****

As the town slid past outside the window, Gemma couldn't stop herself from studying the card in her hand. How had this woman got so close to Ritchie – even spending intimate time with him? Having a meal and wine in her eyes was intimate, and he had never mentioned her. Her flamboyant hair went with her flamboyant name – Indiana, like the state. She was certainly beautiful, with her exotic, emerald green eyes, her low black brows, her unblemished, radiant skin. How well-spoken she was; she must be well educated, too, Gemma guessed.

Why hadn't Ritchie ever spoken of her, especially if they had spent so much time together? Gemma remembered the odd night he had worked away. 'Boring hotel, nothing to do', he'd said. Surely it had been the truth?

Longing to hear what this mysterious beauty had to say left Gemma wanting to meet her. She was intrigued by both her intelligence and beauty, and her curious relationship with her late husband had left her with a desire to get to know her. Like Ritchie had done.

"How did she know my name?" Maria asked.

"Ritchie told her we were best friends."

"Why?"

"I don't know," said Gemma. "That's why I need to meet her, to find out more."

Maria tutted. "Why do that to yourself? Just leave it as it is."

"I can't, there's something not quite right about Miss Indiana Manors," said Gemma, though she couldn't work it out.

"Like what?"

She could tell from her friend's voice that Maria was beginning to lose patience with her.

"I can't put my finger on it, but my instinct tells me there's more to her than she's letting on."

The car pulled up outside the house. Gemma sighed. Home looked so much less inviting than it usually did. This would be the first time she would enter it alone, with no expectation of him ever coming home. After the hardest day of her life, she just wanted to be on her own. Maria was dead set against the idea – she wanted to stay with Gemma to make sure she was okay, but Gemma had been adamant. After all, she was going to have to face it sometime.

"Call me if you need me, anytime, it doesn't matter." Maria hugged Gemma tightly.

Gemma knew she was worried, so she managed a smile for her. "I will, I promise. I will be fine, so stop worrying."

"Ring you tomorrow, lovely."

"Speak tomorrow."

Gemma shut the car door and paused for a minute, waving to Maria as she disappeared down the road. She put the key in the lock and an eerie silence greeted her when she opened the door. The house seemed cold and grey. Pulling off her uncomfortable shoes, she made her way to the fridge, where a bottle of wine was waiting to be opened. She poured out a large glass, taking two gulps that saw half of it off, then took the rest of the wine upstairs. She padded into the bedroom, placing the glass delicately on the bedside table, next to her favourite photo of Ritchie.

With a deep sigh, she picked the photo frame up and held it close to her chest. "I love you," she said.

After a long soak in the bath, Gemma slipped into her pyjamas and reached for the blue, chunky V-neck cashmere jumper Ritchie always threw on when he returned home from work. She screwed it up and held it to her nose; it still smelled of him. With her eyes shut, Gemma could touch him, smell him and see him there beside her. Laying down on the empty bed, the jumper became her comforter. She fell into a deep sleep, her dreams telling her Ritchie was still by her side.

Waking early left her restless and feeling empty, the pain of her husband not being there still fresh after spending the night with him in her dreams. She rolled over and stared at the ceiling, wondering what the day was going to bring. Perhaps she would ring the woman from the funeral, Indiana Manors. What would be the outcome? There was no way she could wait any longer. The need to talk to her was a persistent worry. She had given her nothing but unanswered questions, and Gemma knew that they would bother her until she had the answers. The rainbow-coloured business card in her hand reminded her of the time her husband had worked for Abacus Recruitment. She ran her finger over the logo, thinking of happier times. She had to know. She had to meet with this woman. Normally, it would take her some time to trust someone enough for her to call them a friend, but this time she and this stranger had a common interest – Ritchie.

She picked up her phone and dialled the number.

"Indiana Manors speaking."

A sudden panic set in. Gemma hadn't really expected her to answer.

"Er – this is Gemma Peacock. I wondered if we could meet up," Gemma said, keeping it brief.

"Oh, hi Gemma! Yes, of course – when were you thinking of?"

"Whenever you're not busy. My days are free at the moment, as you have probably guessed. I have a few months off work." Gemma frowned at herself. She hadn't meant to tell her that.

Why am I being so open with her? she wondered.

"I can do tomorrow afternoon, if you'd like. Say, two o'clock at the café on Mount Road? It's not too far from you."

"Yes okay. See you then."

"See you tomorrow, Gemma."

Gemma hung up, puzzled. How had Indiana known the café on Mount Road was near to her house? She didn't know her address... did she?

She was beginning to think she was too hasty in contacting her. She should've waited. Got her head around what she really wanted to meet her for. What was she doing, acting so irrationally?

No, she decided, taking a steadying breath. It would be fine.

She needed to meet her to find out why she felt obliged to come to Ritchie's funeral. How well had she really known him? In all their years of marriage, Ritchie and Gemma had never had any secrets – at least that's what she had thought. Why hadn't he told her he had met a woman like Indiana Manors? Let alone that they had been such close friends?

It just didn't make any sense.

*****

The café was busy, full of workers rushing to get their lunch. Sitting at the scratched wooden table Gemma considered whether to leave and return later. It was another thirty minutes before she was due to meet Indiana Manors for the second time and Gemma had arrived early, eager to get to the bottom of things. As the minutes ticked by, the young waitress started to give Gemma a friendly smile every time she passed by her table.

She probably thinks I've been stood up, Gemma thought, *sitting here all by myself, obviously waiting for someone to arrive.*

She stared into her coffee cup – her second of the day – and wondered what questions to ask Indiana. The night before, she'd had it all sorted in her head. Now, when their meeting was imminent, she wasn't sure.

"Gemma."

Gemma looked up – and there she was. Her long red hair covered by a black cowboy hat. Dressed casually in a black oversized jumper bearing a white NY logo, skinny black jeans and thigh high boots, she still looked like she could have been lifted straight from the pages of a magazine. Immediately, Gemma felt intimidated by her. She felt distinctly inadequate in her black polo jumper and tartan skirt, and began to feel she looked more like a teenager than a mature woman.

"Hi Indiana, would you like a coffee?" Gemma asked, gesturing to the chair opposite her.

Indiana pulled the chair from under the table with elegance – Gemma was in awe. "Freshly squeezed orange juice, please. I'm still on a detox."

Gemma beckoned the waitress over to order two orange juices; any more coffee today and Gemma knew she'd be jittery, and that wouldn't help her keep her cool.

"Thank you for coming," Gemma said.

"No, thank you for agreeing to meet me. How are you doing? It must be pretty hard for you at the moment. It's still only days since you lost Ritchie."

Instantly, the hairs on the back of Gemma's neck stood up. She could hear how close Indiana had been to her husband in the way his name rolled off the woman's tongue. The immaculate make-up, perfectly painted nails and lingering aroma of her expensive perfume had Gemma staring at her. Indiana had obviously wanted to make a good impression – and she had.

"I'm just taking it all one day at a time," she said cautiously. "I can't seem to think beyond that."

"They say time is a great healer, but those are probably not the words you need to hear right now," said Indiana, with sympathy. "I know from past experience what it's like to lose someone you're close to."

Indiana's eyes glistened with unshed tears, unconsciously, Gemma leaned forward, feeling empathetic.

"I'm sorry for your loss," she said. "Was it a family member or a partner?"

"My sister," Indiana told her. "She died of leukaemia when I was a young child. It destroyed my parents."

"How awful! It must have been tough on you."

"I've learnt to block it out," said Indiana, with an air of inner strength. "Anyway, let's not talk about me – we're here to talk about Ritchie. I assume that's why you wanted to meet up."

Indiana removed her hat, placing it on the chair beside her – next to her Prada handbag. She put a lock of hair behind her ear with a practiced motion. For a second, Gemma thought she seemed nervous, though she couldn't imagine why. The waitress brought their orange juices to the table and gave Gemma another big smile. Pleased, perhaps, that she had company now.

"I suppose I would like to know how well you knew Ritchie," said Gemma.

"Does it matter how we became such good friends?"

"It does since he never mentioned you to me," Gemma replied.

Indiana gave Gemma a half-smile as she picked up her glass of orange juice, leaving an outline of bright red lipstick around the lip of the glass, and began her story.

"Well, it was the end of my first week of work and I was pretty stressed out – you know how it is," she said. "I was still trying to find my way around, and I'd gone out for lunch before a big meeting. I was coming back up the stairs when I realised I'd forgotten my key card. I couldn't believe I'd been so stupid!"

She took another sip. "Anyway, there I was, standing outside the doors to the office, mortified and panicking, and up walks Ritchie and lets me in – the perfect gentleman."

Gemma smiled. She could imagine him doing it, trying to help someone out of a sticky situation. It was exactly the kind of man he was. The smile faded a little; the kind of man he had been.

Indiana told her how he'd helped her out that day and she'd bought him a coffee to say thank you, and they'd just started talking about anything and everything. Gemma hung on her every word. It was as if Indiana had brought him back to life for her, just for a few hours. Before she knew it, the café was closing and they were arranging to meet up a third time – just the way

Indiana had said she and Ritchie had, for a meal and a glass of wine.

She waved goodbye at the end of Mount Road, walking quickly away in her high heeled boots, leaving Gemma to make her way more slowly (and infinitely less gracefully) home. They had talked, she realised, non-stop for hours. It felt like she'd known Indiana her whole life – no wonder Ritchie had opened up to her, she clearly had a way of putting people at their ease. For the first time in years, Gemma had felt compelled to pour her heart out to someone. She couldn't remember the last time she had been able to trust someone so completely.

It was refreshing.

Indiana had let her talk about Ritchie – everything from how his absence made her feel like the world was ending, to the way he'd used to whistle to himself as he pottered about in the garden – and because she'd known him, been close to him, it felt good. Finally, someone understood.

Maria had been a great help, but she hadn't known Ritchie the way she and Indiana had. Indiana had been friends with Ritchie and nothing more than that, and that made her someone she could trust entirely. Although she had never had cause not to trust her husband, the fact that he had never mentioned Indiana had made Gemma fear the worst; assurance from her new friend that nothing physical had ever happened between them was a relief.

It was so good to be able to put her trust in someone again.

Chapter 3

May 2016

Six months had passed since Ritchie's death and Gemma found herself gradually coming to terms with losing him. Her friendship with Indiana had grown into a wonderful relationship and now they were almost like blood sisters. Having Ritchie as common ground with another person was heart-warming for Gemma. Both women were able to share their thoughts and memories of him together, as if they were keeping a small part of him alive.

Now, Indiana was in the process of persuading Gemma to accompany her on a well-earned holiday. Gemma, who had never been on holiday without her husband beside her, was reluctant at first, but Indiana assured her it would be fun. A break from the stress of living alone, without Ritchie, before she had to go back to work. Her compassionate leave was coming to an end, and the idea of returning to a more normal life was a little daunting. Two weeks in Hersonissos, Crete, away from it all might be what she needed. But then, Crete was the largest and most populous of the Greek islands, and while that was exactly why Indiana chose it, it made Gemma feel a little uncomfortable.

"I suppose it would be nice to get some May sunshine and relax," Gemma said, unconvinced.

Indiana laughed. "It will be an exciting adventure, I can assure you of that."

"I don't want an exciting adventure, I just want a relaxing time. The last chance to recharge my batteries before I return to work," Gemma argued.

Over the course of their friendship, Gemma had noticed how Indiana had an enthusiasm for adventure, acting upon it in everything she did. It was probably why she was so successful, turning her hand to anything she felt like, and leaving it behind without a second glance when she was done. Looking at her now, her remarkable long red hair cascading down her shoulders, she looked like the ideal woman – someone she felt she ought to aspire to be. She was so beautiful, but sometimes there was an edge of something stiff and austere, just beneath the surface. Gemma couldn't work out why. She would find out the answer one day, she was sure.

"Alright then, I'll go."

"Yes! You won't regret this, Gemma, I promise!"

Gemma smiled, though she didn't feel sure. Perhaps a bit of adventure wouldn't be so bad – and if not she could spend the rest of the holiday relaxing by the pool or on the beach.

Checking in their bags at the airport, a sense of excitement began to build inside Gemma. It was the first time she had felt so eager about anything for months. Indiana had persuaded her to change her usual style and wear baggy tracksuit bottoms, t-shirt, trainers and a baseball cap. Gemma liked her new look, not only was it comfortable for the flight, but also quite trendy. Of course,

Indiana outdid her, looking like a supermodel in her Capri trousers and linen blouse, but Gemma noticed that for once her friend wasn't the only one receiving admiring glances from the opposite sex.

After going through passport control they headed for the bar. A glass of wine to settle their nerves was ideal, since neither enjoyed flying. The cosy bar was filled with people ready to embark on their holidays.

Gemma sank into the soft leather sofa, waiting for Indiana to return from the bar. She watched her friend flirt with the barman, his face turning a deep crimson when she spoke to him. He was good looking. Gemma quickly shook the thought from her mind; how could she even think of such a thing? She didn't want to start thinking of men in that way – it was far too soon since losing Ritchie... or was it?

She shook her head. Time did have to move on, but it would be far too difficult for her to follow it yet. Healing took time, after all.

"Got this bottle of wine free," Indiana declared, coming back over. "Amazing what a few chat up lines can do!" Indiana placed the ice bucket and two glasses down on the oak table.

"I only want one glass, not a whole bottle," Gemma laughed.

"You're not having a whole bottle, we are sharing," Indiana said, sitting down across from her.

"Well, I don't want to be drunk on the plane," said Gemma, reaching for her glass all the same. "You know they chuck you off the plane if you're drunk."

"Oh Gemma, you *are* funny," Indiana droned. "We're not going to be drunk – a couple of glasses of wine will be fine. Now, sit back and relax, and here's to a happy holiday."

They chinked glasses.

An hour later, the bottle stood empty. Gemma felt a little tipsy. She wasn't used to drinking in the day. Indiana, of course, was still her usual composed self. Checking the departures board, Indiana announced they were to go to gate twenty-four to get ready to board the plane. A throng of people were making a mad rush, hoping to be the first in the queue, but instead of joining them, Indiana wanted to buy a holiday hat. Apparently she had no intention of making her way to the gate just yet.

"But we might be too late if you're going hat shopping," Gemma protested, feeling a degree of panic. "Can't you wait until we arrive in Crete?" She always liked to be punctual and if she'd had the guts to say it, she would have liked to be the first one in the queue.

"There's plenty of time," Indiana told her, unconcerned. "We will only be standing in a queue for thirty minutes, what's the point of that?"

"Well, if you're sure," said Gemma, uncertainly. "But let's not be too long."

Gemma wondered why she kept letting herself be dominated by Indiana. It wasn't like that when she was with all her other friends. Maria always seemed to follow her, letting her make the decisions. Indiana was different. Gemma sighed, trailing after her glamorous friend on her quest for a hat. Really, it was a pity Maria couldn't come. She hadn't had as much chance to meet up with her since Indiana had come into her life, but Maria's boss had declined her idea of two weeks of unpaid leave. It would've been a good opportunity for Maria to get to know Indiana properly. Gemma knew Maria didn't like her, and she had hoped if they just had the chance to socialise a bit more they might become friends.

Ah well, she thought. *You can't argue with the boss!*

*****

One month earlier:

"Hi Maria, its Indiana."

Maria frowned, surprised. Never once before had Indiana called her, probably aware of her mild dislike for her. What could she possibly want?

"Hi there, is there something wrong? Is Gemma okay?" Maria asked.

"Gemma is fine," Indiana assured her. "Well, sort of. She's feeling a bit upset – you see, she doesn't want to tell you it might be best if you didn't come with us to Crete. She feels she wants a break from you, as you are the main link between Ritchie and her, and she wants to move on. She doesn't want to talk about Ritchie at all on this holiday. She looks at you and sees Ritchie all the time."

Maria sat down at her kitchen table, hurt. "Really?" she asked, a touch defensively. "She hasn't mentioned this to me."

"She didn't like to, for fear of upsetting you."

That didn't sound like Gemma, but then you never knew what grief would do to a person, and she had been through a lot this year.

"I will speak to her," said Maria.

"No need," said Indiana, hurriedly. "I don't really want her to get upset about it again. This holiday will do her the world of good. Hopefully when she returns, she will be able to move on."

"Oh…well, if you think that's what she wants, then of course I will do what's best for her," said Maria, feeling a little betrayed. She'd been friends with Gemma long before Indiana had come along, and yet here she was, being pushed out of her life. "I'm slightly upset she didn't think she could talk to me directly."

"It's a little awkward, but Gemma doesn't know that I'm ringing you," said Indiana. "She would be even more upset if she knew."

Maria sighed. Hurting Gemma was the last thing she wanted to do, and she suspected Indiana knew it. "So, what do you want me to say to her?"

"Tell her your boss will not allow you the time off work," said Indiana at once, as though she'd already given this some thought. "You are too busy."

"I will ring her tomorrow, Indiana. Was there anything else?"

"No, nothing else." Maria frowned. There was a note of triumph in the other woman's voice that she didn't like one bit. "I hope you are not too upset. I will make sure she has a good time."

"Look after her," said Maria.

And if you don't...

"I will. Goodbye, Maria."

"Goodbye, Indiana."

Maria put the phone down feeling baffled and hurt. Why hadn't Gemma spoken to her about the way she felt? They usually shared everything – had done for years. Until Indiana. Maria frowned. She had had her reservations about Indiana, but as Gemma was so friendly with her, Maria had kept them to herself. Now she wondered whether that had been the right decision.

*****

"Gemma Peacock and Indiana Manors, please make your way to gate twenty-four to board the plane to Hersonissos – immediately. This is your final call."

Gemma's face reddened as she listened to the announcement over the tannoy. Indiana looked at Gemma and burst out laughing.

"Your face is a picture!"

"Indiana, this is not funny. Come on, we need to run, or we'll miss our flight!"

Gemma grabbed Indiana's arm and dragged her along to the nearest escalator.

"What about my hat?" Indiana protested.

"You can buy one when we get to Crete, just liked I told you to do in the first place!" Gemma snapped. "If you'd listened to me before we wouldn't be late."

Indiana giggled all the way to gate twenty-four. She plainly thought Gemma's panic and frustration was hilarious, as if this was all part of some big joke. They were met by two very disgruntled stewardesses who told them both off, implying they'd acted irresponsibly. Which, Gemma thought, they had.

Indiana was never one to back down from confrontation and she wasn't about to now. Before Gemma could stop her, she was already squaring up to them.

"We apologise for being late, but I don't expect to be spoken to in that way," she said smugly. "We were looking for a present for my sister, who is dying from leukaemia. That's why we are making this trip – to be with her in her last few days. She wanted an airline mascot toy to go with her collection."

Gemma's eyes widened and fell to the floor; the two stewardesses didn't know where to look.

A tear rolled down Indiana's cheek. Looking in her handbag she pulled out a tissue, which she dabbed at her eyes.

How had she learned to lie like that? Gemma wondered. It had seemed so natural.

The petite blonde stewardess, who could not be much older than twenty-five, was completely taken in. She stuttered as she spoke. "I – I... I'm so sorry, madam. Please make your way to the rear of the aircraft, where your seats are." Her face reddened with embarrassment.

"Thank you," Gemma said as she took their tickets and passport back from the young lady.

Indiana walked beside Gemma, keeping her head down sniffling into the tissue. Gemma could hear the two stewardesses whispering, but she wasn't able to make out what they were saying. She knew for sure they were talking about them, however.

"You are unbelievable, why did you make up that story?" Gemma asked, astonished.

"I didn't make it up," Indiana protested. "My sister did die of leukaemia, as you well know."

"Yes but years ago. Why would you say that?" Gemma could not hide her shock and total disbelief at her friend's bizarre actions.

"I wanted to wipe the smirk off those two bitches' faces," she said flippantly. "Talking to us like we were a couple of school kids! I showed them. I put them in their place, jumped up tarts."

"They had a right to be cross with us," Gemma pointed out. "We *are* late."

They both neared the rear of the aircraft slightly out of breath.

"I don't bloody care and I didn't get my hat," Indiana complained, sounding particularly petulant.

"Oh, grow up, Indiana." Gemma clutched the rail of the steps leading up to the aircraft. She felt her face grow hot. She knew she was going to have to face the stewardesses on the plane again – and the passengers who were probably seething because she and Indiana had made them late taking off.

"Don't say anything." Gemma turned to Indiana. "Leave this to me."

"Yes boss!" Indiana giggled, giving a mock salute.

Gemma gave the booking stub to the stewardess, explaining at the same time how sorry they were for being late. The stewardess gave her a sympathetic nod. Gemma thought she must have heard the story Indiana had made up. News like that travelled fast.

They made their way to their seats amongst the mumbling of passengers displaying their distaste at them. A middle-aged man with receding grey hair was in the aisle seat. He was wearing beige cargo trousers with a Ralph Lauren black polo shirt. To Gemma's surprise, he smiled at them and didn't seem to mind at all that Gemma and Indiana had to disturb him so they could get to their seats.

"Oh, would you mind if we swapped seats?" Indiana asked, out of the blue. "I like to sit in the aisle seat. I detest sitting in the middle, and I'm a nervous passenger so I hate sitting by the window." Indiana flicked her hair and gave a beaming smile to the middle-aged man, who smiled back.

Astonished, Gemma looked at her and in return Indiana gave her a wink.

"Of course not, that would be fine," the man said. I don't mind sitting in the middle."

"But…" Gemma tried to protest, but it was already too late.

"You will be fine by the window, Gemma," Indiana said, waving her hand up and down, coaxing Gemma to sit down.

Gemma hunched her shoulders, making it clear she wasn't happy. She hadn't anticipated sitting next to a stranger for the four hour flight. She desperately wanted to sit next to Indiana, to enjoy the flight and begin making plans of what they were going to do on their holiday. But by now both of them were waiting for her to take her seat – not to mention the rest of the passengers on the plane – and Gemma's politeness won out. She sat down and gazed out of the window, watching the other planes taxiing up and down the runway.

She was largely left to her own thoughts until they were in the air. Indiana's high, teasing laugh made Gemma turn abruptly towards her. Indiana's right arm was placed on the man's leg – he seemed to be enjoying the unexpected attention. It made Gemma want to roll her eyes. She felt totally ignored until the man asked her if she would like a drink.

"I'm Leon, nice to meet you," he said, holding out his hand for Gemma to shake. Reluctantly, she shook it, his firm grip making her wince.

"Thank you – I will have a gin and tonic, please."

Gemma didn't really fancy a drink, not after the bottle of wine she'd already shared with Indiana, but finding herself in this horrible situation, she needed one – a large one. She didn't like the look of Leon – there was a coldness in his eyes.

The constant muttering and giggling between Indiana and Leon unnerved her. Indiana hadn't spoken one word to her since they'd boarded the plane. It was as if she was consciously neglecting her, cutting her off. Confused, Gemma nursed her gin and tonic. This was not how she had expected the holiday to start out. Why was Indiana acting this way?

Put out, Gemma sipped at her drink, deciding to finish it and then have a sleep. At least that way the time would pass more quickly and she wouldn't have to make polite talk with Leon. Both he and Indiana were beginning to get on her nerves.

As she pressed the button to release the head rest, a vision of Ritchie sprang into her head, his face wearing a bright smile.

They were walking together in Hyde Park. It was the day they'd travelled to London together to sightsee, only a few, short years before. After visiting all the popular tourist attractions, Ritchie had suggested a walk in Hyde Park, one of the old royal parks in London. They had seen Diana, Princess of Wales', memorial fountain there, along with three hundred and fifty acres of beautiful scenery. On such a sunny day it was alive with lovers, runners and dog walkers. For a time, surrounded by such beauty, they had sat on a bench, people watching, wondering what sort of lives the people who passed them lived. Theirs was so idyllic; they were so happy and content together – soul mates. Ritchie kissed Gemma lovingly on the lips, his hand on her thigh. She loved nothing more than his touch – his soft, caring touch. It told her how much he loved her, more than words ever could –

though, of course, she loved to hear him say those words, too.

She lost herself to the memory as sleep overtook her.

"Come on, Gemma, let's get an ice-cream," said Ritchie, as he pulled her to her feet, slapping her bottom as she stood up. She slapped him back as she ran off and Ritchie chased after her, eventually catching her up and holding on to her tightly.

"Love you, Mrs Peacock."

"Love you too, Mr Peacock," she replied, laughing.

"I love you more!"

"No I love *you* more!"

Onlookers stared as they passionately kissed, but neither of them paid the passers by any mind. Breaking away from each other, they both gasped for air. Ritchie grabbed Gemma's hand – sweetly kissing the back of it, before escorting her to the ice cream van. They strolled around the park, enjoying their ice-creams and the natural splendour surrounding them. Time seemed to evaporate quickly and the shadows of dusk soon began to fall, prompting them to wander back towards civilisation.

Since it was a warm, humid evening they both decided to enjoy a glass of red wine outside a cosy bar in Kensington. Their fellow tourists also frequented the bar – it was close to local landmarks. Gemma revelled in the intoxicating atmosphere, inhaling the different cultures around her. She stared at Ritchie, thinking how lucky she was to have him in her life. They had already enjoyed years of blissful marriage, but it still felt like they were newlyweds. Ritchie's sweet charisma enveloped her. She tried to imagine him in old age: his quiff of hair would be a silvery grey, his grey eyebrows bushy and curled. He would be a distinguished, handsome pensioner. Both the image and looking forward to many more happy years together brought a smile to Gemma's face.

"What're you smiling at, love?" Ritchie asked fondly, watching her expression.

"Just you."

"What about me?" he asked, resting his arm on the table, leaning in closer.

She smiled. "Imagining what you will look like when you're old."

"Good, I expect," he declared, chuckling as he said it.

"What about me?" she asked, and he grinned.

"You will look like a beautiful princess – with lots of beautiful wrinkles."

"Thanks," she giggled.

"We will be a couple of old wrinklies together," he laughed.

"I like that thought."

"So do I," he said, seeing off the last of his wine. "Shall we go?"

"Yes – I would like to take you to bed," Gemma said flirtatiously.

"Yes, please!" Ritchie stood up and took Gemma's hand. "Come on then – take me to bed."

"Walk this way."

They left the pub, which was by now beginning to fill up with regulars.

As they took the short walk back to the hotel, Gemma managed to drag her gaze away from Ritchie to look up at the night sky for just a moment. The wonderful afternoon they had just shared promised to turn into a magical evening and she shivered a little at the thought of just how much more special it was going to be once she and Ritchie were alone.

On their way into the hotel lobby, they passed a group of young people, obviously just starting their night out and full of excitement. Gemma smiled at their enthusiasm, but forgot them as soon as Ritchie took advantage of the moment of privacy getting into the lift afforded them and turned her into his arms to kiss her. The feel of his lips on hers made her tremble from head to toe, as they always did. He released her and took a small step away and she figured out why he'd stopped driving her crazy with his kiss when she heard people approaching. The doors to the lift were open again – she hadn't even noticed.

Ritchie tugged at her hand and began to walk towards their room; obviously impatient to get her somewhere they would not be disturbed. He unlocked the door and held it open for Gemma as he ushered her through, the perfect gentleman.

The décor in the room was tasteful and very romantic, though Gemma expected no less for the price she knew Ritchie had paid.

The walls were a subtle shade of cream, providing a perfect backdrop for a large canvas adorned with a painting of a deep red poppy. The focus of the room was a huge four poster bed, dressed with crisp white sheets and a pretty throw, embroidered with red roses. Gemma smiled to herself. It was all so achingly romantic.

She heard Ritchie close the door behind her and she gasped when he scooped her up into his arms, planting her softly down on the bed. He joined her there, bracing his weight over her body with one hand as he used the other to tenderly smooth her fringe away from her brow. Gemma reached for him, wrapping her arms around his neck, lacing her fingers together to hold him there so he couldn't pull away even if he wanted to. Ritchie made it clear he had no intention of going anywhere as his face drew nearer and she felt his warm breath caress her face. The sweet, heady aroma of the wine they'd drunk together teased at her nostrils and she felt her lips part, eager for a kiss she knew would taste just as sweet.

Ritchie did not keep her waiting. Their lips met and she trembled, overwhelmed by both his touch and in anticipation of what was to come. Gemma could barely wait to feel their bodies entwined and the memory of how good each session of lovemaking over their happy relationship had felt, made her impatient. She unlatched the fingers she had locked around Ritchie's neck and reached down to find the button on his jeans, fumbling a little from the intensity of her desire for him. The button gave way easily and she unzipped his jeans, thrusting the fabric out of the way with impatient fingers, sliding them inside his briefs. She began to stroke up and down, tightening her grip on him when he moaned with pleasure into her mouth, telling her without words how much he loved her touch.

Ritchie trembled above her for a moment longer and then groaned as he pulled away to sit her up. He began to undress her, equally impatient. Her top and bra were quickly disposed of and she felt the cool night air tickle across her heated flesh. Gemma struggled to help him, desperate to be fully naked and pressed beneath him as she wriggled free of the lace skirt that had bunched around her thighs in their excitement.

He stood up to remove his jeans and slip off his shirt. Gemma's breath caught in her throat as her eyes travelled greedily over his tanned and tautly muscled torso. He was a thing of beauty in all his naked glory.

When she looked up at his face, she saw him smiling down at her and knew that he understood how much looking at him turned her on. He leaned forward and pulled her to the edge of the bed with a gentle but firm grip on her ankles, sliding his hands up her calves and over her thighs to grasp the lace panties she wore and tug them off. He spread her legs wide apart and knelt in the space beneath them, laying his body over hers once more as he kissed her again. Ritchie leaned to the side, bracing his weight on an elbow while his hand played over the tips of her breasts, driving her crazy as he teased her taut body with each gentle caress. His fingers moved lower, tracing the shape of her abdomen and then dipping between her thighs where she ached for his touch the most. He played her body expertly, using his lips, his tongue, his fingers and even just the sensation of his breath on her heated flesh to give her one powerful release after another.

Just when she thought she could take no more, he set her free and stood up to flip her over onto her front. Gemma rested her weight on trembling elbows and knees, her muscles still not quite recovered from Ritchie's expert touch. She arched her back and bit her lip when she felt his hands clasp her hips and knew she wouldn't have to wait much longer to have him inside her.

Ritchie entered her in one strong, powerful thrust, making Gemma groan aloud and push back against him. He pulled out straight away and pushed into her again and again, going deeper each time, setting a pace he knew from experience that she loved. His thrusts were quick and hard, and in the last part of her brain still functioning, Gemma knew she was not far away from heightened euphoria and that they would climax together, as they usually did. When she felt his grip tighten almost painfully on her body, and heard his ragged panting get louder and louder she tumbled over the edge with him, her cries blending with his.

*****

Gemma woke up to find Leon tugging at her arm.

"Get off me!" she cried, shocked.

"Gemma, he's only waking you up because we're landing," Indiana told her curtly. "My God, what's the matter with you?"

"Sorry, for a moment I forgot where I was. I must have fallen asleep." Gemma wasn't about to disclose what she'd been dreaming about. She wanted to cherish the dream.

"You've been asleep for nearly the whole flight – and you were talking in your sleep. *'Oh, Ritchie! Oh, Ritchie'!"* Indiana sniggered and Leon joined in.

"Oh shut up, Indiana! Just shut up!"

Gemma had tears in her eyes. How could Indiana be so cruel? Gemma wanted to be at home – home alone. She now realised going on holiday with Indiana was a terrible mistake. Gemma wished Maria was here. She would never have treated her this badly – nor would she have allowed Indiana to. If only her boss had given her the time off to be here. Fresh tears sprung into her eyes. She wiped them away, trying to conceal them from her so-called friend and the creep in the seat next to her.

As the plane met the tarmac, all the other passengers on the flight gave a squeal of delight. A safe landing had them all wearing a bright smile, all except Gemma. She couldn't help thinking this holiday was going to be a disaster. She realised she didn't know Indiana at all, for all their deep conversations. Did anyone?

Indiana stood up flicking her hair from side to side – aware men were staring at her and making the most of it. Gemma watched as she arched her back seductively to pick up her bag. Oh, she knew how to make all the right moves, alright.

"Come on then, Gemma, this is the start of two weeks of mayhem. Nice to meet you, Leon," she added provocatively to their neighbour. "Thanks for entertaining me on the flight." Indiana bent over and pecked him on the cheek.

"It's been a pleasure meeting you," he replied, flattered. "Can I take your number so we could maybe meet up again, one day?"

"No, I don't give my number out," said Indiana, without a trace of regret. "And anyway, I don't think our paths will cross again."

Gemma looked at Indiana, startled. Indiana sent her a wink, which was now becoming quite an irritating habit. Indiana grabbed Gemma's hand, forcing her to squeeze past Leon and into the aisle, before pulling her along the gangway of the plane. She didn't get the chance to say goodbye to him so she just smiled helplessly, the flabbergasted expression on Leon's face barely registering as they followed other eager passengers to the exit of the plane. The cabin crew thanked them for their custom and then the hot, humid, Aegean air hit them as they stepped onto Greek soil. Gemma immediately began to feel better – now that Indiana was away from that creep, Leon, she seemed to be acting more normally again. She was in two minds about speaking to her about her strange behaviour on the plane. She decided she would wait and see if Indiana mentioned it first.

When they were passing through passport control, Indiana spoke her first words to Gemma since landing.

"Sorry for ignoring you on the plane, Gemma." Indiana hung her head, apparently embarrassed.

"Why were you so cruel to me?" Gemma asked, with a frown.

"I don't know," said Indiana, sounding sincere. "Please forgive me. I want our holiday to be so much fun and I just ruined the start of it. Sorry."

"I will forget it for now, but I'm not sure I can forgive you," Gemma told her. "How could you make fun of me about the dream I had? And laughing at me with a stranger, too! Why on earth did you want to be around that Leon guy, anyway?" Gemma found herself becoming irate.

"I don't know – truly I don't," Indiana said and sniffled, as if she were about to start crying.

They made their way to belt six to collect their cases in silence. The carousel creaked as the first cases made their way along the winding belt. Indiana's arrived first, and with the huge red bow tied to the handle, it couldn't be missed. It was as flamboyant as its owner. Shortly afterwards, Gemma's much more demure case arrived. Indiana was still snivelling into her tissue as she pulled it off the carousel, so Gemma hugged her, promising that everything was forgotten. Reconciled, they were both ready to embark on their holiday adventure.

Indiana suppressed a laugh, a wicked smile growing on her face as they hugged. Once again, her plan to keep Gemma Peacock wrapped around her little finger had worked. Vonny whispered in her ear to keep calm – things were beginning to come together.

Chapter 4

The *Hotel Ramos* sign was emblazoned with bright sparkling lights, the blue clear water of the pool picked out with glowing tea lights. It looked simply idyllic. Gemma knew she'd be happy to reside here for two weeks, even if all she did was stay at the hotel and lounge by the pool. They entered the reception area, where they were met by a tall, slim man with a tanned, leathery face, spectacles perched on top of his head. Not a face you would call handsome, but a face you could tell had lived a full life.

"Hello ladies, I'm Stavros," he declared warmly. "Welcome to the *Hotel Ramos.*"

"Oh, hi, thank you. I'm Indiana and this is Gemma," said Indiana, giving him one of her bright smiles.

"Hello," Gemma said, more reservedly.

"Have you stayed here before, Indiana?" Stavros asked, studying Indiana closely. "Your face looks… familiar? Is that how you say it? Sorry, my English is not the best."

"No, I have never been to Crete before," she said lightly. "You must be mistaking me for somebody else."

"Ah, yes, that must be so." Stavros continued to peer at Indiana for a moment, then shrugged and placed the room key in

Indiana's hand. "Enjoy your stay here."

"Thank you, Stavros," said Indiana. "We intend to."

As he turned away, Gemma could have sworn Indiana looked agitated, but she chose to ignore it. Not everyone travelled well, and she hadn't slept on the plane. Yes, she was probably just tired.

Making their way to their apartment, Gemma noticed several groups of men huddled at the bar, all turning to look at them as they passed. She felt very uneasy following Indiana as her friend sashayed across the floor, always ready and able to impress. Gemma thought it must be a strain to maintain the performances Indiana carried out in front of the opposite sex. As Indiana put the key in the lock she turned to Gemma and raised her eyebrows.

"What was that look for?" Gemma said, perplexed.

"That Stavros," Indiana remarked. "What an arsehole."

Gemma stared at her, surprised. "I thought he was very charming."

"Well, you would," Indiana chided.

"What's that supposed to mean?"

Indiana ignored the question, instead making her way into the apartment and letting the door slam shut on Gemma.

"Thanks for holding the door," Gemma grumbled.

She grappled with her case, scraping it against the wall. She managed to hold the heavy hotel door open with her free hand, dragging the suitcase in with the other. Once she was in and had pushed her short hair out of her eyes, she was a little surprised at how small the apartment was. There was a small lounge area with a kitchenette to the left hand side, a bathroom so small you weren't likely to stay in it for too long, and the bedroom! It was like a cubicle, with two single beds nearly touching each other. Not quite what she had had in mind when she had left England, but it would have to do. She wasn't planning on being in the apartment for long, anyhow.

Gemma watched Indiana as she silently unpacked her suitcase. There was a tense atmosphere in the bedroom – one Gemma didn't like. What was the matter with Indiana now? Her mood swings were beginning to annoy her.

"Is everything okay?" Gemma asked.

"What do you think?" Indiana slammed her suitcase shut, her clothes slung all over the bed in a heap.

"Well, that's why I'm asking you. This holiday is supposed to be fun, but it seems like you are in a bad mood and I wondered why," Gemma replied, her tone deepening.

Indiana thrust a hand through her long red hair. "Sorry, it's just that I wanted everything to be perfect for you and it's not."

"Oh, Indiana…" Gemma put her arm around Indiana and explained to her that everything was fine.

Soon, they were laughing over the bizarre day they had just spent together.

Anticipating their plans to explore the local nightlife that evening, Indiana ordered a bottle of wine to the room, and when it arrived they happily sipped a glass each, getting ready for a girly night out. Laughing and talking together, they slipped on their skimpy summer dresses and heels. Gemma smiled at her reflection in the mirror. This was the first time Gemma had felt enthusiastic about a night out in a long time. She chose not to dwell on that fact, knowing it was time to make small steps towards getting her life back on track. Ritchie's smiling face popped into her mind as she smoothed the light fabric over her hips, but this time she just smiled to herself.

Before long, the bottle of wine lay left empty on the balcony table and both women were enjoying the confident buzz it gave them. Gemma knew she was the one that needed pre-party drinks, since Indiana was confident enough without any at all, but it was pleasant to be in understanding company. They left the apartment and made their way down to the bar terrace. The heat of the day was subsiding a little now, and the quaint terrace looked inviting, with small, comfy, rattan chairs and tables adorned with tiny lanterns. It was both magical and homely at once. Stavros served them a small shot of Raki, Crete's national spirit, on the house – a welcome drink.

In high spirits, Gemma and Indiana made their way towards the strip. It was bustling with holiday makers and locals, the perfect setting for a mad night on the town. The bars were filled with partygoers enjoying the flow of alcohol and loud music. A neon blue light sign caught their eye – *Bailey's Bar*. Indiana said she liked the look of the small, compact bar, with only a few occupants spread around. It meant they would be able to have a conversation and still be heard.

Together, they walked up to the bar, where a guy who must have been well over six foot tall was waiting to greet them. His long, brown hair was tied back into a pony tail and a bushy beard covered his tanned face. "Hi ladies, what can I get you?" His Aussie accent was quite pronounced.

"Can we have two Sex on the Beaches, please?" Gemma said, feeling far more confident than usual.

Indiana nudged Gemma in the ribs, a smirk on her face. Generally, Indiana liked to take control of a situation, especially where men were concerned, but this time she felt a moment of glee at Gemma's forwardness.

"I'm Mick Delaney," said the barman. "I hope you two will become regulars." Mick handed them their drinks, giving Gemma a long, lingering stare as he did so.

"I'm sure we will be," Indiana remarked, interrupting the obvious sexual attraction between them. She led the way to a quiet table in the corner of the bar. "Well he's hot."

"Not bad," Gemma replied, surprised at herself. Mick was the first man she'd felt even a slight attraction to since Ritchie's death.

"We could give him a nickname, as I'm sure we will be returning here every night," Indiana suggested mischievously.

"Yes! Let's think… I like this game," Gemma declared,

entertained.

"I know, how about 'Skippy'?" Indiana laughed.

"I like it." Gemma tipped her head back, laughing uncontrollably.

Mick worked the bar, distracted. He couldn't take his eyes off the woman with the short, brown hair who had ordered a cocktail earlier. She was sitting with her bubbly friend in the corner, both laughing at some private joke. He hadn't found a woman as attractive as her in the six weeks he'd been in Greece. She was so feminine and beautiful, but he thought he had glimpsed sadness in her eyes. Interested, he felt compelled to find out what that sadness was. In his break, he walked over to their table and sat in the vacant chair next to the woman with the stylish bob-cut.

"Would you ladies like a refill?" Technically, he had asked them both, but it was clear to all three of them he was focusing all his attention on the object of his affections.

She blushed. "Yes please. One for the road, Indiana."

"One for the road?" Indiana repeated, raising an eyebrow. "I don't intend to go home just yet."

"Where is home?" Mick asked.

"Hotel Ramos – for the next two weeks, at least," said Indiana, before her pretty friend could stop her.

Mick caught the slightest movement beneath the table, suggesting that Indiana had just been kicked on the shin.

"What a small world, that's where I'm living for the next six months," Mick said, trying to make his smile reassuring. "I'll probably see you around more than I'd thought."

"Probably will, then," said the woman, returning the smile. "I'm Gemma and this is Indiana."

"Nice to meet you both. I'll get your drinks." Mick stood up and grinned like a Cheshire Cat as he left the table.

"Wow, the chemistry between you two is really hot," Indiana smirked.

"Don't be silly. You're imagining it," Gemma said, though she couldn't quite keep the smile off her face.

Mick bought over their drinks just in time to overhear and revelled a little. He liked that the girls were talking about him.

"Hey, if you've not got plans tomorrow, there's a small party I'm heading to with a few friends at Star Beach," he said, setting the cocktails down.

Star Beach was one of the most relaxed locations on the island, a place where you could chill, have a drink and sunbathe next to the Olympic sized pool. He held his breath, desperately hoping Gemma would agree to go too.

Exchanging amused looks, the two women agreed, finished their drinks and said goodnight. Mick returned to the bar, his spirits soaring. Things were looking up.

*****

When dawn broke the following day, Gemma was the first to

wake. A full day of travel, several more drinks than she was accustomed to and a bad night's sleep had left her with a pounding head. She fished about in the first aid box in the tiny kitchen and picked up a packet of paracetamol, hoping it wouldn't be long before they worked their magic. Looking out over the pristine pool below, Gemma thought a swim might clear her head. She put on her red bikini and grabbed her towel, closing the door behind her quietly, so as not to wake Indiana.

The clear blue water looked so inviting. Gemma dived into the pool with urgency, the ripples leaving an outline behind her. She loved the quietness of the empty pool; it was like her own, private world and she was glad no other swimmers were around this early in the day. Her lithe body darted in and out of the water like a fish and some of the aches of the day before began to leave her. She made a pledge to herself she would do this every morning of the holiday.

Ten lengths of the pool and Gemma was ready to retire. Climbing the steps, water cascading off her body, she spotted Stavros walking towards her. Quickly grabbing her towel, she pulled it around her to shield her modesty, holding it tight. Ordinarily, she might not have minded people seeing her in her bikini, but it was just Stavros out here and she didn't want him to get the wrong idea.

"Good morning, um…early bird," Stavros stuttered, obviously enjoying the view she had allowed him.

"Good morning," said Gemma hurriedly. "Yes, I thought I would have a nice quiet swim to wake myself up."

"It's very nice this time of the morning, yes." Stavros looked over the top of his glasses at Gemma, and it made her feel a little uncomfortable.

"Lovely. I must be going – Indiana is preparing breakfast, thought we would have a fruit medley on the balcony," Gemma smiled tightly as she walked past him, wanting to put some space between them. She felt uncomfortable standing there in her bikini with just a small hand towel wrapped around her. She wished she'd brought the larger beach towel down with her.

"Ah Indiana, yes," Stavros said thoughtfully. "I know her from around four years ago when she was here. She say she never been here before, but it was her. I don't forget a face."

"Really? She did say she thought you must be mistaken," Gemma replied, a little startled.

"No, I'd remember that face anywhere. She came with a young man last time. Nice man, he was."

"A man, what was his name?" Gemma asked, curious.

"Can't quite remember," Stavros laughed, rubbing his head. "Ah his name I think is Robert, no – Ricky? No, not that. I will remember – my memory no good."

"I will ask her, but she told me she's never visited Crete before," said Gemma, feeling puzzled.

"Have a good day, Gemma," Stavros said as he walked away, leaving Gemma alone with her thoughts.

Gemma walked slowly back to the apartment. Her headache had

gone, but instead she was left with an uneasy feeling as she tried to digest what Stavros had said. If it was true, if Indiana had been here before, why would she lie about it?

She spied Indiana out on the balcony laying out a fruit banquet that could have fed an army. It looked delicious. Gemma slipped on a baggy t-shirt and joined her. She tucked into a fruit salad and thanked Indiana for preparing it.

"What were you and Stavros talking about by the pool?" Indiana asked sternly, not looking up from the bowl of strawberries she was eating.

"He was just wishing me good morning and asking what we were going to do today," Gemma lied.

"Oh – but it seemed like you were shocked by something he said," Indiana said, subjecting her to a long, cool stare that was a little unnerving.

Had Indiana been watching her from the balcony?

"I couldn't work out what he'd said – his English isn't very good," she said, as lightly as she could. "Do you find that, Indiana?"

As little as she enjoyed lying, something was telling Gemma not to reveal the truth.

"I think his English is good," Indiana said, with a shrug. "Anyway, are you looking forward to meeting Mr Skippy man – Mick – today?"

"We are both meeting Mr Skippy man," Gemma laughed.

"The Star Beach sounds good, doesn't it?"

"Yes, it should be fun." Gemma thought Indiana looked anxious; she wasn't her usual, buoyant self today. She looked drawn in the face and her mind seemed to be elsewhere – where, she didn't know.

After breakfast, they both showered and changed. Indiana looked stunning in a lemon sundress, brown wedges, a brown trilby and a large pair of sunglasses. Next to her, Gemma felt inadequate; her white lace skirt and black camisole seemed dull in comparison. She wanted to change, but Indiana talked her out of it saying she looked beautiful. Gemma was excited about meeting Mick, but apprehensive at the same time. She thought it would be nice to have a friend of the opposite sex whilst on holiday, though where it might lead, she was unsure.

They left the apartment and made the short walk to the Star Beach, Gemma remembering the directions Mick had given her the night before. Soon, they spotted the 'Free Admission' sign that marked its entrance. As they entered, in the midst of a steady trickle of fellow sun worshippers, Gemma and Indiana scoured the place to see if Mick had already arrived. He wasn't there yet, so they agreed to make a base on the grassy area near the pool. Making themselves comfortable on the sun loungers provided, Indiana wasted no time before ordering drinks at the bar. Gemma was reluctant to start drinking so early in the day, but Indiana ignored her protests.

"Holidays are for enjoying yourself and doing things you wouldn't do at home," she lectured Gemma.

Gemma realised she had no choice in the matter, so she agreed. She decided if Indiana dozed off while they were sunbathing she could go to the bar for something softer.

Drinking their second cocktail of the day, Gemma spotted Mick and a group of men walking through the entrance. She counted eight of them. She nudged Indiana, who had her eyes shut, catching the hot rays. Indiana stared across in the direction Gemma was indicating and sighed appreciatively.

"There are some hot men with Mick," Indiana remarked, sitting up straight to admire eight muscular alpha males.

"Shall we go over?" Gemma asked.

"No, let them find us. Please be a little cool Gemma." Indiana looked irritated. She laid back down on the sun lounger without saying another word.

Wondering what was wrong with her this time, Gemma took out her compact mirror and lipstick from her beach bag, applying more bright red gloss to her lips. She brushed her fringe with her fingers and dabbed the sweat from her forehead. As she finished, she looked up to find Mick walking towards her. Suddenly nervous, she fidgeted about in her bag – pretending she was looking for something.

"Hi, glad you made it. Have you been here long?" Mick asked, making meaningful eye contact with Gemma.

"Hello," said Gemma, smiling up at him. "No, only about an hour." Gemma felt her cheeks grow warm. It was impossible not to notice the attraction between them, undiminished from the previous evening.

Mick sat down on the grass beside her, beckoning the other men to join him. Indiana sat up and smiled at Mick.

"Hi Mick, I see you brought an army of followers with you." Indiana stood up, posing in her white bikini, knowing full well she would attract at least one man from the eight. She hadn't decided which one she was going to opt for yet, but Gemma suspected it probably didn't matter.

The men introduced themselves one by one, and Indiana quickly singled out Liam, who was about five years her junior, Gemma reckoned. His big brown eyes and long black lashes made quite a statement, and she could see why her friend liked him. Tall and muscular, with a baby face, Gemma had a shrewd suspicion he wouldn't be getting away from her any time soon. Indiana made her move, talking to Liam with her legs astride and hands on hips. Gemma watched Indiana flirt, already used to the effortless charm Indiana exuded. Liam looked utterly spellbound, not taking his eyes off Indiana for a second.

Mick noticed, too. "Looks like they're hitting it off."

"Indiana gets what she wants, and at this moment in time it's Liam," Gemma said boldly.

"And what do you want this moment in time?"

"A good holiday is all I want," she replied, looking away from Mick's stare.

"You have deep sadness in your eyes Gemma Peacock," he said

softly. "Can I help you get some happiness back into those eyes?"

"How do you know my name is Peacock?" Gemma asked, a little too abruptly.

"You told me last night, you were a bit tipsy."

"That explains my headache this morning. I had to go for an early swim to clear it. Did I say anything else?"

"You said a lot of things," he told her, with a grin.

"I hope I didn't bore you."

"Far from it." Mick stood up and grabbed Gemma's hand. "Come on, lets go to the bar, I think you need a refill."

Gemma felt anxious about what she might have revealed to Mick. Had she told him about Ritchie? Had she told him she was married? Whatever she'd said, Mick seemed to like her still, and that was nice. She liked that he held her hand all the way to the bar.

Drinking at the bar for the next hour with Mick and his friends had them all in a party mood. Before long, Indiana was seductively dancing with Liam – the eyes of the whole group upon her. Gemma, more reserved, mingled with Mick's friends. They seemed a lovely bunch of men, all with a great admiration for Mick. As she laughed and joked with them, she was aware that Mick was watching her every move, she felt his eyes constantly on her. Several hours of drinking was beginning to make her head spin and she didn't feel completely in control anymore, so she tore Indiana away from Liam to go to the toilet with her and catch up on what was happening between them. Indiana wasn't backwards in her intentions.

"Well, what do you think's going to happen," she asked a startled Gemma. "I'm going to get laid tonight, and Liam looks like just the man for the job."

Gemma was shocked. How could she just meet a guy and intend to end up in bed with him. Gemma had never done that before in her life. "Indiana!" she exclaimed, shocked, but her friend simply brushed her off.

"God, Gemma, it's not a big deal," she berated her. "You can be such a prude sometimes."

"Hey, just because I've never done it doesn't mean I think it's wrong," Gemma protested. "It just feels a bit sudden, that is all."

"This is what holidays are *for*," Indiana reminded her. "Enjoying the local nightlife and making new… friends!"

"We're moving on in a bit, Star Beach is closing soon," said Indiana, putting on more lip gloss and smacking her lips in the mirror. "The boys were thinking of heading to *Bailey's Bar* for cocktails, that is – if it's not too adventurous for you."

"No, I like *Bailey's Bar*," said Gemma, with a small smile.

And the barman, she added, privately, following Indiana out of the toilets and back to their new friends.

Indiana was beginning to sway a little as she walked hand in hand with Liam along the narrow path towards the main strip. Gemma hadn't seen her so drunk before, which worried her a little. Indiana was usually so in control; she needed to drink water not more alcohol. They arrived at *Bailey's Bar* and nabbed the high stools at the tables outside. Mick and his friends went inside to buy drinks. While they were gone, Gemma tried to get her friend to drink some water, but Indiana ignored her. She was hunched up on her bar stool, staring at the space beside her, muttering urgently to herself. Gemma frowned. It wasn't the first time she had noticed her talking to herself, but up until now, Gemma had chosen to overlook it. Not this time.

"Who are you talking to, Indiana?" Gemma asked, aware that since she was tipsy she might be more open to talking about herself.

"No one – why?"

"I thought I heard you," said Gemma, wondering why she was lying about it. "And your lips were definitely moving."

"Who would I be talking to?" Indiana asked. "There's no one here but you, and we weren't having a conversation. What is your problem, Gemma?" Indiana was cross, Gemma could tell.

"There's no problem with me Indiana. Are you okay?"

"I couldn't be better. And I'm going to get laid tonight. Thank you for asking," Indiana retorted, staggering off and leaving Gemma alone.

She watched her go, feeling uneasy. It was only the second day of the holiday and Gemma felt confused. She looked out to the clear blue sea, shimmering in the moonlight, and thought of

Ritchie. Oh, how she wished he was here. A tear escaped her eye and rolled slowly down her cheek.

What am I doing here? She wondered, brushing it away.

She wondered if she had a sound mind. Maybe she hadn't given herself enough time to grieve. Ever since she'd left England she had been questioning her actions. Why had she felt the need to come on holiday with Indiana? Before they'd come to Crete she had felt so close to her flamboyant friend, but now... she still felt an inexplicable connection with her, and that didn't seem to be about to disappear, but Indiana's odd behaviour kept resurfacing, and it made Gemma both uncomfortable (she was sharing a very small room with her, after all) and undeniably intrigued.

Needing a steadying influence, Gemma took out her phone from her bag and walked down the steps to a gangway. She wanted to speak to Maria. She knew the time difference would make it one o'clock in the morning in England, but she was sure Maria wouldn't mind her ringing. She felt compelled to talk to a friend, and as she dialled the number she hoped Maria would pick up.

After about a minute, a sleepy voice spoke. "Hello Gemma."

"Hi Maria, sorry, I know it's late, but I need to talk you," Gemma said, surprised at how upset her own voice sounded.

"What's wrong, Hun?"

"It's Indiana... she's acting really strange – this holiday is not what I was expecting."

"What were you expecting, Gemma?" Maria's tone was unusually blunt.

"I don't know, but I wish your boss had agreed to let you have time off work so you could be here with me," she said. "I miss you."

There was a pause before Maria spoke again. "It wasn't my boss not letting me go," she said slowly. "Indiana rang me to say it was in your best interest that I didn't come. She told me I remind you of Ritchie too much and you didn't like it. She made me lie to you, Gemma." Now it was Maria's turn to sound upset.

"What?" Gemma exclaimed, shocked. "I don't get it! I never told her that, I would never say I didn't want you to come on holiday with us! You are my best friend! What the hell is she playing at? Oh, Maria I'm so sorry."

"Don't worry, Gemma I knew you were under a lot of stress," said Maria soothingly. "You'd just lost Ritchie, for God's sake."

"It doesn't make any sense, any of it." Gemma began to pace up and down. "Why didn't you tell me?"

"She was so convincing, Gemma."

"I'm so sorry," she said again. "I'm going to find out what the hell is going on, I promise." Gemma ended the call, put her phone in her bag and went to seek Indiana out.

Chapter 5

Indiana exited the bar and staggered over to their table, Liam right on her tail. She steadied herself as she climbed onto the high bar stool, clinging onto the table for support, obviously several more drinks down. She rummaged around in her bag for a couple of minutes, sighing with pleasure as she took the cigarette out of the red packet. Indiana put it to her lips and lit it inhaling deeply.

Gemma studied her; she was amazed that she had never known Indiana smoked.

"What's the matter *now*, Gemma?" Indiana asked, noticing her attention.

"I didn't know you smoked."

"There's a lot of things you don't know about me, Little Miss Perfect," she chided, an unpleasant expression on her face.

"Indiana, why are you being like this?" Gemma demanded, fuming.

"Like what?" Indiana snapped. "You don't like it because I'm not boring – like you." She laughed as she put out her half-smoked cigarette in the silver porcelain ashtray; her laugh changed pitch oddly. She lifted the ashtray off the table and threw it down onto the floor with so much force it smashed to smithereens. Not content with breaking one ashtray, she picked up another, and another, until there were broken pieces of porcelain all over the floor.

Liam, who was obviously marginally less drunk, pulled her off the stool, holding onto her hand securely so she couldn't cause more trouble. The bar manager came scuttling out to see what the commotion was. He told Liam to take her home and not to return. Gemma watched, appalled and dumbfounded, as Liam led her away. Not one word had been uttered during the entire episode; there was something about the deliberate look on Indiana's face as she smashed things that made the others uneasy.

"What was that all about?" Mick asked, looking perplexed.

"I really don't know. The woman is insane," Gemma replied, just realising the truth of this herself.

"Well, that's put a dampener on the night," he reflected.

Gemma nodded. "I think I will call it a night, Mick. I'm not sure I really want to be near Indiana tonight. Hopefully she's gone to Liam's."

"I'll walk you to the hotel," he offered gallantly.

"Thank you."

Gemma walked alongside Mick, happy he was there. She didn't pay much attention to what he was saying – her mind was elsewhere. She couldn't get the vision of Indiana smashing the ashtrays out of her head.

"Gemma?" Mick raised his voice as he said her name.

"Sorry Mick, my mind was elsewhere – Indiana," she apologised, realising he'd asked her a question.

"You can always stay in my apartment tonight – no strings attached," Mick offered calmly.

"No – I will be fine. Thanks for the offer though," Gemma said, a little too abruptly.

"I promise I won't jump on you," Mick laughed.

"I didn't think for a minute you would," she assured him, laughing a little to herself. "No, honestly, I will be fine."

"If you're sure." Mick gave Gemma a cheeky wink and she chuckled.

They walked on in silence until they arrived at Gemma's apartment door, which was ajar. Frowning, Mick decided to enter first, while Gemma waited nervously outside. When he came out again, he looked a little flushed, as if he'd just seen something he'd rather he hadn't.

"I think you'd better stay in my apartment tonight," Mick said, hurriedly taking Gemma's hand.

"Why? What's wrong?" Gemma asked, worried.

"Indiana and Liam are... er... passed out asleep," he said, and she thought that perhaps he wasn't being entirely truthful about that. Frankly, though, she didn't want to know. "I don't think you want to be in there, do you?"

"No – I would not. I accept your offer then, Mick, if you really don't mind me staying the night in your apartment?"

Mick gave her another cheeky wink, making her stomach flutter. She hadn't realised how gorgeous Mick was until that moment. Yes, her first impression had been that he was handsome, but now, having spent more time with him and seeing how gentle and caring he was, she found him all the more attractive. Mick's apartment was on the opposite side of the building to Gemma's and two floors higher. Gemma was pleasantly surprised at how clean and tidy it was. She sat down and perched herself on the end of a two-seater settee, the checked brown and cream material identical to the one in her apartment. Gemma supposed every apartment must have the same décor. Before she'd seen Mick's apartment she thought they might be decorated differently. She didn't know why.

"Would you like a drink?" Mick asked.

"Yes please, I think I need one after tonight," Gemma replied.

"Red wine okay?"

"Yes, that's fine."

Gemma watched Mick as he removed two large wine glasses from the kitchenette cupboard, poured the red wine, filling the glasses halfway, and brought her a glass. He grabbed a kitchen stool, setting it down opposite her. He sat on the stool with his legs astride, leaning on the back of the chair. Gemma wondered why he didn't just sit down beside her. It was almost intimidating, Mick sat opposite staring straight at her. It unnerved her a little.

"So, tell me, Ms Peacock, why did you decide to visit Crete with your unstable friend?" he asked cheerily, and then frowned. "Sorry, I shouldn't say that, but tonight she did display some odd behaviour."

"I'm beginning to ask myself the same question," Gemma admitted quietly.

"Sorry I didn't mean to pry," said Mick, sensing her discomfort. "Here, let me refill your glass." Mick jumped off the stool to fetch the bottle of Merlot and filled Gemma's glass, which she had barely touched, to the top.

"I've only known her about six months and I've been finding out quite a few things I don't like about her since we got here." The wine was beginning to loosen Gemma's tongue. "Her mood swings are a cause for concern."

"How did you become friends?"

That was a question Gemma didn't really want to answer. She wasn't ready to disclose anything about Ritchie just yet. She was relieved she hadn't spoken of Ritchie the night before, when she'd been tipsy enough to let loose a little. Perhaps she had, and Mick was just playing games with her, but he didn't seem the sort.

"At a funeral, believe it or not." Gemma pursed her lips and took another sip of wine. She couldn't believe she had just said that.

Mick raised his eyebrows, surprised. "Whose funeral?"

"My husband's... Ritchie's." It was suddenly hard getting words out; Gemma looked at the floor.

Mick was quiet, though. For a moment he seemed to be pondering what to do. Then he stood up and sat next to her, putting his arm around her shoulder and giving it a gentle squeeze.

"I'm sorry, Gemma. It must be so hard for you," he said sympathetically.

"It is, but I'm gradually coming to terms with it," she admitted, appreciating the way he was trying to take care of her. "I thought this holiday would be the break I needed to – I don't know, to get my life back together, I suppose. It isn't turning out how I expected it to."

Gemma's eyes began to water but she was determined not to cry. Instead, she rolled another gulp of wine around her tongue, the warmth it gave her dulling the pain a little.

"You'll get there," he said, and the way he said it made her wonder who Mick had lost to make him so understanding. "It just takes time. Would you like another drink?"

Gemma looked down, surprised to discover that she'd finished the whole glass.

"No, I think I've had enough, thanks," she said quietly. "In fact, I'm quite tired. I think I might get some sleep, so I will wake up fresh in the morning."

"You can have my bed, I'll sleep here." Mick patted the settee.

"No, don't be silly. I'll sleep on the settee. I can't take your bed,"

Gemma stood up, feeling slightly embarrassed.

"Well, if it bothers you, we could share the bed, no strings," Mick offered, holding up his hands as if he was apologising.

Gemma surveyed him for a moment, considering. "Okay then, if you're sure."

Gemma felt the need to feel close to someone tonight and she wanted it to be Mick. He had been so kind to her. She had no reservations about Mick being a gentleman, she felt entirely safe in his presence.

Gemma went to the bathroom. She picked up Mick's toothpaste from the dolphin beaker on the wash basin, squeezed a pea size amount out onto her finger and used it to give her teeth a basic – if not thorough - brush. As this was a spontaneous occurrence, she hadn't come well-prepared, but she was thankful she had some face wipes in her handbag, at least. Cleaning the makeup off her face, she sighed. At least she was going to have fresh breath, if nothing else. She would have to worry about anything else in the morning. Gemma found Mick sitting up in bed, waiting for her, and fleetingly she wondered what he was wearing under that black, silk sheet. Nervously, she removed her white, lace skirt, keeping her camisole on, and hopped into bed. She turned to face Mick, feeling much more confident now she had fresh breath.

"Thanks for this, Mick," she said. "I really didn't want to be near Indiana tonight." She gave him a peck on the cheek. Night."

She turned away from him and rested her head gently on the pillow.

"Goodnight, Gemma," Mick answered and clicked the light switch, plunging them both into darkness.

*****

The bright sunlight shone through the bedroom and hit Gemma in the face. For a brief moment she wondered where she was. She felt an arm wrapped around her and froze, suddenly scared to move. She had been hoping she'd be able to sneak out of bed and rush back to her apartment without waking Mick, although she knew it wasn't the right thing to do as Mick had been so kind to her. The minutes stretched on as she lay there, not daring to move. She focused on keeping her breathing shallow; how long was she going to have to lie here? It wasn't exactly comfortable, with Mick's heavy, muscled arm heavily draped across her.

Finally, she felt a movement. Mick removed his arm and climbed out of bed; she gave a quiet sigh of relief. Gemma climbed out of bed, grabbed her skirt and quickly slipped it on. She would shower at her apartment, she decided. She wanted to get back. She should never have stayed here, and wouldn't have if Indiana and the wine she had drunk hadn't forced her to. She felt awkward, even though she'd done nothing to be ashamed of. Mick had been the perfect gentlemen. She met him in the doorway.

"I was just bringing you breakfast," he said, with a smile.

"Thanks, but I need to get back." Gemma pushed past Mick.

"Hang on what's the rush?" he asked, looking puzzled.

"Sorry, Mick!" Gemma slammed the front door on her way out.

Gemma hurried to her apartment. She looked up at the bright blue sky for a second. It was almost perfect, the way it had looked in the brochure, with only a few fluffy white clouds marring it. A good time to take a swim, she thought. It would clear her throbbing head. Two hangovers in two days was significantly more than she was used to. She unlocked the door to the apartment cautiously, wondering if Indiana would be in there and what mood she would find her in. Gemma's nose was met by an aroma of stale cigarettes and booze which made her wince for a second. The balcony door was wide open and she could just make out the silhouette slightly hidden behind the curtain. Liam. She walked towards him.

"Morning Liam, is everything okay?" she asked, noticing how tense the young man's shoulders were.

"Hi Gemma," he said, turning. "Well it was last night... not so sure now."

"What's happened? Where's Indiana?" Gemma asked, looking around.

"She left over an hour ago," he told her. "Just packed her things and left."

"Left?" Gemma gaped. "Where has she gone?"

"Caught the next available flight home, wherever that is." Liam stared out of the balcony, obviously feeling pretty dejected.

"Flight home?" Gemma echoed, beginning to panic. "You mean she just upped and left me?"

"Looks like it," he said apologetically. "Is she alright, Gemma? I mean, Last night she was acting really strangely."

"How do you mean?" Gemma sat down on the brown rattan chair next to him.

"After the ashtray throwing she started crying," he said slowly. "Then, when we arrived here, she was all over me – she was insatiable." He looked away, embarrassed about what he was saying, his face flushing a reddish colour. "She went berserk, shouting and screaming that I attacked her. She came at me with a hate in her eyes I cannot describe. Look." Liam lifted his T-shirt revealing deep red scratches all the way down his back.

"Oh my God, Liam!" Gemma could not hide her shock. She felt awful for him and immediately stood up, before hesitating, unsure if he wanted her to show him any sympathy or not. He turned towards her and they embraced.

"I really did like her Gemma," he said, when they separated. "When I met her at the beach bar yesterday, I thought straight away there was a strong connection. How wrong was I?"

He gave a playful laugh.

"Don't be too hard on yourself, Liam," said Gemma gently. "You weren't to know she had mental health issues. At times she can hide it well. I'm only finding out for myself, now, and I've known her for six months."

"What are you going to do?" Liam asked with genuine concern.

"Catch the next available flight home and see what the little madam has to say for herself," Gemma said, with determination. "I'm not letting her get away with all the havoc she has caused. I don't even know why she wanted to be my friend, but something about this doesn't add up."

"Wish you luck, Gemma." Liam kissed Gemma on the cheek and left.

She locked the apartment door and sat down to think for a while. She couldn't quite believe how events had turned out these last couple of days. Again, she wondered why she'd agreed to come on holiday with Indiana – after all she hadn't really known her that long, and now she seemed a total stranger. She shook her head. There was definitely something wrong here – if only she could figure out what.

Deciding to push it all to the back of her mind for a short time, Gemma decided to go for one last swim before packing and sorting out a flight home. She changed into her red bikini and grabbed her towel, looking forward to being in the cool water of the pool as the heat of the morning began to rise. It was going to be a scorching hot day and she wanted to make the most of it while she still could. She wanted to clear her head of all the troubles that lay in front of her.

Gemma dived into the pool, immersing beneath the water of the deep end, swimming under the glorious azure water until she had no breath left. Surfacing, she swam the length of the pool until her body ached, telling her it was time to retire. She pulled herself out of the water with some regret; she would miss the early morning dips, even if the rest of the holiday hadn't been exactly what she'd signed up for.

Walking slowly up the steps from the pool she noticed Stavros walking towards her, an echo of the morning before. She hurriedly picked up her towel, glad she had brought the larger one this time. Stavros made her feel nervous.

"Hello, Ms Gemma," Stavros greeted her with a smile.

"Morning, Stavros," Gemma replied.

She was about to walk past him, making it obvious she didn't want to hold a conversation with him, when his words stopped her in her tracks. She had to ask him to repeat what he'd said. Not because of his broken English – because of what she'd heard.

"I remember name of the gentleman Indiana was here with," he repeated cheerfully. "A man called Ritchie. Ah, see? I know I'd remember."

It felt like the world had shifted sideways.

"Are you sure?" Gemma knew she was repeating what she'd already said, but she was in denial. She felt like she was going to collapse.

"You okay, Ms Gemma?"

"Yes, I'm fine," she lied, and ran off leaving Stavros standing by the pool, bewildered.

She didn't remember getting back to the apartment, though she knew she must have run all the way, given how out of breath she was. Numbly, she poured a glass of water, her trembling hands hardly able to raise the glass to her mouth. Water dripped from her mouth as she gulped it down. Her breathing was shallow and it took all of her strength to make it to her bed, where she simply spread herself face-down on the pillow and sobbed. The image of Ritchie that surfaced in her head made her sob even louder.

It couldn't be true. It just couldn't.

Hours later, Gemma woke with a throbbing headache. She rolled over, feeling betrayed and emotionally drained. She made her way to the shower, slipped off her bikini and let the steaming hot water caress her body, bringing her back to life. She washed her tear stained face, relaxing a little, now the worst of her shock had passed. Feeling slightly better, she thought she'd make the effort to look half decent to say goodbye to Mick. She knew she could just leave without seeing him again, but she didn't want that, especially since he had been so sweet to her. Dressing slowly, she reconsidered. The deep vulnerability she felt right now meant it probably wasn't the best thing to do – she didn't want to give him the wrong idea. No, she would pop a note under his apartment door explaining why she had to leave so urgently.

Yes. That would be the best option.

Gemma arranged the flight home, picking a night flight, so she didn't have to rush; she still had packing to do. She took her coffee out onto the balcony and began to reflect on the chaotic three days she had spent with the person she had considered her friend. The questions in her mind were jumping around, all muddling into one. Why had Ritchie been here with Indiana and why, if that was true, did Indiana bring her here? Nothing made sense. Were they having an affair? That thought made her shudder.

She stared out at the glimmering pool beneath the balcony, wondering what on earth she was going to do. By the time she'd finished her coffee, she had made up her mind, when she landed back in England she was going to hunt Indiana down and find out what was going on, once and for all.

Glumly, Gemma popped the note under Mick's door. She knew she wouldn't be seeing him again. It had been surprisingly easy to compose a relatively amiable note outlining what had made her leave prematurely. She hoped Mick would understand. She knew he had a fondness for her and she didn't want to hurt him.

From the back of the taxi, Gemma took one last look at the *Hotel Ramos* sign then turned away. What was supposed to have been an idyllic holiday had turned into a nightmare. The only good thing to come out of it was meeting Mick, and she knew it would be a long time before she could get him out of her head. It was a real shame that she wasn't going to see him again and she couldn't help feeling a small pang of sadness. This was the first time Gemma had looked twice at another man since Ritchie's death.

Ritchie.

The image of her late husband rose voluntary in her mind, joined by one of Indiana's blinding grins. Had he been living a double life? Surely, she would have noticed? Or would she? Gemma knew she was blinkered when it came to Ritchie – after all, he'd been her first love. Hell, he'd been her whole world. Even now, she didn't want to dwell on the fact Ritchie had lied to her.

She wanted Indiana to explain why she and Ritchie had been in

Crete before she jumped to conclusions, but it was hard to keep her mind straight.

The taxi journey to the airport seemed to pass in a blur. The aged Greek driver kept glancing at Gemma, probably wondering why she hadn't spoken throughout the whole transfer to Heraklion. She paid him and smiled as he passed her suitcase to her when she got out. None of her mental or emotional turmoil was his fault, after all.

Gemma walked into the airport with renewed purpose. As distasteful as the things she knew she would have to face were, it was good to have something practical to do. She checked the board, relieved to find her flight was on time. With the urgency Stavros's revelation had stirred in her, she hadn't wanted to face a delay. She wouldn't reach Indiana's house until six a.m., even without a delay. If you included the two hour time difference as well, it was going to be a long night.

Still, she thought, with a slightly unpleasant smile on her face, *it's got to be a better flight than the one on the way out here!*

She turned towards a coffee shop, determined now. She was looking forward to seeing Indiana's expression when she opened the door to her!

*****

Mick arrived at his apartment feeling shattered by a twelve hour shift serving a boisterous, holiday crowd had seen to that. He just wanted to sleep – working eight until eight was taking its toll on him, as much as he was enjoying living in Crete. As he stepped inside and switched on the light, the white envelope lying on the charcoal doormat stood out. Mick picked it up, curious, and sank into the sofa, unable to believe what his eyes were reading.

Dear Mick,

Firstly, I'd like to say what a pleasure it has been meeting you. I've enjoyed the time we spent together and would like to thank you for being the perfect gentleman.

I'm sorry that I won't be able to say goodbye to you in person but it is with regret that I have to leave immediately. I am booked on a flight tonight returning to England. Indiana has left suddenly and I need to know what is going on. I found out some shocking news about her, so my intention is to turn up unannounced and get to the bottom of whatever secrets she has been harbouring. I feel like she's up to something, and I want to know why she felt the need to involve me.

If you are ever in England (not very likely, I know), please call on me for a visit.

27 Eden Road,

Croydon,

London,

CR1 7SF

I wish you all the best,

Gemma

X

He read it through a second time, at a bit of a loss, before tossing the note aside and grabbing his car keys. It was a good hour's drive to the airport, so he would be cutting it fine, but if this was his only chance of seeing Gemma again, he had to try. Even though he had only known her a couple of days, he guessed Gemma would have aimed to arrive at the airport at least two hours before her flight, as the airline advised; she didn't strike him as someone who willingly left things to the last minute. There was just the slightest chance he could catch her before she went through security.

Mick was careful not to go over the speed limit, but even so, he knew he was driving faster than he'd ever driven before. The picturesque scenery was usually a distraction to be enjoyed, but not this time. His blood was pumping fast around his body, making him sweat.

How this woman had got so completely under his skin, he didn't know. What he did know was that from the first moment he had met her he felt a spark. Gemma was special. He'd wished now he'd pursued her more attentively, though he knew that her confidence in the bar that night had been largely down to tipsiness. She wasn't ready for that though – he could tell. He thought he'd have more time to woo her; he wasn't expecting her to take off and run home.

Mick frantically searched the airport car park for a parking space, praying he would find one soon. He was losing vital minutes. Couldn't the people here tell it was an emergency? He scowled at a passing pedestrian, his nerves jangling. A car reversing out of a parking space had him screeching to a halt, the driver behind him tooted his horn waving his hands about like a maniac, loudly wondering what the hell Mick was doing. Ignoring him, Mick parked the car dashed out his seat and ran all the way to departures. He scanned the crowded airport, hoping to see Gemma, but there was no sign of her.

Then, as he took one last look around, his heart jumped in his chest. His eyes lit upon the back of her short brown bob. He instinctively knew it was her. She was already walking towards security and he didn't have much time to catch her.

"Gemma!" he shouted at the top of his lungs, but a voice over the tannoy drowned him out. He watched as she vanished from his sight.

Goodbye, Gemma, he thought sadly. *I love you.*

Gemma turned around. For a moment, she thought someone had called her name, but who could have? She shrugged, deciding she must have been mistaken. Carrying on through security, Gemma wondered if Mick had received her note yet. She hoped he wouldn't be too upset. It surprised her how difficult she was finding it to come to terms with the emptiness she felt inside at leaving him behind. Her longing to see Mick again wouldn't subside, even though she had only known him for a few, short days. She knew it was ridiculous; he only had four and a half months left in Greece then he'd be returning to Australia. No, she wouldn't be seeing Mick again. The sooner she got that into her head, the better, she told herself sternly.

No sooner had the plane taken off, Gemma fell into a deep, dreamless sleep. She was amazed when she woke to find that in forty minutes she would be landing. She replayed the conversation she was going to have with Indiana in her head. Soon the questions the ill-advised trip had left her with would hopefully be answered.

Chapter 6

In all the time Gemma had known Indiana, she'd never been invited to her home. Indiana had always given excuses. Either the house wasn't tidy, or she'd mislaid her keys. Gemma never thought anything of it before, but now, after the other woman's perplexing behaviour, she was intrigued to see where Indiana lived. Luckily, she could remember the address: 24 Hillside Close. She gave the address to the driver, considering her next move. Within the hour she would be there, hoping Indiana would be in (given the early hour) and be surprised to see her on her doorstep. This time she'd be prepared for any lies Indiana would throw at her.

At ten minutes past six in the morning, Gemma found herself on Indiana's doorstep. The small, compact semi with its olive green lawn looked surprisingly inviting.

Trust her to have an immaculate garden, Gemma thought. She was reluctant to ring the doorbell for a minute and stayed at the end of the path, taking her surroundings in.

The more she looked around, everything she'd thought of to say evaporated from her mind. Amidst the turmoil, the little hand-painted gnome on the garden step caught her eye. It brought a smile to her face. Of all the people in the world, she hadn't expected Indiana to have one of these. It seemed a little crass for her usually high-brow tastes. Oddly comforted by its ugly little face, Gemma braced herself and lifted her hand up to the doorbell where she rested her finger lightly on the brass. It took her another few minutes before she actually pressed it.

She listened eagerly. No lights came on and no noise of anyone coming to answer greeted her ears. Frowning, Gemma pressed it again and again. Indiana didn't seem to be in.

What was she supposed to do now? She could always wait, but that didn't seem a good idea, she was already tired from all the travelling and she had no way of knowing when the woman might return. She would have to come back later. She still wanted to turn up unannounced, to throw Indiana off course, but now was clearly not the time.

House sparrows were beginning to break into song, their sounds carrying further due to the lack of noise. Gemma listened to their voices for a moment, remembering the time when she had gone camping with Ritchie. They had both loved listening to the birds sing first thing in the morning. So much had happened since his death. Standing on the front doorstep of the woman who might very well have had an affair with her husband, it all seemed so surreal. Gemma stooped to pick up her suitcase and was about to leave when a flicker of light illuminated the porch. She heard faint footsteps coming towards her. For a second, she panicked, but quickly composed herself; she didn't want to start off on the back foot. She waited anxiously for the door to open.

"Well, well, well, – if it isn't little Miss Florence Nightingale," Indiana sneered. "To what do I owe this pleasure at such an ungodly time in the morning?"

Indiana stood there in all her glory, hands on hips, looking immaculate in her matching pyjamas and dressing gown, hair tied up into a top knot. Gemma could hardly believe the woman had been in bed only moments before.

How rude, she thought, aggrieved.

"Can I come in?" Gemma asked assuredly, refusing to give away how insecure she felt inside.

"Please do, Gemma." Indiana motioned her inside, waving her arm in a curtsy and moving aside to allow Gemma past.

Immediately, Gemma noticed the barren décor: bright white walls, no pictures or ornaments in sight; the laminated flooring gleamed around the circular beige mohair mat. A brown leather sofa was awkwardly positioned along the small alcove in the wall. Either Indiana didn't spend much time here, or this was a rented place she had only just moved to.

Gemma gently placed her suitcase down onto the shiny floor, careful not to scratch it with the unbalanced wheels. She felt uncomfortable standing there in the silence, wishing the moment would hurry up and go away. It didn't take much longer for the silence to be broken. A black and white spaniel appeared from nowhere and began to sniff around her ankles. Smiling, Gemma bent down to stroke him. He was utterly adorable with its clean fur stood up on end.

"Don't you dare touch him!" Indiana snapped, the venom in her voice making Gemma jump. "Barney, here boy." Barney raced towards his mistress – she picked him up and nuzzled into his neck. Barney whimpered with delight, gazing adoringly up at his owner. Enthusiastically, he started licking Indiana's face.

"I wasn't going to hurt him," Gemma remarked, distressed. "Jesus Christ, Indiana, whatever's the matter with you? Why did you abandon me in Crete? Why did you behave so irrationally from day one? Why did you even ask me to go away with you? Why did you even want to be friends? I have so many questions I don't know where to begin!" She startled herself with her outburst, annoyed that she'd lost control already.

"So many questions, Gemma," Indiana purred. Gemma was infuriated to see how much she was enjoying this. "Are you really that flummoxed by me?"

"What do you mean?" Without asking Gemma went and sat down on the sofa. Indiana didn't object. She was pacing up and down the small floor of the lounge; Gemma realised she was witnessing something she'd never witnessed before – Indiana looking stressed.

Barney barked as Indiana lowered him to the floor. She clapped her hands at him and he obeyed her by scuttling out the room.

"If you are that dim, Gemma, I will spell it out to you!" she hissed. "Did you genuinely think that you'd be the sort of person *I* would want as a friend? I couldn't believe Ritchie would pick someone like you to be his soulmate. I was most..." She paused and then sneered at her. "Put out. The first time I saw you with Ritchie I was in denial. I didn't think it was true, both of you looking so happy – even though you'd been married for years. Who stays happily married, for God's sake? It was supposed to be *me and him* together. *I* was the one who was going to love him forever, to be with him every day. Not you! You stole that away from me!"

"Indiana, what are you talking about?" Gemma sprang up from the sofa, grabbed the woman by the shoulders and shouted, "TELL ME!"

"I love Ritchie – I loved Ritchie," Indiana sobbed.

She embraced Gemma; Gemma responded automatically to her touch and pulled Indiana close to her. "So did I."

Indiana made coffee for them both with shaking hands and they carried their cups back to the living room, where they sat side by side on the sofa, coffee in their hands. Gemma didn't really know what she should do next, but what she did know was that she couldn't leave Indiana – not now. She was afraid she might do something stupid.

So, she mused, *this was a case of unrequited love.*

Ritchie hadn't loved Indiana, he'd loved her, as she'd always thought he had. Gemma was elated about that, but absolutely distraught that Ritchie had failed to mention he'd had a stalker in tow. Hadn't he thought she could help – at the very least by listening to him and helping carry that burden. She hardly knew what to feel, and those turbulent emotions weren't allowing Gemma to think clearly. The only conclusion she could come to was that even though he had been faithful to her, Ritchie was not the man she'd thought he was.

"So what now?" Indiana asked, almost meekly.

Gemma wasn't used to being in control over Indiana – up until now, it had always been the other way around.

"How about I stay with you for a while?" Gemma suggested, against her better judgement.

"That would be lovely, Gemma. Thank you." Indiana put down her coffee cup and embraced Gemma, concealing the wicked smile of triumph on her face.

The next few days passed by in a blur for Gemma. She was finding it difficult to come to terms with the dilemma she'd found herself in. Indiana seemed a new person now she'd explained everything to her.

She told her that Ritchie had naively become friends with her when they'd worked together – five years ago. He innocently listened to Indiana's problems and she mistakenly took this as a sign that he had feelings for her. She fell in love with him, but knew she couldn't have him when she saw Gemma and Ritchie together. Instead, she'd flung herself into any relationship going, including the man she'd gone to Crete with. Ritchie wasn't the man Stavros had met in Crete – and Gemma thanked her lucky stars for that – instead it was a man named Rudi, who had a passing resemblance to Gemma's husband and reminded Indiana of him. Indiana showed her a photo of him; it was strange, really. He had the same hair - even the quiff of blond hair Ritchie had been so proud of.

*****

A few days after she'd agreed to stay with Indiana, Gemma went out to meet Maria. She knew she'd been neglecting her and they still hadn't had a proper conversation about the phone call in Crete, so Gemma was feeling a little apprehensive about meeting her. She'd lied to Indiana, telling her she was going into town to do some shopping. She didn't want any more conflict between them, knowing that Indiana had manipulated Maria before, so she kept it quiet. Something told her that Indiana wouldn't want her meeting up with her old friend.

On the bus journey to town, Gemma rubbed the condensation away from the window and watched the passers-by. Everything outside the bus seemed so ordinary. It seemed odd to her that people were going about their daily business, looking like they didn't have a care in the world, while her mind was caught in a whirlwind of turmoil – and at its centre: Indiana. Her life was standing still, orbiting around this strange, possibly broken woman and her obsession with Gemma's late husband.

She sighed.

What was she going to tell Maria? It was time to be completely honest with her, she decided. After all, Maria had been her friend long before Indiana had stormed into her life. In particular, Gemma was hoping that she could start to mend the gaping hole that had come between them. Not Maria's fault – just hers. And Indiana's. Damn that woman. If she hadn't been so obviously messed up about Ritchie, Gemma could have simply gone home, chalked it up to experience and tried to move on with her life. But the way Indiana had spent the last few days sobbing into her shoulder told her that she couldn't be left entirely alone just yet, and as much heartache as the woman had caused her, Gemma couldn't in good conscience leave her without support.

Gemma jumped up from her seat; she had nearly missed her stop due to her daydreaming. Hitting the button just in time, she thanked the driver as she hopped off the bus. As soon as her feet hit the pavement, her mood improved. Now she felt quite jubilant and excited to be seeing her best friend. Gemma briskly walked to the little coffee shop situated on the corner of the high street, which was quickly becoming busy with shoppers.

It's only nine o'clock in the morning, she thought, hurrying through the crowd. *Don't people have better things to do?*

Shopping always seemed a complete chore to her, she couldn't imagine ever choosing to do it for fun. Bending her head to look into the small, cottage-style window of the café Gemma instantly noticed Maria, sitting at a table in the corner, waiting for her. A huge smile spread across Gemma's face and she almost skipped through the café door, elated to see her friend.

Maria rose from her chair as soon as she spotted Gemma and the two women immediately put their arms around one another in a tight bear hug.

"Maria – how wonderful to see you, you look amazing!" Gemma couldn't take her eyes off her, noting her small, thin frame. Surely she hadn't been away that long? When had that happened? Her weight loss was dramatic.

"Hi, Gemma," Maria said reservedly.

They both sat down. An older grey-haired lady behind the counter shouted out, "Yes please," not giving them any time to get up to give their order.

Maria shouted back, "A skinny latte and a cappuccino, please."

It was their usual. It felt deliciously normal to Gemma, who couldn't help but grin.

"Be with you in a jiffy," beamed the old lady.

"So, how are you Maria?" Gemma asked, eager to hear all the news. "Oh, how I've missed you!"

"Have you?" Maria retorted scathingly. "I thought you'd found a new friend to replace me."

"No, never!" Gemma exclaimed, horrified that her friend would think such a thing. "Why would you say that, Maria?" She swallowed, feeling strangely uncertain.

"Well, let's see," said Maria, ticking items off on her fingers. "You met Indiana just after Ritchie's death. You made a connection with her, even went on holiday with her, only six months after knowing her. You completely lost touch with me until something went horribly wrong and you needed someone to talk to. You've been back, what? Four days and you didn't bother to ring me until yesterday. Now you're living with Indiana. Do I need to continue?"

Gemma was totally taken aback. She'd never expected such an angry outburst from Maria.

"I'm so sorry, Maria. I didn't realise you felt like this," she said sincerely. "I would never knowingly do anything to hurt you or upset you."

"But you have."

Gemma couldn't believe what she was hearing; her best friend was essentially calling her a traitor. She desperately wanted Maria to understand why she'd become so close to Indiana. She needed her to realise that any link to Ritchie was a lifeline to her. Looking back she knew she'd been in denial over Ritchie's death, and as a result, she had treated Maria shabbily.

How was she going to put this right?

Taking Maria's hand, Gemma began to pour her heart out, starting with the way losing Ritchie had felt like the end of the world, and how Indiana's connection to him had made her feel more rooted. Maria listened intently, her eyes watering. A single tear rolled down her cheek, and somehow Gemma knew that her friend had understood.

"I'm sorry, Gemma," said Maria, her voice thick with emotion. "I was too harsh on you before. Your friendship means the world to me, and the thought that I'd lost it hurt more than I can explain."

"I'm so sorry, Maria – I think my grief for Ritchie must have made me blind to anyone else's suffering. I –"

"It's forgotten," said Maria, interrupting.

"Thank you," Gemma said, grateful that her friend had chosen to forgive her. "There's more I need to tell you – if you'll listen?"

"Of course I will," Maria assured her. "What are friends for?"

The two women smiled weakly at one another, taking a moment to dry their tears and composing themselves before Gemma continued, telling her all about Indiana, and how her behaviour had deteriorated so completely in Crete.

Maria stared at Gemma in open shock; Gemma stared back, wondering what her friend was going to say. There was an eerie silence, the two friends were looking at each other like strangers.

"Why on earth are you staying with that woman, Gemma?" Maria blurted out. "Come and stay with me. That woman is dangerous."

"Oh, can I? Are you sure, Maria? I'm so sorry," she said again. "I don't know what's been happening to me."

"Of course I mean it!" Maria exclaimed. "You need to get away from that woman, the quicker the better."

Maria stood up, holding open arms out to Gemma. Gemma rushed straight into them, her friend's comforting scent enveloping her.

"Right, we need to come up with a plan. Indiana isn't going to let you go without a fight," said Maria, squeezing Gemma's arm.

"I have an idea," said Gemma, after a moment's thought. They sat back down, still holding hands. "I will tell her I'm going to stay with you, as you're unwell. She won't be able to refuse."

Gemma rubbed her hands like it was the best hatched plan ever. She felt better than she had in days.

"That will do," Maria agreed. "You need to go and pack your things and come to mine tonight."

"Tonight?" Gemma gasped. "But I'd better give Indiana a chance to get used to the idea. I'll pack tonight and come tomorrow."

"No, tonight Gemma, it needs to be tonight," Maria snapped, and Gemma saw genuine concern spread across her features. "I don't want you around that woman a minute longer."

"Tonight it is, then," Gemma said gratefully. "Thank you, Maria."

"What for?" she asked, looking puzzled.

"Just for being you." They both smiled, both enjoying the moment. They felt they'd got their friendship back.

*****

Shakily Gemma put the key in the lock of Indiana's front door, afraid of what mood she would find the woman in. To Gemma's relief, the door opened to an empty house. Indiana was nowhere to be seen. A note left on the kitchen table told her that Indiana wouldn't be returning until eight o'clock that evening.

She heaved a sigh of relief. If she packed quickly, she would be able to get out of here without having to deal with her at all.

It gave her six hours to do what she had to do. She hurried upstairs to the guest bedroom, grabbing her things from the bathroom as she went. Busily packing, it occurred to Gemma that this was the first time she'd been alone in Indiana's house. Stunned by this sudden realisation, she let the blouse she had been folding fall back into her case.

If she was alone, then no one could stop her looking around –

and she might finally be able to make some sense of this whole mess. She looked up, feeling a sudden compulsion to explore Indiana's bedroom – she hadn't been in there before, and Indiana always made excuses for her not to.

Gemma felt slightly uncomfortable about entering a room that she knew she wasn't supposed to, but she yielded to temptation. With the door already ajar, she squeezed through and stopped, staring around, startled by the blood red colour on the walls. Not just the walls – the ceiling too, and the carpet, the curtains, the bedspread. All of it. It was unsettling. Gemma sat herself down on the bed; Indiana's bed. The scarlet duvet cover engulfed her as the waterbed conformed unexpectedly to the shape of her body. Gemma had never laid on a water bed before. She quite liked it. She rubbed her hands up and down her face, gathering her thoughts. What was she doing here?

Looking for clues, right...

The double wardrobe seemed a good place to start and besides, Gemma was curious to see what Indiana had in there. She imagined it was full of designer gear. She opened it and discovered she was correct. There was just so much of it. She ran her eyes over the bright array of expensive clothing, wondering what occasions Indiana had had to wear them. Her gaze fell on a wicker basket jammed underneath the clothes. She froze.

On the top was a black and white photograph of Ritchie.

What the hell?

It looked like a newspaper clipping. Gemma composed herself and took the basket from the wardrobe, tipping the contents out onto the bed. Newspaper cuttings covered the blood red fabric. Gemma stared at them, unable to understand what was going on. She delved through the cuttings, not really believing what she was reading. They were all cuttings on one particular subject, every one of them: Ritchie Peacock. There was an article about how successful his company was, and an interview with him – his face smiled out at her – a photo of various dignitaries shaking hands, Ritchie among them, atop an article about positive workplace behaviour; a picture taken at the golf club, when they'd had that charity game; more besides. She flicked through them, feeling slightly nauseous.

Reeling, she picked up her late husband's obituary. Gemma studied the articles she held in her shaking hands, each one a moment in Ritchie's life. She studied them for almost five minutes, dumbfounded, before scooping up all the newspaper clippings and stuffing them back into the basket, all but one. Ritchie's obituary was going to remain with her. This one, she wasn't going to leave behind.

In a state of shock she slipped back out of Indiana's bedroom. Numbly, Gemma managed to continue with her packing, although her mind was preoccupied with what she had uncovered. It didn't seem comprehensible. What could Indiana have possibly been doing with those clippings? It boggled the mind. Why did Indiana have an obituary of Ritchie? Perhaps that was understandable, if what she'd said about having an obsession with him was true.

Once again Indiana had so many questions to answer. At this moment, however, Gemma didn't want to see her. Really, the only conclusion she could come to was that Indiana was either some kind of confidence trickster, or else she'd had a much more significant relationship with Ritchie than Gemma had thought. She shuddered. Either way, Maria was right about Indiana: she was dangerous. Gemma threw her things untidily into her case. She had to get out of here, had to escape this nightmare. With her suitcase packed, she shut the front door and didn't look back.

The next time she set foot back in that house, she vowed, it would not be alone.

Chapter 7

"What's wrong, Gemma? You look white as a sheet!" Maria held the door open and Gemma walked straight past her without saying a word, still too shaken to think properly. "Gemma, what is wrong?" There was fear in Maria's voice.

Gemma handed her Ritchie's obituary, still not saying a word.

Her friend looked down at the article in her hands and then back up at Gemma's face. "What does this mean? Why have you got this, Gemma?"

"It was in a basket in Indiana's wardrobe with at least ten other clippings about him. Indiana was out so I went for a snoop in her bedroom," Gemma said breathlessly. She hadn't realised quite how angry she was on the way over to Maria's, but now her whole frame was shaking with suppressed emotion. "Do you know what? Her bedroom is completely red. Everything is the colour of blood."

"I don't understand."

"And you think I do?" Gemma scoffed. "Nothing about this makes sense." She started to pace up and down. "Actually, some of it does. Indiana has Ritchie's obituary, which was how she knew when the funeral was, and how she came to be there to meet and become friends with me. I don't know why, but that must be what happened. She went to Crete with someone who looked similar to Ritchie, four years ago. My thinking is that it *was* him. Ritchie was with Indiana in Crete."

"Why would Ritchie be in Crete with Indiana?" Maria asked, puzzled. "And when is this supposed to have happened? Ritchie never used to leave you on your own."

"I know, but remember when I stayed with you that time when Ritchie had to go away on a business trip?" Gemma said hotly. "That was four years ago, too. Meeting other recruitment agencies at a seminar in Brussels, he said. *He lied, more like!*"

"You don't know that, Gemma," said Maria harmoniously.

"I know I don't, but I'm beginning to build a picture in my mind," she argued. "All these things that have been happening – they are starting to piece together."

"Yes, but are you sure that you aren't putting two and two together and getting five?" Gemma ignored her, and Maria shook her head. "I knew that Indiana was trouble. The first time I set eyes on her, I didn't like her."

"I should have listened to you, Maria. I'm so sorry." They hugged each other tightly. "What am I going to do?" Gemma sobbed.

"Right, what we're going to do is this," said Maria, leading her to the sofa. "Both of us will confront Indiana. We'll back her into a corner until she explains the reason behind her irrational behaviour, how she really knew Ritchie, and whether she did go to Crete with him."

"What if she lies?" Gemma mumbled, her face in her hands. "I don't think I can take much more of this."

"Yes you can," said Maria, with such complete certainty that Gemma began to believe her. "You are a strong person, Gemma. You always have been. You do want to hear the truth, don't you? Even if it's not what you want to hear," Maria said gently.

Gemma looked up at her friend's kind face and recognised that she had her emotional well-being at heart.

"Yes, I need to know."

Both women were up bright and early the following morning. They had a plan sorted in their heads now, and that helped rather a lot. Considering they had stayed up most of the night plotting out exactly what they had to do to deal with Indiana, they didn't feel too bad.

Stirring her tea in Maria's bright, homely kitchen, Gemma hoped that the day would bring all the answers she needed. Maybe, after today, she would actually be able to move on with her life. The thought of moving on immediately brought the image of Mick Delaney to mind, but she was quick to dismiss it. This was not the time to be thinking of him. She didn't want any distractions today. Nervously, Gemma applied her makeup, knowing how important it was for her to look good. If makeup was a mask people wore to hide their emotions, she had never had more need of it. The act she was about to put on in front of Indiana would have to be flawless in order to work, and Gemma was unaccustomed to performance. Still, it would work – it had to. There was no way Indiana was going to outwit her this time.

"Ready, Gemma?" Maria asked, calmly.

"I think I need to do this on my own, Maria," Gemma took Maria's hand and gave it a tight squeeze.

"Why? I don't think you're capable of doing this on your own," said Maria. "I don't mean that in a belittling way," she added hurriedly. "But Indiana is a skilled manipulator. She could easily run circles around you – like she has done before. If I'm there, I can protect you from that, at least."

"No, my mind is made up," said Gemma, though she appreciated that Maria had her back. "I need to do this myself – on my own."

"Well, if you're sure," said Maria reluctantly. "I'm not going to stop you, but please be careful. Ring me if anything goes wrong."

"I will." Gemma kissed Maria on the cheek. "I promise."

She left her standing in her front doorway, looking very worried.

The bus journey to Indiana's house seemed to take forever. Her fellow passengers looked like they didn't have a care in the world. Gemma envied them. She wished she could have just one day like them. Not to have to think of anything so complex or so painful for a day would be bliss. Gemma couldn't remember the last time she had a day without anxiety intruding somewhere. It was exhausting.

She arrived at Indiana's front door and paused on the step, feeling uneasiness creep in. She wasn't expecting to be entering Indiana's house again, particularly not on her own. Perhaps asking Maria to let her do this on her own had been a mistake.

She took a deep breath as she pressed the doorbell, the jingle resounding eerily in her ears. Deciding not to use her own key this time, it just might surprise Indiana. The feeling of Déjà vu swept over her. Gemma waited and waited, listening for any sign of movement until she plucked up enough courage to ring again.

Please make her answer, she whispered. *I need this to end.*

The door suddenly opened, but Indiana was not there to greet her. She frowned. Cautiously, she walked in and shut the door behind her.

"Do you want a coffee? You stayed longer at Maria's than you thought, huh? Would've been nice if you'd let me know," Indiana yelled from the kitchen.

The statement flustered Gemma. Why was she acting as though nothing had happened? And how did she know Gemma had gone to Maria's? She bit her lip, calming herself down enough to be able to walk into the kitchen and smile.

The gleaming white tiles were polished mirror-bright; Indiana liked her kitchen to be spotless. There wasn't a mark or smear on the kitchen worktops. Like her exterior, Gemma thought, suddenly.

"I need to talk to you, Indiana. Come and sit down." Gemma's voice betrayed a slight waver.

"I haven't got time to sit down and have a cosy chat. I need to get myself into gear and go into work. You can't return here and make demands." Indiana chided.

"I'm not demanding you do anything, Indiana. I just need to talk to you. I need to know how you knew Ritchie," she told her. "No more lies, Indiana I need the truth."

Indiana was astounded. For a moment, she was quiet, her mouth slightly ajar.

"What do you mean, Gemma?" She walked past Gemma, not looking her in the eye.

"I found Ritchie's obituary, along with several others, in your wardrobe," said Gemma, following her, the words she had been afraid to ask rolling off her tongue. "What are you playing at, Indiana?"

"Alright, you want the truth?" Indiana spat, agitated. "I'll give you the bloody truth – but don't come crying to me when you don't like it, Little Miss Perfect!"

Ignoring the insults, Gemma motioned for her to continue.

"I told you I'd fallen for Ritchie – that much was true. He was good and kind, and a perfect gentleman, and he kept resisting my charms." She pushed her fiery hair back. "Well, there's nothing more infuriating than that! The more I saw him – and the more I saw him out with *you* – the more I wanted him. I knew I had to have him."

Gemma watched the woman as she started to pace around the living room, hanging on her every word.

"I knew he wouldn't give up without a fight, so I came up with a plan. He was going to be mine, he just didn't know it yet. It took me months of going out with everyone at his office, luring myself into his life. He was too damn polite. I knew I was going to have to push him, so I did." She grinned, and Gemma shuddered. It wasn't a pleasant smile.

"I pretended that I'd split up with my boyfriend," said Indiana, obviously enjoying her own shrewdness. "I was inconsolable, I'd wanted to spend the rest of my life with him – the usual emotional blather. Anyway, Ritchie being Ritchie, he listened. He tried to look after me."

That sounded like her husband, Gemma thought, painfully.

"I was drinking, and of course I can hold my drink better than men think," Indiana went on, relentlessly. "He tried to keep up with me at first, before he realised just how broken up *poor, pitiful, abandoned Indiana* was," she said, screwing up her face and voice as she spoke. "Then, of course, he tried to get me to slow down. By then I had him, though. He was already three sheets to the wind."

Gemma felt her expression sour, and Indiana cackled. "That's right! Your precious Ritchie was drunk! And I knew just what to do with him. Chivalrous as ever, he offered to escort me home, so I got him in a taxi and I brought him here, all the time having to listen to all the reasons why he should be a good boy and be faithful to his wonderful wife." She sneered. "But after all that – and after another glass of Shiraz – he seemed happy enough to ravage me. He took me right there, Gemma. Right there on the sofa."

Brutally, Indiana pointed to the spot where, only two nights previously, the two women had shared a pizza and a bottle of wine, watching rubbish on the TV together like old friends.

Gemma felt sick.

"It was bliss! After all those months of lusting after him, I finally had him!" The look of triumph on her face eroded a little. "Of course, as soon as he was sober again the next morning, he was all anguish. Begging me not to tell you, telling me it could never happen again – but of course, I told him if he tried to break it off with me I'd tell you everything. Eventually he agreed to continue seeing me – if only to save your precious marriage!"

Gemma's head was spinning. She was dumbstruck. Ritchie had obviously got himself into something so deep he didn't know how to disentangle himself from it. Blinkered by the emotional tirade of helplessness from Indiana, he'd fallen for it hook, line and sinker. He'd felt compassion for her, as that was just the person he was. Ritchie never passed up an opportunity to help someone in distress.

"I got him to agree to come to Crete with me. I couldn't wait!" Indiana crowed. "I had him all to myself for a whole week! And your name was forbidden – he was all mine! Oh, it was so romantic, Gemma," said Indiana, apparently delighting in rubbing salt in the wound. "We took long walks on the sand, watched the sun go down together, and made love in our hotel room all night long. It was exhilarating, having someone who wasn't mine to keep, just on loan."

Gemma didn't want to listen. "That's enough, I don't want to hear any more about Crete."

"Fine," said Indiana. Then, unexpectedly, her tone turned softer. "That was the last time we were together," she said. "I promise. The last time we were intimate – you've got to believe me."

Gemma did. She sank into a chair, brain sagging under the weight of what she had heard. Indiana had blackmailed her husband for months.

He was too frightened to tell me of his betrayal, she realised. *He probably suspected I would not want to listen and leave. Would I have done that?* She wondered. *I'm not sure.*

She sighed. Deep down within herself, she knew she'd have to forgive Ritchie for his infidelity. Carrying around those painful thoughts forever would be too harrowing.

Across from her, Indiana had also taken a seat. She was watching Gemma, motionless, in the exact spot where she had first slept with Ritchie. It was more than a little disconcerting. Her expression showed a hint of an apology, and as Gemma studied her, she noticed that her usual youthful complexion had vanished – she had been left with a dull, lined face. It looked like she'd aged ten years in the course of her tirade.

Try as she might, though, she couldn't bring herself to hate this woman, even after everything she had done.

"You need help, Indiana." Gemma spoke with empathy in her voice.

"I think you might be right for once," Indiana said heavily. "What do you suggest? Do you think anything will help me or am I a lost cause? Why won't you give up on me Gemma? Other people would." Indiana shook her head, looking distraught. "After all I've done to you. Are you a martyr? Sorry," she said, noticing Gemma's expression. "I do appreciate what you are doing, but I don't think you can help me. No one can."

Gemma shook her head. "Is that what you want? To push everyone away, so there's no one to care about you, no one wanting to help you? You still want to feel rejected and lonely, like you did all those years ago, in your childhood."

"Don't mention that," Indiana snapped.

"Why? I know it hurts, Indiana, but you need to face this," Gemma told her. "If you are serious about getting better, you need to revert back to your childhood memories and figure out why you're compelled to act this way."

"Those memories are not good ones, Gemma," Indiana admitted. She gave a hollow laugh. "I can't believe this, it's the first time in my life I have spoken to anyone about my childhood. Except for *Vonny,* of course."

"Who's Vonny?" Gemma asked, confused.

"Vonny is my only true friend," Indiana explained. "She has been since my sister died. She is the only one that helps me."

"Where is she now then?" Gemma asked, a little concerned that she was getting in over her head.

"She's right here." Indiana pointed her index finger to the side of her head. "She is telling me to be quiet and not tell you any secrets."

"Oh, Indiana! Stop it!" Gemma cried, alarmed. "You need to stop this."

The other woman burst into tears; Gemma went over to Indiana and cradled her in her arms. Indiana rocked back and forth and gently sobbed.

For reasons she could not explain, Gemma felt compassion for this woman. She would not be able to rest easy if she left her to destroy her life, and the lives of those around her any longer. Indiana was a victim, although she seemed unable to see that herself. She needed kindness and humanity and Gemma was going to give her that. It would be her way of forgiving her. This woman had severe mental health issues and Gemma felt an overwhelming sense of protectiveness towards her.

Now that feeling had taken root, a steely determination rose within her to get Indiana the help she so desperately needed. Where she was going to start she didn't know – not yet. But she would find a way.

When Indiana had gone to work, Gemma texted Maria, letting her know she was coming back over to collect her stuff – and that she would explain everything later. Maria wasn't happy about it, but she did understand Gemma's drive to help people – even if she couldn't fathom why she would want to help the woman who had stolen her husband.

Maria had made her promise to call if she needed help, and not to fall out of touch like she had after the funeral.

Settling back in at Indiana's house had been strange, after everything she had learned about her.

Once she had unpacked and made herself a cup of tea, Gemma opened her laptop and typed in 'Bipolar Disorder', which she had a sneaking suspicion might be what Indiana was suffering from. At once, she was bombarded with a baffling array of information. A few clicks took her to an authoritative looking website.

"Bipolar disorder, formerly known as manic depression, is a condition that affects your moods, which can swing from one extreme to another," she read aloud. "People with bipolar disorder have periods or episodes of depression – feeling very low and lethargic – and mania – feeling very high and overactive. Less severe mania is known as hypomania."

She had to admit, that sounded a lot like Indiana. She ran a finger down the list of symptoms, mentally ticking them off against examples of her friend's disturbed behaviour.

Symptoms of bipolar disorder depend on which mood you're experiencing. Unlike simple mood swings, each extreme episode of bipolar disorder can last for several weeks (or even longer), and some people may not experience a "normal" mood very often.

Gemma took a sip of her tea, thinking back to Indiana's strange moods. That fit, too. She read on:

Depression and Mania

You may initially be diagnosed with clinical depression before having a future manic episode (sometimes years later), after which you may be diagnosed with bipolar disorder.

During an episode of depression, you may have overwhelming feelings of worthlessness, which can potentially lead to thoughts of suicide.

During a manic phase of bipolar disorder, you may feel very happy and have lots of energy, ambitious plans and ideas. You may spend large amounts of money on things you can't afford and wouldn't normally want.

Not feeling like eating or sleeping, talking quickly and becoming annoyed easily are also common characteristics of this phase.

You may feel very creative and view the manic phase of bipolar as a positive experience. However, you may also experience symptoms of psychosis, where you see or hear things that aren't there or become convinced of things that aren't true.

Gemma nodded to herself. That would explain Vonny – and Indiana's mad, adventurous plans. She thought back to her enthusiasm for going to Crete and the smashing of the ashtrays.

Well, she thought, *if I can figure out what it is, I might be able to help her.*

She scrolled down the page to the next section and read on:

Living with bipolar disorder

The high and low phases of bipolar disorder are often so extreme that they interfere with everyday life.

However, there are several options for treating bipolar disorder that can make a difference. They aim to control the effects of an episode and help someone with bipolar disorder live life as normally as possible.

The following treatment options are available:

- *medication to prevent episodes of mania, hypomania (less severe mania) and depression – these are known as mood stabilisers and are taken every day on a long-term basis*

- *medication to treat the main symptoms of depression and mania when they occur*

- *learning to recognise the triggers and signs of an episode of depression or mania*

- *psychological treatment – such as talking therapy, which can help you deal with depression, and provides advice about how to improve your relationships*

- *lifestyle advice – such as doing regular exercise, planning activities you enjoy that give you a sense of achievement, as well as advice on improving your diet and getting more sleep*

"Right," she said aloud. "Then we need to get her to the doctor's."

She called the nearest surgery, where she suspected Indiana was registered, and arranged a doctors' appointment with the overly bubbly receptionist for Indiana, to which she would escort her. She couldn't be trusted to attend on her own; Gemma was under no illusion that she would resist the changes she needed in her life and she didn't want to give her the chance to back out of appointments.

There was a very long way to go before Indiana would be able to gain any trust from her again.

*****

The doctors' appointment went as well as could be expected.

Doctor Archibald was a gentleman of elder years. He was certainly charismatic and had a pleasant tone to his voice, the sort you could listen to for hours and not get bored. He put Indiana immediately at ease, which was a relief for Gemma, who had been expecting pandemonium.

Unexpectedly, Indiana was on her best behaviour and Gemma actually thought she was glad to be there, to be getting help and advice to put her on the road to recovery. The doctor listened to Indiana's concerns – and Gemma's – and treated her with unusual delicacy and sympathy. Finally, he recommended talking therapy, one to one, to kick start her off. Doctor Archibald stressed that talking therapies could help all sorts of people in lots of different situations. Gemma had also heard of them.

"Yes, that sounds good, doesn't it, Indiana?" she said.

Indiana remained silent.

Doctor Archibald smiled encouragingly. "Indiana, it would be a good start to talk to a therapist about your thoughts and feelings, just to help you understand them better," he explained in his pleasant tone. "You can talk about things that are troubling you and how to explore your feelings. You may well feel anxious or distressed because you might prefer to ignore things that seem painful or overwhelming. I can put you in touch with Mr. King – he's a talking therapy counsellor, and very good at his job, I might add."

He made a note on his computer, bringing up a fresh window to check the counsellor's availability. "I think he'll be able to fit you in from next week, actually. You will meet for fifty minutes in his office, once a week for ten weeks. I will also prescribe you a maintenance medication, which is nothing to worry about. It's just a mood stabilizer, to make day-to-day life a little less stressful for you. I'll also give you a medication to treat acute episodes." He checked a couple of boxes on his computer. "Yes, I will prescribe a combination medication called Travil which will include Amitriptyline and Perphenazine – your medical history gives no indication that you would have any trouble with those. You will need to take them as directed, Indiana, but in no circumstance should you stop taking your medication without consulting me first," he said sternly, turning to face her. "Do you understand, Indiana?"

Indiana nodded in agreement. Gemma thought she must have lost her voice – she'd hardly spoken a word since they entered the doctors' surgery.

"Good. I would like a follow up appointment with you in a month's time," he said. "Just to see how the medication is going and if the sessions with Mr King are helping you. I'll book it in with the receptionist for you. Have you any questions, Indiana?"

Indiana shook her head. She stood up and shook Doctor Archibald's hand. In a quiet voice that didn't sound like her at all, she said, "Thank you."

"Thank you again, Doctor." Gemma shook his hand, too.

Back at Indiana's, you could cut the atmosphere with a knife. Indiana refused to talk about what they'd just sat through and Gemma quickly became frustrated at her for not answering her questions. The eerie silence their disagreement created did nothing to alter their moods. Gemma decided it might be a good idea to let Indiana have some space and return to Maria's for a few days.

"No, you can't leave me now, not after what you just put me through!" screamed Indiana.

"What do you mean, what I put you through?" Gemma demanded.

"Being spoken to in that condescending way by the decrepit Doctor Archibald!" she retorted. "Who did he think he was, speaking to me like that? I only kept quiet as I knew I would lose my temper!"

"He was trying to help you, Indiana," Gemma said, exasperated. "He's put you in touch with a therapist to help you overcome your illness."

Indiana scowled. "What's a therapist going to do?"

"Well, at least see if it helps. Don't lose faith now, Indiana," Gemma admonished. "I thought you were being positive about the treatment you're going to receive."

"Yes, I know…" she said, fiddling with the hem of her sleeve. "I do want you to stay, Gemma. I don't want to be on my own. I'm scared."

"Scared, what of?" Gemma asked, putting an arm around her shoulders.

"Of – myself."

Chapter 8

Gemma waited with Indiana until it was time for her appointment. She was glad Indiana was trying to do everything Doctor Archibald suggested. That's all she could ask of her.

The door to the therapist room opened. Gemma couldn't believe how handsome the man that came out to greet them was. When did therapists become so young? She had been expecting an older man, nearer retirement age. Suddenly, Indiana didn't seem quite so unhappy to be there.

"Indiana Manors?" Jonathan King said, looking at both women in turn.

Indiana stood up and gave Gemma a half smile.

"Good luck," Gemma said, and left to meet Maria, pleased things were going so well.

Indiana took a seat in the uncomfortable chair opposite Mr King, feeling surprisingly optimistic. She was glad it was a man who sat opposite her in the black leather swivel chair. A man, she could work with. He looked like he was in his late thirties. His blond hair was shaved at the sides with a fringe that lay over his left eye. His big brown eyes were going to prove a distraction, she could tell already, and hid a smile.

He held a notebook in his lap, a pen in his left hand. Indiana stared at him. His body language suggested he was uncomfortable in her presence, which stirred her to shift position slightly. He was expecting helplessness, and she could give him that. Indiana had known for many years about the effect she could have on men. Once again, she was ready to play the game.

Perhaps this 'treatment' wouldn't be a total loss, after all.

Mr King cleared his throat. "I want you to feel like this is a safe space for you to speak your mind. Feel free to interrupt me at any time, but I want you to be honest with me – and with yourself." He gave her a comforting smile. "So, what brings you here, Indiana?"

Indiana studied Mr King's face, not taking her eyes off him for one second. She was going to have to use a very careful strategy here. Say what he wanted to hear.

"What brings me here today – let me think?" she said, placing a finger on the side of her chin in thought. "Well, it was Doctor Archibald who recommended you. He seems to think I need a counsellor."

Indiana crossed her legs, deliberately allowing her skirt to rise a little too much up her thigh. She stood, aware that his eyes were following her movements, and pulled her skirt down slightly before sitting back down.

"And you don't think you do?"

Indiana played along. She didn't want to be caught out just yet.

"I don't *think* I do, I *know* I do, Mr King," she said, playing the perfect patient.

"Indiana, please call me Jonathan, there's no need to be too formal," he said kindly, rewarding her frankness.

"I'd prefer to call you Mr King, if you don't mind," she replied.

"That is not a problem. Have you ever seen a counsellor before, Indiana?" he asked. "You seem pretty comfortable and confident coming in here."

"No, never."

"From your point of view, why do you 'know' you need to see a counsellor?" he prompted. "I'm here to create positive changes as quickly as possible, without you feeling rushed."

"I always hurt people," she said simply.

Mr King raised an eyebrow, but didn't otherwise comment. "How do you get along with people at work?"

"I keep my distance until I allow them to become closer."

"How would you describe your personality?"

"When I'm having an acute episode, or when I'm normal?" she asked flippantly.

Indiana was finding it easy to answer all the questions he was firing at her. She could keep this up no problem. It was quite enjoyable, really – just another kind of game.

"Both."

"Outgoing, excitable, intelligent, happy, ambitious and energetic," she reeled off.

"When you're having an episode or when you're feeling normal?" Mr King asked.

She put her head to one side flirtatiously and smiled. "Both."

Jonathan King laughed, showing off his white veneers as he did so. Indiana was always attracted to men who had bright white clean teeth; she thought of it as a positive trait: clean teeth, clean mind, body and soul. Her smile widened.

"What are three of your biggest life accomplishments, Indiana?" he asked, making a note.

"Graduating from university, becoming a successful business woman and becoming a mother," she said, at once.

"How does your disorder typically make you feel?"

"Sad and lonely." Indiana searched in her handbag for a tissue, figuring this would be a good time as any to shed a few crocodile tears. The man was already half on her side – and she knew exactly how to play to the protective glimmer she saw in his deep brown eyes.

"Would you like to stop now, Indiana?" Jonathan King asked, concerned.

"No I will be fine, just give me a minute." Indiana blew her nose into the tissue, and gave Jonathan King a nod to proceed.

"What do you expect to get out of this counselling process?" he asked her, watching her face carefully. "Everyone who comes here expects something different, Indiana."

"Someone who listens to me and doesn't judge me." She shrugged, and he nodded.

"Well, I like to hope that that's what you'll get," he smiled. "Overall, how would you describe your mood today?"

"Blue."

"Okay. Do you use drugs, alcohol, sex, money, or other 'mood soothers' to make you feel better?" he asked, moving through his notes.

"All of those," she admitted.

And why not? Life is about having fun, isn't it? Vonny whispered in her ear.

Indiana smiled.

"What has been a major life disappointment?"

"Oh, that's easy," she said. "People."

Mr King raised an eyebrow. "Do you feel mad when you don't get your own way or lose control?"

"Yes."

"Do you consider yourself to have a low, average or high interpersonal IQ?"

"Low." Indiana knew it wasn't low, but she had to keep this

façade up. Her brief, confident word answers were working; she could see it in Jonathan King's eyes.

"How would you best describe your relationship with your parents?"

Here we go, Indiana thought. She had been expecting this question. The next one would be 'how do you get along with your siblings?'

"Icy."

He made another note.

"Do you get along with your siblings?"

Bingo!

"No, because they're dead." Indiana broke down into entirely convincing tears and cried into her tissue.

"Right, well, I think we will leave it there for now, Indiana," Jonathan King said quietly. He sent a sweet smile her way as he reached over to give her shoulder a gentle squeeze.

His hand lingered a little too long on her shoulder and he let his thumb brush down her bare arm. Indiana smiled back, managing to look at once grateful and seductive. Vonny whispered in her ear that she had him right where she wanted him. Mr King was all hers.

Indiana bit her lip, allowing her eyes to drop to his mouth, then back up to his eyes. He swallowed, and that was all the encouragement she needed. She uncrossed her legs and stood up fast, sending the chair crashing to the floor behind her. Her eyes lingered on Jonathan's face and this time, he didn't look away, locking his eyes with hers. Indiana's heart began to beat faster as she walked over to him, feeling sensual and seductive. She leaned over him to balance her weight against the back of the chair and climbed onto his lap, placing her legs either side of his body to straddle him. The swivel chair slid a little on the laminate floor when she lowered her lips to kiss him.

There was a momentary struggle of wills, where he obviously considered the ethical and professional rules he was breaking, but not too much of one. Clearly his training hadn't prepared him for someone like her.

Good, thought Indiana, as his hands came up to press her closer. *He doesn't mind breaking the rules, either.*

Jonathan wrapped his hands around her torso and stood up, lifting her weight easily as he pivoted around and placed her none-too-gently down on the chaise longue. His hasty fingers made short work of the buttons of her silk blouse, and he slid it off her body, exposing her to his gaze.

He groaned as he looked at her and reached forward, more impatient now, to rip off her white, lace, plunge bra with one hard tug, exposing her breasts. His attention focused on her nipples and she arched her back as he teased them between his thumb and index finger. Indiana moaned, delighting at his touch. He dragged his hot mouth down her torso to flick his tongue in and around her navel, making her abdomen tense and her body tremble as she cried out at the sensation. He grasped one of her breasts, flicking at her nipple as he moved downwards.

She wanted him right now, right this minute; surely she was going to climax soon if the exquisite torture his hands and mouth was subjecting her body to continued for much longer.

Jonathan removed her skirt and then her panties, and then stood up to look down at her, naked and unashamed. They stared at one another, eyes full of lust, before he pulled Indiana to her feet and reclined on the chaise longue, inviting her to undress him the way he had done for her. She complied immediately, her trembling hands moving quickly to strip him of his clothing.

Her lips trailed an erotic path over his body and he groaned, responded to her touch with trails of goose bumps forming on his skin, following the path her mouth had taken. His husky panting made her feel powerful and in control. She liked the idea of screwing a professional – particularly one who was supposed to be responsible for her. Indiana had him in the palm of her hand, so to speak, from the first time they'd laid eyes on each other.

Jonathan writhed about on the chaise, almost falling off it, as her services continued. His husky voice broke the silence.

"Stop, Indiana," he breathed. "I don't want to climax yet." He gave her a wicked grin as she relented. "I want to bury myself deep inside you."

Pleased, Indiana slid over him, straddling him once more, and slowly lowered her weight until the full, hard length of him filled her completely. They both moaned in appreciation.

He placed his hands around her hips, lifting her up and down. Very quickly they found a fast, satisfying pace; it was the pace he wanted and the pace she needed. Indiana tossed her head back and groaned with delight as her body responded to his hard, frenzied thrusts.

Focused on the pleasurable tension the friction between them was eliciting in her abdomen, she gasped in surprise when he suddenly lifted her off him and in one swift motion, slid out from under her to kneel behind her. His hands encouraged her up onto her knees and Indiana eagerly complied, impressed at his prowess and arching her back in anticipation as she rested her weight on her palms.

Jonathan looked down at Indiana's svelte body, taking a moment to enjoy the view. She looked over her shoulder, enjoying watching him watch her. She knew she had the body of a much younger woman – she had worked at it every day of her adult life – and he allowed his hands to roam freely over her soft, supple skin. Indiana bit her lip, relishing the feel of his fingers moving over her creamy flesh. When she trembled beneath him, touching her was no longer enough for the counsellor. He needed to taste her. Jonathan leaned over her again, pressing his tongue against her hot skin as he licked her all over, tracing lazy circles down her spine and between her buttocks, making her shudder and squirm as his tongue moved lower.

When he could wait no longer – and Indiana was groaning with need – he penetrated her deep and hard, pausing for a moment when he had filled her completely. While he was eager to be inside her, at the same time, he wanted this feeling to last forever.

Indiana ground her hips against him impatiently, desperate for release. It stirred him to action once more, and he resumed the punishing pace they had set themselves. Her moans were coming faster now, and he could feel her pushing hard against him. Jonathan had never experienced ecstasy like it.

He felt Indiana's body tremble around him and he smiled, knowing she was almost there.

It took every ounce of his self-control to do it, but he pulled out of her, just as the first tremors of her climax began. She whined in complaint, but he ignored her. Indiana was a tease - he'd figured that out from the first moment she'd strutted in through the door of his office, crossing her legs provocatively and deliberately drawing attention to how short her skirt was. She wasn't like anyone he'd ever met before. Indiana oozed sensuality. The way she tucked her hair behind her ear, the way she crossed her sinfully long legs, and especially the way she licked her lips after she answered a question, had swiftly driven him crazy with lust.

Everything she did was very erotic, and she knew it. God only knew how he'd managed to remain professional until she'd climbed into his lap.

Yes, Indiana was a tease. Well, now she would learn that he liked to do a little teasing of his own. It turned him on to stop right in the middle of fucking a woman who was about to climax, withholding her pleasure and making her beg for more. Right now, she might think of him as cruel, but he knew from experience that the orgasm he eventually gave Indiana would be much, much more intense as a result.

Seeing that her arching back and searching hands were getting her nowhere, Indiana cried out in frustration, sounding almost as if she was in pain. She turned to look at him, irritation showing on her beautiful face until she caught the glimmer of mischief in his eyes and smiled.

"You're a bastard, Mr King," she said, with every trace of joyful anticipation in her voice. She laughed, her voice soft, low, and husky with desire. The sound made his whole body tighten and he knew he wouldn't be able to stay away from her for long.

Jonathan picked her up and carried her across the room, laying her across his desk. He'd fantasised about taking a beautiful woman here, and Indiana more than fit the bill. He wasn't about to pass up the opportunity when it threw itself at him.

Indiana lay beneath him, her skin glistening with sweat, and he couldn't tease her any longer. He entered her quickly, with one savage thrust; she trembled beneath him, her body begging for release. Jonathan could feel the way she convulsed around him and knew she was aching to reach her climax. Hooking her legs over his shoulders, he powered into her hard and fast, over and over again, driving them both over the edge.

Their cries of pure ecstasy combined, filling the air, as they shouted each other's names.

He collapsed on top of her, gasping for breath, his head resting on her panting chest. When his body returned to normality, he fell away from her to sit on the floor and watch as she quietly put on her clothes, swung her fur coat around her shoulders, and left him sitting, naked, on the floor of his office without so much as a backward glance.

Jonathan King laughed quietly to himself as she closed the door behind her. He couldn't wait for the next meeting with Indiana.

*****

How did it go? Gemma eagerly asked.

"Mr King was good. He helped me to release some emotion." Indiana gave a wry smile that was evidently lost on the other woman.

"That's good," said Gemma, obviously pleased. "Are you going to continue going?"

"I will be carrying on with his therapy; he knows how to hit all the right spots." Indiana smirked. She was enjoying this.

"That's great news Indiana. Now we've sorted your medication out too, you should be feeling much better soon." Gemma gave her a hug before she passed her by to go into the kitchen. "Want a cuppa?" Gemma asked.

"No thank you, I might go for a little lie down. Mr King has taken all my energy from me today."

First though, Indiana decided to take a shower. Standing in the shower, Indiana noticed the bruising on the top of her thighs. A sudden rush of adrenalin seeped through her body as she recalled exactly how those marks had got there. She ran her hands over her body, suddenly feeling the need to relieve the ache that had resurfaced within her.

She closed her eyes as the hot water cascaded down over her naked body. Her hand wandered down, stirring the tension in her belly once more. This action always managed to relieve her aching, every time. The hot water flowed around her breasts as her breath started to come quicker and quicker, as if the liquid was purposefully caressing her. Her release came, as she began to remember the feel of Mr King making love to her.

She stayed in the shower, letting the water soothe her and for once she felt alive. She hadn't felt this invigorated since being with Ritchie Peacock.

Stepping out of the shower, Indiana reached into her bathrobe pocket for the tablets she'd hidden and threw them into the toilet bowl; feeling triumphant, she pulled the flush handle, and watched them disappear. She was aware Gemma was watching her every move, so she had been careful to conceal what she was doing with the stupid pills the doctor had prescribed. It wasn't like she needed them, anyway. Every morning she would place her tablets next to her cup of strong coffee and pop them into her mouth, just to please Gemma. When her friend turned away, she'd spit the tablets into a tissue, which she would quickly place into her bathrobe pocket. When the opportunity arose, she would make her way to the bathroom and dispose of them.

Gemma seemed satisfied that she was still taking them, and Indiana's acting skills had thus far enabled her to disguise any acute episodes of bipolar disorder with ease. Gemma was none the wiser. Of course, Indiana still spoke to Vonny during times of real desperation, but she didn't have as many opportunities as she would have liked. Gemma saw to that. She was playing a waiting game with that woman, allowing her to think she was in control, making all the decisions.

What a fool she was.

*****

On Saturday mornings, Indiana would go on her usual outing across town. She hardly ever missed a Saturday. Missing one would have brought on an attack of her disorder, and now that she had a name for it, she needed to keep it down, otherwise Gemma would grow suspicious.

She always looked forward to the time she spent with him. He was the only one she had ever given all her love to, in her whole life. She had never experienced feelings like those she had for him, and she was determined to remain strong for this reason alone.

It was a frosty morning, and she'd dressed accordingly. Her long beige trench coat suited her, she decided, assessing her appearance in the hall mirror. When Indiana was ready to leave the house, the white mohair hat and gloves looking striking against her olive skin, Gemma stuck her head out of the kitchen.

"Where you off to this early?" she asked. "Every Saturday you seem to be gone all day."

"Only across town," said Indiana, with a small shrug.

"Wait ten minutes and I can come with you," Gemma said, and her tone was almost one of pleading.

"No it's okay. I'm about to leave," said Indiana hurriedly. "Sometimes, Gemma, I need time on my own."

"Oh, sorry, I didn't think. I understand. Maybe another time then?"

"Maybe, bye."

Indiana hurried down the garden path, feeling Gemma's eyes on her all the way down the road.

Chapter 9

November 2016

Wıth the holiday season finally over in Crete, Mick had decided what he wanted to do.

He'd given it a great deal of thought over the last few months; this was the biggest decision he'd ever taken. He had never been the kind to be impulsive, which was why he'd been contemplating his next move for over a month. After having lost her at the airport, Gemma had never been far from his thoughts. Never before had a woman left such a powerful impact on him. Remembering Gemma always made him smile. The night they'd spent together had been sweet.

Although nothing sexual had happened between them, he couldn't forget it, and that was a first for Mick. To have slept with a woman and not have touched her, was a new experience. She'd looked beautiful as she had lain in his bed, and for a while he had simply admired her as she slept. Her black camisole had risen up while she was sleeping, displaying her flawless skin. With her face half hidden under the duvet, her nose wrinkled like a sleeping baby's, her mouth was slightly open, showing her perfect white teeth – he had known right then that she was special.

Today would be the day he was going to be impulsive for the

first time in his life. Mick felt a rush of thrilling excitement as he stepped into the travel agent's office. Forty minutes later, he held in his hand a flight ticket to England, to pursue a woman he'd only known for two days, and who he hadn't seen in months. It was madness, pure and simple.

He wasn't even sure how she felt about him. It had been five months since she'd left Crete. He just knew he couldn't let her go and not see her ever again. It felt like he was on some big adventure, slightly daunting but exciting. He had been daydreaming about buying a ticket to England ever since she'd slipped away, instead of going back home to Australia, and now he had done it.

Mick had already rung his parents to let them know he was extending his time away. He explained to them how he'd decided to continue travelling around Europe, omitting the fact it was on account of a woman. No, instead he'd told them he had met a nice bunch of lads who asked him to travel Europe with them. His parents were disappointed; Mick was their only son and they missed him. They completely understood, however. He'd had a thirst for travelling ever since he was a young boy. They had bought him a globe for his tenth birthday and that was it. He'd sit for ages just staring at the countries, working out which ones he would visit first, when he was old enough to travel on his own.

He awoke on the plane; he had been dreaming about Gemma again. Mick sat up and stretched out the kink in his neck. He looked out of the window and saw they were flying over land – they were nearly there. Mick couldn't believe he was about to land in England in ten minutes. It had all been a bit of a whirlwind arranging all the details to his trip, and now he was nearly here he felt nervous and excited.

He couldn't wait to see Gemma again.

He guarded the note she had left him carefully; it was one he wasn't about to lose. Since that ill-fated trip to the airport, all those months ago, he'd kept it folded up into four, tucked into the small pocket of his wallet.

He remembered the words she had written:

If you are ever in England (not very likely, I know) please call on me for a visit.

He'd read it over and over, feeling closer to Gemma when he did. It was going to be such a surprise for Gemma when he showed up. One he hoped she'd like – even love.

He booked a room at a Travelodge in Southwark, London. It was about an hour away from Croydon, where Gemma's note told him she lived. Mick paced around the small hotel room, wondering what his next step ought to be. He wasn't sure whether to completely surprise Gemma by turning up on her doorstep out of the blue, or give her a heads up beforehand. Although he didn't want to shock her, he also didn't want her to talk herself out of meeting up with him. He wished he'd had her phone number so he could ring her, but that would have given her the opportunity to say no. There was a good chance she would refuse to see him, anyhow.

No… the best thing to do would be to send her a postcard. He peered out into the city; London was certainly a busy place, bustling with people. On the short ride from the airport to the hotel, he had seen hundreds of tourists, with their cameras at the ready, intent on capturing pictures of London's greatest attractions; people rushing home from work, all fighting for a seat on the tube; school kids weaving in and out between the grownups, engaged in their own mischief; street hawkers selling everything from mobile phone covers to balloons. Mick could sense the frenzy in the manic city, even from inside the taxi, passing through. He wasn't sure whether he liked it or not. He was used to a slower, more measured pace of living. One you could relax in. But he was an explorer at heart, and while he was here he decided he would embrace it. It wasn't like he was ever going to live here.

Meanwhile, across town, Gemma was thinking about whether she should return to her abandoned home. It had been months, now, since she had come back from Crete and decided to try to help Indiana with her mental health issues, and she hadn't been back to her house in a while. In some ways it was easier, because going back there always reminded her of Ritchie, but not going back at all seemed very foolish. She'd returned a couple of times since moving in with Indiana, and although she'd found it safe and secure, there was no getting away from the fact that it looked like no one lived there – and that was just asking for trouble.

It was probably time, she decided, to move back home and gain her independence back. Also she needed to meet up with Maria, who she had fallen out of touch with again. Indiana's condition was quite demanding to keep up with at times, though she was trying so hard to manage it and stay optimistic. She needed to explain what kept her away for so long to her old friend. They hadn't even spoken on the phone, recently. Gemma missed Maria. She knew she'd neglected her and felt lousy about it, but she told herself it was for a good cause – and Indiana really did seem to be improving.

Now she felt able to leave Indiana on her own, she planned to put her long absence in Maria's life right.

In two days time, it would be the first anniversary of Ritchie's death, and as it got nearer, the more she ached to be alone. To remember him, her way. She wanted to visit his grave, lay some flowers down and talk to him for a while, on her own. No Indiana in sight; no Indiana to remind her of his infidelity. She didn't want to feel anger towards Ritchie on his anniversary. She wanted to remember him as her loyal, loving husband. To recall how happy they'd been and how much they'd loved each other.

It had seemed impossible at the funeral, but the year following his death had passed quickly. So many things had materialised in that year. Truths and non-truths had surfaced, Indiana and her constant pathological lying being one of them. Gemma didn't know if Indiana knew it was Ritchie's anniversary, but she wasn't going to be the one to tell her.

Instead, Gemma decided to leave Indiana a note. She didn't want to tell her face to face she was leaving, because Indiana would try to stop her. She picked up the note pad and pen from the coffee table and scribbled a quick few lines:

Dear Indiana,

It's time I returned home. I need to check everything at my house is in order. I think we both need to get back to normality. I'm always at the end of the phone if you need me, but I'm sure you won't. You are doing so well now, you don't need me to be watching over you. See you soon.

G x

Gemma placed the note on the kitchen worktop, next to Indiana's pint-sized mug. She would catch sight of it instantly. Indiana always reached for a mug of coffee when she arrived home. Come to think of it, Gemma thought, Indiana drank far too much coffee. She might even have an addiction to caffeine, along with all her other vices. As she shut the door behind her, Gemma wondered if she should post her keys back through the letterbox. Maybe it would be best to keep them. Other dilemmas could easily crop up; it wasn't like Indiana was suddenly going to become normal. Was it?

Walking down the garden path, she hated that last thought, but it was true. Being bipolar wasn't something that just went away – it could only be managed.

Gemma entered her house and was immediately welcomed with the stale odour of unaired, unoccupied rooms. Not feeling ready to unpack just yet, she dropped her luggage in the bedroom and left it there. The familiar picture of Ritchie on the bedside table made her smile. It was good to be home. Glad that she'd stopped to pick up groceries, she threw those that needed to be chilled into the fridge and began to relax. She didn't feel like going back out again. She was ready to have a hot bath, a glass of red, and relax in front of the TV. She flicked the hot water and central heating button to on. In thirty minutes it would be ready.

Throwing the windows open for the rooms to air, Gemma

unpacked her belongings then sifted through the pile of unopened letters she'd collected from the doormat on her way in. There was quite a substantial pile of post since she'd been away. Nothing of real importance, by the looks of things, just bank statements, store card reminders, credit card balances. Everything was on time, so none of it looked ominous. She picked all the letters up and tried to shuffle them together. A picture of Buckingham Palace caught her attention; it was on the front of a postcard.

Who sent postcards anymore? She wondered. She turned it over and read:

Dear Gemma,

You did say to look you up when I was in England. So, here I am. I arrived a few days ago. Would love to meet up with you at The Shard, 32 London Bridge Street. I'd like to take you to the fifty second floor, to the cocktail bar, GONG, on the twenty-ninth of November. I will meet you outside at seven thirty p.m. If you are not there, I will understand.

Mick

X

Gemma gasped. She couldn't believe it. There were butterflies in her stomach; she felt both nervous and excited all at once. She checked the date on her phone. The date Mick said he wanted to meet was today — tonight. It must have been fate. If she hadn't returned home today, she wouldn't have seen the postcard in time and she would've missed the meeting with Mick. She might never have seen him again. What were the chances?

She couldn't believe Mick was in London. Gemma felt dizzy with excitement, and slightly light-headed. Looking at the *Route 66* American clock hanging above the fireplace told her it was now five thirty. She felt a jolt like electricity pass through her – what was she going to do? If she was going to meet Mick at seven thirty, she would only have an hour to get ready, and it would take her at least another hour to get across town. Saturday traffic would not be kind to her.

Calm down Gemma, she told herself.

Right, first thing's first: shower. Yes, the hot water would be ready by now. She hurried into the shower, letting the hot water revive her. She felt like she wanted to stay there for longer, but knew she couldn't. She didn't have time. When she'd showered, washed her hair, and shaved her legs and arms she rushed back into the bedroom, considering what to wear. From her wardrobe, Gemma pulled out dress after dress after dress. She threw them all onto the bed, holding each one up individually against her body, looking in the mirror and tersely saying, "No," to each one.

She must have tried on at least ten dresses before giving up, but not one fitted properly. A cocktail bar at the `Shard` was going to be trendy – she had to look her best.

Think, Gemma, think, she thought desperately.

In the end, she decided on black leather trousers with a white, cold-shoulder blouse, high heels and black pashmina. Gemma felt chic and comfortable. Her natural looking make-up looked slightly bare, so she added thick, black eyeliner, more mascara and bright, red lipstick, which gave her a more glamorous look. Adding a few curls to her usual straight bob was the finishing touch. She raised her eyebrows, surprised. Surely, the woman staring back at her in the mirror couldn't be her. This woman looked stunning, confident and sultry; how had she managed that? And in just under an hour, too. She complimented herself.

Picking up her keys and placing them in her black Chanel bag, her phone started to vibrate. She looked at the screen: *Indiana calling*. Gemma ignored it. Tonight was her time. Indiana would have to wait.

*****

Indiana arrived home wearing a smile that hadn't left her face since she'd said goodbye to him. She'd had such a special day. Yes, it was sad she wouldn't be seeing him again for a week, but for now she only wanted to remember the lovely day they had spent together. She put the kettle on, needing her caffeine fix. She hadn't had a coffee all day.

The house was quiet, which was surprising. She wondered where Gemma was.

It was then, when she reached for her mug, that she spotted the note. She read it, sighing, before picking up her phone and dialling Gemma's number. No answer.

Two can play at this game, she told Vonny. *And I shall win.*

*****

On the bus, Gemma felt uncomfortable. People seemed to be staring at her. Perhaps it was just her nerves, but it made her feel a little uneasy. Gemma got out her phone. Three missed calls.

She put the phone back into her bag. This was her night, and Indiana wasn't about to ruin it for her. It was seven fifteen and she was almost there. Her nerves were beginning to make her feel tingly and nauseous, but in a nice way, if that was possible. She couldn't wait to see Mick. She liked that she was excited about seeing him again. She hoped he would be excited to see her, too. After all, he had sent her that postcard and invited her out.

Her stop was the next one. She didn't need to press the orange button to let the driver know, somebody else had done that. Wrapping the pashmina around her shoulders she stood up and walked to the front of the bus without falling over – always a minor victory in and of itself. The bus stopped and off she jumped. It was only a five minute walk to the Shard from her stop. The distance would make her exactly on time; Gemma always liked to be punctual. It would also give her a chance to clear her head.

She spotted him as soon as she turned the corner, the familiar pony tail, bushy beard and tanned face she remembered so well from her time in Crete. He looked so handsome in his black and white jacket, black t-shirt and skinny jeans.

And all six foot of him, looking attractive, waiting for me, she realised, with a jolt of excitement.

His face lit up as soon as he saw her, though Gemma felt embarrassed walking up to him, his eyes looking her up and down. He kissed her on both cheeks, like a Parisian.

"Hi, Gemma Peacock," Mick said, with obvious excitement.

"Hi, Mick Delaney." Gemma smiled back at him.

"I can't believe you're here!" Mick declared, before picking her up, swinging her in a circle then putting her down, both of them laughing.

"I can't believe *you're* here," Gemma said. "Sorry, I don't mean to keep copying what you're saying." Gemma laughed again, covering her mouth with her hand.

It felt like an age since she had last laughed. It felt good to do it again.

"Come on, beautiful lady." Mick took hold of her hand and led the way through the double doors. "We need to go to level fifty-two to get to the cocktail bar, but first I want you to see something."

They arrived on floor seventy-two and Mick led her to the viewing area. Gemma could not believe what she was looking at. It was the highest and best view you could see of London. The three hundred and sixty degree view was breath-taking. She could see the entire city from there – and beyond it, where the grey suburbs began to be broken up with little islands of green. A notice on the window told her she could see as far as forty miles on a clear day. Gemma believed it. Awed, Gemma could hardly speak. She was totally spellbound. She'd heard things about the Shard, but never imagined it would be such an amazing experience.

"Thank you, Mick, for bringing me here. It's incredible," she breathed.

"No problem," he said, a hand on the small of her back. "As soon as I saw it, I knew I had to share it with you. Come on, let's head back down to *Gong*."

Gong, one of the most fashionable cocktail bars in London, was on level fifty-two of the Shard. Its romantic atmosphere with intimate chambers where you could continue to view the dramatic back drop of London's skyline was breathtaking. Its décor had a traditional Chinese flavour; there were brown pouffes and tables placed beside comfortable blue sofas. All very modern and tastefully done.

"This place is stunning," said Gemma, gazing around.

"Glad you like it." Mick handed Gemma a flute of champagne.

"Like it? I *love* it," she told him. "Who wouldn't love this view?" Once again, Gemma looked out across the vast city of London. The splendour of the lights sparkling below her made her feel intoxicated. "So, Mick, how are you enjoying your stay here in England?" She asked, turning back to him.

She was already feeling the effects of the champagne.

"It's a little colder than I thought," he admitted, with a laugh. "I almost had to buy an entire new wardrobe. It's so good to see you, Gemma. I have to admit that I raced to the airport after I found your note. I tried to catch you up, to persuade you to stay."

Gemma stared at him, astonished. "You really did that?"

"Yes. I called out your name just as you were about to go

through security. You turned around, but then you were gone."

"That was you?" she cried, surprised. "I remember now, I thought I heard someone call my name."

Mick took the champagne flute out of her hand and placed it down onto the table. He wrapped his arms around her waist, pulling her in close, ready to take a chance. He placed his lips on hers, kissing her gently. After a moment's surprise, she responded by kissing him back. Their kiss was a passionate one; both seeking out each other's tongues. They broke away from each other, and for a second they simply stood staring at each other, and both burst out laughing.

"Okay let's swap phone numbers," Mick said, with concern. "I don't want to lose you ever again."

After entering the digits into their phones, Mick took her hand and kissed the back of it. It made her skin tingle pleasantly.

"Come on," he said, voice a little huskier than usual. "I'll take you home. Let's grab a taxi."

"Alright."

She liked the way he was taking charge. She'd missed that of late. Always having to make decisions by herself, it was nice to be led for a little while. She felt she wanted to share this, now. She was ready – dare she say it – to move on.

Gemma didn't know if she was doing the right thing, but this did feel right. She didn't want to let Mick go. The taxi ride home took hardly any time at all, they were so wrapped up in one another. Before they knew it, the car had come to a halt outside her house; Mick climbed out of the car and ran round to open her door.

"You can come in," Gemma whispered into Mick's ear.

"Are you sure?" Mick said, slightly surprised.

"Never been so sure," she told him, smiling.

Mick paid the cab fare and Gemma took Mick's hand; this time she led the way. She turned the key in the lock, her hand still in his. Pressing the dimmer switch on a touch, just enough to see the silhouette of each other, she turned to him. For a moment, both stood in silence, staring into one another's eyes. Then Mick put his hands up to her face, kissing her passionately. The taste of him lingered inside her mouth as he released himself from her, his hands resting lightly on his waist. Slowly, Gemma began to undo the buttons to his shirt, revealing the fine, dark hair on his chest. His muscled torso was hard beneath her hands, showing how fit he was.

With Mick enthusiastically following Gemma into the bedroom, she saw the point where Mick noticed the photo on the bedside cabinet, next to the elaborate antique lamp. Gemma observed Mick's tense body language as she followed his eye line to the photo by her bed. Her favourite picture of Ritchie. She knew what she had to do. Gemma picked the photo frame up and put it inside the bedside cabinet drawer, closing it gently. Reminders of Ritchie were dotted all around the house, but she didn't want him on display, and she supposed Mick didn't, either.

But she was ready.

"Sorry, I can't do this, Gemma," said Mick, bringing her train of thought crashing to a halt. "Not here, anyway."

He started to walk out of the room, ready to leave. Gemma grabbed his arm. "Mick, please don't go. I want to be with you," she told him.

"This is not the right time, Gemma," he said gently. "I can't stay here. All your memories with Ritchie are here. Here, in this bedroom. I don't want to be the person who makes love to you and all the while you're thinking of him. I wouldn't want that. I wouldn't want to bring back any painful memories for you." Mick kissed Gemma on the cheek and squeezed her shoulders.

Sadly, Gemma let him go. His last words as he left, were: "I will ring you."

Locking the door behind him, Gemma felt deflated. How could she have been so stupid? Inviting Mick into her bedroom – the bedroom where she had so many intimate moments with her husband. No wonder Mick left; he could probably feel the ghost of Ritchie all around him.

Gemma heard the sound of a message coming through on her phone. She rushed to pick it up, thinking Mick had already sent her one.

"Where are you?"

Disappointed, she tossed the phone down onto the bed. Indiana. She'd forgotten about Indiana. Tonight, Mick had stolen her attention for nearly five, blissful hours. And it had felt good.

Mick felt miserable. A wonderful evening had turned into a wretched situation that he didn't like at all. Had he been right to judge the situation as he did? Gemma seemed at ease, but he didn't. How could he feel relaxed in her bedroom, her husband's eyes spying on him from the photo by her bedside table? It may have been an overreaction on his part, but nonetheless it had felt strange.

He hoped he hadn't ruined things between them. He took out his phone and tapped the screen, writing a message:

Hi Gemma, thank you for a lovely evening, it was lovely to see you. I look forward to the next time. Mick x

His finger hovered above the blue icon to press send, but he withdrew it. No, he would give it a few days. He deleted the message. A little time apart might be what they both needed, now. He just hoped he hadn't blown it with Gemma. Only time would tell. He'd wait to see if Gemma contacted him first.

*****

Sitting numbly on her bed, Gemma sat staring at her phone, willing it to ring or ping with a message. She desperately wanted to know how Mick was feeling. She wrote out a message:

Mick, it was great seeing you tonight. I had a wonderful time. Hope you're not too upset, that wasn't my intention. I understand, fully, how you must be feeling. Would love to see you again soon. Give me a call. Love, G xx

Gemma saved the message, realising she should wait before

contacting him. Give it a few days. She didn't want to seem too needy. Tomorrow would be a new start, she decided, as she got ready for bed. It was time to put Ritchie to rest.

When she rolled over the next morning, the clock told her it was already nine thirty. How had that happened? She never usually slept past eight.

Gemma checked her phone. No missed calls, no texts. Her heart sank for a moment. Deciding that activity was the best way to keep unpleasant thoughts at bay, she pulled back the duvet and jumped out of bed. The grey tracksuit hanging in the wardrobe would be perfect for today. She felt energised wearing the baggy outfit; a run would sort her out. She hadn't been on a run for such a long while.

By the time she got back, her face was bright red, a sheen of sweat over her forehead, neck and chest. She jumped in the shower, knowing exactly what she had to do. As soon as she was dry, she would make a start.

The cardboard box she had pulled out of the attic began to fill up quickly. Gemma hadn't realised how much of Ritchie's things were still about the house. His clothes, which had still been hanging in the wardrobe, had now been removed and bagged up, ready to go to the charity shop in town. After all, most of his clothes were designer labels, the money raised would go to a good cause. This brought a smile to Gemma's face. Remembering how much Ritchie adored his designer labels. Gemma didn't feel at a loss remembering, instead, it warmed her heart. It took a few hours, altogether, and she imagined she'd missed one or two things. When she was finished, she dusted her hands off and looked around the house. There was no sign that Ritchie had lived there at all.

Gemma gasped, that couldn't be right, Ritchie had been a big part of her life and anyone who didn't understand that would not be able to find a place in hers. She put back some of the memorabilia, pictures and items they'd bought together, pieces of bric-a-brac – nothing of much value, just sentimental junk really. Gemma felt better for doing it. It was better than stripping him out of her life entirely. It felt right.

It was Ritchie's anniversary tomorrow and she'd already made plans. Maria had been kind enough to invite her over, even offered to go to the grave with her, but Gemma wanted to be alone. She could do this.

Chapter 10

December 2016

G emma woke feeling slightly lost and lonely. It was Ritchie's one year anniversary and she didn't expect to feel like this, particularly after how energetic and focused she had been the day before.

What was with anniversaries, anyway? She had never understood why the day someone died was commemorated and called an anniversary. It was hardly something to celebrate.

Gemma felt overwhelmed with shock, so much had happened in such a small amount of time.

She realised for the first time in a year, she was no longer Ritchie's wife. She was a single woman. Today wouldn't be about loss, she told herself, but would symbolise something good. Moving on with her life. She thought of Ritchie every day, and that would never change – but it didn't have to control her life. She also felt a sense of guilt. Guilt for liking Mick, guilt for inviting Mick into the home she'd shared with Ritchie, even guilt for probably not being the best wife to him. She knew she was being harsh on herself, but today there was a part of her that wanted to feel pain. She looked at her phone, which had several message alerts. The kindest contacts had let her know they were thinking of her – and her loss. She read friends' support in texts, emails and Facebook messages. Others left phone messages, which she decided she would listen to later, not wanting to engage with the phone today.

She stared at the huge helium balloon she had bought the day before. It wavered in the draught in the living room, the letter she had composed for her late husband lying close by. The letter had taken her five nights to write. It was full of memories they'd shared together; some funny, some sad. When she went to Ritchie's grave later she wanted to read the letter aloud to him, then release the balloon. Pleased she'd found a way to mark his one year anniversary, it made her feel slightly better.

After showering and getting ready, Gemma was all set to visit Ritchie's grave. It was a struggle getting the balloon in the car; it was so eager to escape, at one point she thought she was going to pop it. Why hadn't she bought a smaller one? It hadn't looked so big in the shop. Ritchie would be laughing at her for this, she realised, which brought a bittersweet smile to her face. The balloon was the brightest yellow she could find. She knew yellow represented youth, fun, joy, sunshine and other happy feelings – a cheerful and energetic colour. Perhaps unfitting for a graveyard, but she didn't want a drab colour; it was time to celebrate Ritchie's life.

Arriving at the churchyard with the balloon, letter and a single sunflower, Gemma felt grief stricken. Her tears flowed freely as she slowly walked to where Ritchie had been laid to rest. As she sat there reciting the letter to him, the grief evaporated and she began to enjoy telling Ritchie the memories she'd penned down. It was like something had lifted from her aching heart, releasing her.

By the time she came to the last three words, Gemma had been talking for forty minutes.

"I love you," she told him, kissing the sunflower and placed it down gently on Ritchie's grave. Before she walked away she tied the letter to the balloon and let it go. Watching the balloon slowly rise into the overcast sky, she felt lighter, somehow, as though she had turned a monumental corner. Gemma knew she was changed forever. Grief was never totally resolved, but she finally felt able to put her grief away for a while and deal with the present instead. Her life would carry on and a new chapter was beginning.

*****

In Gemma's absence, Indiana found herself regressing to her childhood, to when she was only five years old. Although she was small, she had known something was seriously wrong with her older sibling. Her parents lavished all their attention on Freya and neglected Indiana, and she was angry. She would act up just for them to notice her, even though it always got her in trouble. Her favourite thing of all was to sit on her daddy's knee, whilst he read her a story. How she loved that time with her father! It had meant everything to her. In her young eyes, she saw her father as a strong, articulate man who would always be there to protect her. It made her feel safe. No men in her later life had ever come close to him. Maybe that was what she was always looking for, her whole life. Someone to make her feel safe and protected.

She had even started disclosing her feelings to Jonathan King in their one-on-one therapy sessions, though she didn't know why.

What she *did* know was that she wanted to carry on. Outlining some of the feelings she'd been harbouring inside for so many years seemed to make her feel easier, more comfortable with herself. Mr King didn't interrupt her. He knew better than to interrupt Indiana Manors.

"Why did my parents love my sister more than me?" she demanded, pacing around the little office. "*I* should have been their favourite, *I* was the youngest. Doesn't the youngest usually get all the attention? I had to put a stop to it. I needed their love more than poor, pitiful Freya did. The only way to gain their attention was to pretend I was different to any other child.

"I would make Freya pay," she said, with relish. "I would do awful things to her. And I enjoyed it. Why did she have to be ill? Needing all the love, care and time from my parents, leaving me with nothing – it was so unfair! The day she died was a godsend. At least I thought it would be."

She paused for a moment, glaring out of the window.

"My parents never really recovered from Freya's death," she continued. "They still had no time for me. They thought my extreme behaviour was because I'd lost my *beloved* sister. Little did they know, I couldn't have been happier when she finally died. They didn't realise all I wanted was their attention. I mean, how could they not know?" she demanded, furious. "I was their daughter too, *I* deserved something, right? But no! Their mourning lasted the rest of their lives, until they took their last breaths on this earth. They died within six months of each other – broken hearted, people claimed. I never attended their funerals, I didn't see the point. They meant nothing to me. When I was notified that my mother had followed my father and sister, I made a decision there and then, never to be like them. Never, ever."

Jonathan King looked surprised. He had no idea Indiana was carrying all this anger around in her head. He gazed at her, remembering their exciting, passionate love making. How he wished for it to happen again, despite his professional ethics. He wouldn't make the first move, though, not while she was in such a fragile state; he would wait patiently for Indiana to show she wanted that as much as him.

Indiana continued ranting about her parents and sister, accompanied by an outburst of expletives. When her anger subsided, it was quickly replaced with hysterical laughter. Eventually, the cackling ended and she spluttered the words, "Bloody pathetic they were, both of them."

Without a second glance, Indiana got up and left without saying another word. King watched her go, making one or two notes on his clipboard. Indiana's childhood trauma was out in the open now, which must help her a little, but the negative impact of it had obviously had a much deeper impact on her. Her personality disorders were bordering on schizophrenia, exacerbated by all that anger and resentment.

He would see what the meeting next week would bring and make his decision then. Indiana was someone he knew you shouldn't mess around with, particularly given how deeply unbalanced she was, but he couldn't help it. He was going to have some fun. Jonathan King vowed he would find a different side to Indiana – it was only a matter of time.

*****

Gemma was glad to hear Indiana was still attending her counselling sessions. She always seemed so much happier after those visits. Not quite as much as she did when she returned on Saturday afternoons, but close. With her therapy sessions and medication, Indiana was sure to be on the way to feeling better. After Gemma left the house, Indiana was the one who had got in touch first. In fact, her relentless phone calls never ceased. In the end, Gemma had no option but to answer, and when she finally did, Indiana begged her to see her right away. She sounded upset – very upset.

Gemma made her way over to Indiana's. She knew Indiana had had an appointment with Jonathan King earlier in the day, so she was hoping her friend would be feeling happier than she was on the phone. Why she was so upset, Gemma didn't know. Indiana had refused to tell her anything useful on the phone.

Indiana was in remarkable form, in fact, not at all how Gemma had expected her to be. If she didn't know any better, Gemma thought she might have been seeing someone, even though Indiana told her she wasn't interested in men at the moment because she wanted to concentrate solely on becoming well. Men were simply not on the agenda – or so she said.

"How was your session today?" Gemma asked Indiana, as they both settled on the sofa.

"Good, thanks. I was able to offload some of my emotional attachment issues to Jonathan. I mean – Mr King." Indiana winced as she let Jonathan's name slip. She was allowing herself to get a little too close to the counsellor.

"That's good, then," said Gemma. "I'm glad it's going well for you."

Indiana was relieved Gemma hadn't picked up on the error she'd just made.

"Why were you so upset earlier, Indiana?"

Indiana sighed. It had been surprisingly easy to bare her soul to Jonathan, but Gemma was a different prospect. But as Indiana explained her torment, Gemma began to feel sorry for her.

Indiana felt so vulnerable, sitting on the sofa, crying into a tissue, but she was damned if she wasn't going to turn this situation to her advantage. She still had the knack of making Gemma feel bad about the way she had left. Gemma returning home had left Indiana having panic attacks, and she wanted her friend to feel bad for her. She didn't like to be left alone anymore. She'd grown to love the company, much to her own astonishment. Somehow, Vonny just wasn't enough. She pleaded with Gemma to return, but although Indiana could tell that Gemma was close to giving in, she refused, telling her that it would do Indiana no good if she succumbed to all of her wishes again.

Gemma explained to her that she needed to be back at home now, to start to lead a new life. It was time for her to move on.

Then, of course, Gemma told Indiana all about the date she'd had with Mick, describing every single detail to her. Indiana listened with interest, eyes never leaving Gemma's face. Every now and then Indiana would interrupt her, encouraging her to tell her more.

When Gemma had finished her story Indiana rested her head on her hand, fixing Gemma with a sharp stare. "Best you stay away from him, then," she said.

Gemma had merely shrugged and turned the conversation to other things. Indiana was under no illusions at all – she had made reading people her life's work, she could tell when one dowdy widow was lying to her. So, when Gemma excused herself to go to the bathroom, Indiana swiped her phone from her handbag. The daft woman hadn't even locked it. She had Mick's number saved on her own mobile and Gemma's phone back in her bag before she'd even been gone a minute.

A smile spread across Indiana's face. She remembered when they'd met Mick for the first time. She'd had her eye on him, but Gemma had taken a liking to him, too. Since it had been the first time Gemma had even looked at another guy since her husband's death, Indiana had decided to break with tradition and let him go.

But now Gemma was trying to leave her, and Indiana couldn't have that. Gemma was hers – not Mick's. She would see to it; she always did.

*****

Mick could hardly take in what Indiana was telling him. He was so sure he had misheard her, he asked her to repeat it.

"Gemma has asked me to contact you," said Indiana calmly. "She wanted to let you know that she doesn't want to see you again. She couldn't bring herself to call you directly, so she asked me to do it."

"But why? I thought we'd got on really well and our relationship was going somewhere," Mick said in amazement, something painful happening in his chest.

"Gemma has realised this is not the right time to get involved with you," Indiana told him, sounding sensitive. "You upset her walking out on her like that the other night. She figured out she's still not over Ritchie, yet. He was obviously a big part of her past and she would like him to remain a part of her future – a future without you in it. Putting his picture in a drawer was like shutting him out of her life completely."

Mick swallowed, feeling panicked. "I'm so sorry if I offended her," he said desperately. "I know Ritchie will always be part of her. I need to see her again, to explain –"

"That would not help," said Indiana quickly. "She wants to be left alone, Mick."

"I can't just give up on her," said Mick, his voice cracking with emotion.

"You have to accept the fact, Mick, that Gemma is just not interested in you. She… she never really was, it's just a fact."

"Thank you, Indiana," said Mick, his heart breaking at her cold words. "Goodbye."

Mick cut Indiana off, the phone hanging limply in his hand.

This surely can't be true, Mick said to himself.

He recalled in his mind the times he'd spent with Gemma. She had seemed so genuine – and when they had kissed...

He shook his head.

He had thought Gemma felt the same way about him as he felt about her. Her past was always going to be part of her, he understood that, he just didn't want all her memories with her husband to be on show. He couldn't cope with that.

It can't be over, it can't be, he told himself. *I don't care what Indiana says!*

He put the phone down on the desk with slightly more force than was necessary.

He needed to see her one last time and hear it first-hand. Until then he wouldn't believe it.

*****

Oliver stared into Indiana's eyes and smiled. He loved the days his mother visited, although it wasn't often enough. He hadn't quite worked out where his mother went on the other days he didn't see her, or why, but for now he was just grateful she was here. They always did great things together, like a visit to the park, going swimming or shopping. His mother always spoilt him. His fifth birthday was going to be so much fun! There would be presents and balloons and cake – everything!

Bridget, his carer, and his Granny Joan looked after him when his mother wasn't around. Bridget was very nice, and as happy as he was to be with her, he loved being with his mother more than anything.

He sometimes wondered where his father was. All the other children at school had a father. Zach's father picked him up from school every day. Zach was his best friend. His mother didn't like him having best friends, so he didn't tell her. Zach was his only friend at school. They shared all their secrets with one another.

Perhaps his father was with his mother when she wasn't with him – that's what Zach thought, anyway. Oliver often asked about his father, but his mother refused to tell him anything about him. However, she did say he loved him very much. Oliver couldn't remember one time he'd seen his father, so he knew that probably wasn't true. People who loved each other saw one another, didn't they? How could you love someone if you hadn't even seen them?

"What do you want to do today, baby?" his mother asked.

Oliver knew his mother was in a good mood when she called him `baby`. He had learned to take advantage of this fact.

"Can we go for a picnic? It's a sunny day!" Oliver jumped up and down on the spot, full of excitement.

"What a wonderful idea," cried his mother. "Yes, let's do that. The fresh air will do us good."

Oliver watched his mother prepare sandwiches, sausage rolls, crisps, apples and orange juice, his stomach rumbling in anticipation. He wanted her to hurry so he could get to the park. Zach might be there, he told him he was going to the park at the weekend, and then they could play together. Maybe his mum wouldn't mind him having a best friend so much if she met Zach in person.

When they arrived, he thought the park was busier than usual for a Saturday afternoon. The lovely sunshine had brought out lots of families to enjoy the good weather. It didn't take Oliver long to find a friend to play with. The small, brown-haired, blue-eyed boy followed Oliver everywhere, happy enough to join in with whatever game Oliver came up with. He wasn't Zach, but he'd have to do, thought Oliver. As he played, Oliver watched his mother relax on the wooden slat bench out of the corner of his eyes. He knew she was watching his every move. Why did mothers worry so much?

*****

She watched her son fondly, his blond quiff of hair blowing slightly in the warm breeze. His opaque blue eyes shone like flying saucers in the night sky. He was tall for his age, making people think he was older than his almost-five years. Indiana loved her son so much. She wished it could be different – that they could be together every day – but she knew it couldn't be. Not yet, anyway.

Oliver came bounding over to her. "Mum, I'm hungry can we have our picnic now?"

"Of course darling, jump up. We can eat our picnic here on this bench." Indiana ruffled the top of Oliver's head with her free hand.

Oliver sat down on the bench leaving just enough room between him and his mother for his lunchbox to fit, looking absolutely thrilled to be eating his picnic out in the sunshine.

"If I eat everything, Mummy, can I have an ice-cream?"

Indiana smiled. "We'll see."

Maria watched the woman and child cautiously. She couldn't believe what she'd just witnessed. The moment she had spied the all too familiar red hair cascading down her back, the thought that Indiana might be here, of all places, had taken her by surprise. But there she was, with a small child – a small child who was looking up at her in adoration. Both of them sitting on a bench, eating lunch in a park. It didn't seem real.

Who was the little boy?

The image that came into her head made her gasp. *No way!*

How on earth was she going to tell Gemma? How had Indiana been able to keep this a secret? Not only did she have an affair with Ritchie, but she had obviously had his baby, too. The resemblance to Ritchie was remarkable. Maria reckoned the boy must be five or six years old – which matched with what Gemma had told her about Indiana taking Ritchie away to Crete.

Oh God, she thought, feeling staggered. *How long did this go on for? Gemma will be devastated!*

Maria had never witnessed this side to Indiana before. It was oddly tender. She hadn't once taken her eyes off the boy in all the time Maria had been watching them. She'd only observed the cold, sombre exterior of Indiana, and the occasional bout of madness. Maria never expected Indiana to have a soft heart at all.

To anyone else, they would look like a normal mother and son on a trip to the park – except Maria knew that Indiana was not normal, far from it.

What was Indiana playing at? Maybe her acting skills were so good she'd been playing a game all along. But why? Why would you pretend you were bipolar? What possible motive could she have?

And, thought Maria, frowning, *more importantly, what did it have to do with Gemma?*

Chapter 11

Five years earlier – 2011

Joan had never been so ecstatic about anything before. This was her chance to set her son up with the perfect girl, unlike the trollop he had married.

Who did Gemma think she was, denying her access to her beloved son? She'd been so close to her only child, a mother and son with the perfect relationship. Then Gemma had come along and spoilt it all. Of course, Joan was the dutiful mother-in-law, but she detested the sight of Gemma. She never got the chance to have her Ritchie to herself anymore, because *that woman* was always around. Ritchie never left her side. He was completely under her spell – and Joan could tell, Gemma enjoyed stealing him away from their family. Eventually, the times they would meet became less and less frequent due to *her* interference.

However, Ritchie did make sure she received a phone call from him once a week – on the quiet, no doubt. Gemma would definitely have put a stop to that, if she'd known.

Ritchie sat in his car outside his parents' house, building himself up to knocking on the door. It wasn't that he didn't love his parents, and he enjoyed their company, but sometimes they made it such hard work to remain cordial.

In many ways, of course, it wasn't his mother's fault that she was the way she was. Joan had lived with her mental health issues all her life. Hiding it to others was a constant strain, though of course Ritchie and his father knew first-hand how unbalanced she could be. His long-suffering father, David, turned a blind eye to her reoccurring episodes, doing his best to conceal his wife's plight. To the outside world they were the perfect couple with an idyllic, middle class lifestyle, full of luxurious evening parties in a magnificent house, lavishly decorated.

The live-in maid, Brenda, helped endlessly, keeping the house running smoothly and in order. Because of her issues, Joan constantly needed to retire to bed, sometimes for days on end; when one of her episodes appeared it was hard on everyone. Brenda never raised an eyebrow at her employer's strange behaviour, for which Ritchie and David were both grateful. She was paid a well-deserved monthly wage, so being discrete was not a problem for her. Ritchie suspected she would have loved to have gossiped about them, but her job was worth keeping.

Joan was an attractive sixty-two year old woman. All the cosmetic surgery she'd undergone had seen to that. Her waistline would make any twenty-year old jealous. Looking immaculate to others was her primary aim. She was obsessed with the image that she – and, by extension, the rest of her family – presented to the world. She adored the attention of her female friends, the envy in their eyes. They all wanted to be just like her, which was a powerfully addictive feeling. The attention of men never really interested her. To Joan, men were only good for one thing: sex – and they didn't care where they got that from.

Her son, of course, was a different prospect altogether. Ritchie was aware that he was perfect in his mother's eyes, which he found put a tremendous amount of pressure on him. Sometimes he wondered if she loved him at all, or he was just another accessory to make her friends envy her.

It was Ritchie's afternoon off and he was already regretting the arrangement he'd made with his mother. She had strictly forbidden him to tell his wife that he was meeting her, which made him feel distinctly uncomfortable. He thought for a moment that he might tell Gemma, but decided not to in the end – it would only cause an argument. His mother and wife had never really hit it off. They seemed to clash on most things, both being headstrong women. Ritchie loved them both. He didn't want to pick sides, so he always found ways to keep both of them content. His strategies worked every time.

He looked up at his parents' house, wondering what his mother wanted this time. She only called him when she was in need of something, or having one of her episodes. Ritchie often found her in bed in a deep slumber when she'd invited him round. When she awoke, he would have to sit there and listen to his mother telling him how much she missed him and demanding how her only son could abandon her like that. He would leave full of guilt, promising more frequent visits, at which she would immediately feel better, recover enough to get out of bed and continue with her day, like nothing had happened.

This afternoon, there was a familiar black mini parked in the driveway. He knew who it belonged to, of course: Indiana Manors. Why was she here, visiting his mother?

He'd been working with Indiana for the last year and they knew each other pretty well; he'd always found her polite, a conscientious worker with a good sense of humour – just what you needed in their profession. He knew his mother had met Indiana a few times, but he hadn't realised they were on such friendly terms. His mother would often pop into his workplace unannounced to catch him for a quick coffee, or chat. She took it upon herself to become acquainted with other members of staff in his office – part of her determination to force herself into every aspect of his life. Apparently, his mother had taken a liking to her. He wished she could be like that with Gemma, but he knew that would never happen. She had never got over the fact that Ritchie could love a woman that wasn't her.

Ritchie had his own, seldom used key. Most of the time, his mother would be on the doorstep to greet him before he even had time to put the key in the lock. This time was no different.

"My dear Ritchie, how good it is to see you!" she enthused, kissing him on both cheeks and linking her arm with his. "Come into the dining room, Indiana is here." Joan led the way, practically dragging Ritchie along.

Ritchie noticed the cocktails lined up on the silver salver tray, perfectly placed in the centre of the black ash coffee table. He made his way over to Indiana, who was perched awkwardly on the edge of the leather four-seater sofa. Indiana stood up, smiling up at Ritchie. Her eyes were twinkling, making her face look radiant. Ritchie kissed her on both cheeks, as he had been brought up to, then they both sat down on the sofa while Joan brought over the cocktails. Ritchie thought his mother was being unusually extravagant. It was only three o'clock in the afternoon and the two of them had driven here – and would presumably need to drive off. Still, he sipped his cocktail like the dutiful son he was. Even his mother was indulging, though she never usually drank.

Conversation flowed freely between all three of them, with no embarrassing silences or awkward pauses. After cocktail number two, Ritchie found his tongue loosening. He hadn't felt this relaxed for a while. The more he drank, the more he found himself becoming animated by Indiana – her looks and her pleasant, slightly shy persona were quite attractive, even to a happily married man.

Ritchie felt guilty about even thinking it.

Before he knew it, his afternoon off had disappeared entirely. Where had the time gone? A glance at the clock told him it was six o'clock in the evening and the cocktails were still flowing. Ritchie still didn't know why Indiana was really there, but he was enjoying her company, nonetheless. After several cocktails, he didn't care too much. It was a pleasant way to while away the afternoon, but now he felt tired and tipsy, and he ought to go home to his wife.

Ritchie stood up, swaying slightly to his right, brushing his leg against Indiana's. They both laughed, acknowledging to each other that they'd probably had too much to drink.

"And on that note, I should probably think about leaving," said Indiana. "I have an early meeting in the morning and I want to be on top form for it."

"Well, I don't think either of you should drive after all those cocktails," said Joan, with some concern. "I know, I'll call a taxi and Ritchie can escort you home first, then carry on in the taxi."

"Are you sure?" Indiana asked. "That would be very kind of you."

"What about our cars?" Ritchie pointed out. "I'll need to get to work in the morning."

"Oh, they'll be fine on the drive, darling," said Joan, dismissing his concern out of hand. "And catching the tube and walking for once won't do you any harm."

Ritchie raised his eyebrows, surprised to see his mother so obviously in control. It was unusual. Still, at least it gave him more time with Indiana.

Not that anything will happen, he thought happily. *She's not interested in me and I'm a happily married man. She's just pleasant company.*

The taxi pulled up outside Indiana's small compact semi in what seemed like no time at all. Ritchie frowned; he hadn't wanted this car ride to end.

The taxi driver turned to look at Ritchie. "Twelve pound fifty, mate, please." He turned back around not waiting for a reply.

Ritchie fumbled in his pocket for cash.

"Would you like to come in for a coffee?" Indiana whispered in Ritchie's ear.

"Best not, I should be getting home. Thanks."

"Okay," said Indiana, looking very disappointed. "If you are sure."

He hated seeing a woman so sad – and besides, he didn't actually want to go home just now.

"Well, I don't suppose a quick coffee would hurt," he said, with a grin.

Ritchie handed the driver a twenty pound note. "Keep the change."

In return, the driver gave him a wink, which Ritchie ignored. After all, nothing was going to happen.

Indiana unlocked the door, welcoming Ritchie in with a hand gesture. Both of them stood in the kitchen in silence for a minute until Indiana spoke.

"Make yourself at home, Ritchie." Indiana pointed to the sofa. She busied herself in the kitchen making a cafetiere of coffee.

In the living room, Ritchie was grateful of the aroma of coffee hitting his nostrils. He needed to sober up; the coffee would do the trick.

However, when she brought the coffee through, she left it on the coffee table, untouched.

"Sod the coffee," she said. "Would you like a nightcap? I have brandy in the cabinet. I only use it on special occasions – and this is one."

He watched as she walked slowly over to the drinks cabinet and pulled the handle to reveal an impressive stash of alcohol.

"Maybe a small one, then," said Ritchie, feeling he ought to be polite.

Indiana poured the liquid into the brandy glasses, filling them to the top. She passed a glass to Ritchie. It seemed to him that she took her time to release it into his hand, enabling their hands to remain in contact for longer. It was probably just his imagination.

"So, why were you at my mother's today?" Ritchie asked.

"It's a mystery to me," Indiana admitted. "She asked me if I would like to view some prints of Cezanne she has in her art collection. Of course, I jumped at the chance. I visit art galleries every time I'm in a different city or country."

"Really?" he said surprised. "You don't look like the sort of person who would like art."

"What sort of person do I look like then?" she asked, throwing her head back, allowing her long, red hair to flow loosely around her shoulders.

"Well, I could say a catwalk model," said Ritchie, after a moment's thought. "No, in fact I *will* say a catwalk model."

"Oh, please! You are being so generous, Ritchie," she exclaimed playfully. "Top up?"

Indiana took his glass before he had a chance to answer and he was surprised to see he had almost drained the glass.

"What made you work in recruitment then?" Ritchie asked. "I mean, if you're so interested in art, why not look for work in a gallery?"

"I like meeting different people," she told him, with a smile. "I find people fascinating. I like nothing better than placing them in employment. It is rewarding to know you have the power to help someone."

"I think you are too nice for this job." Ritchie took the glass from her hand. Once again, he was feeling the effects of the alcohol he'd drank. "You need to be ruthless."

"I disagree," said Indiana. "You can go places if you treat people the way you would like to be treated."

"Are you treated nicely by a Mr Manors, then?" Ritchie studied her, hoping her answer would be no, all thoughts of his wife vanishing..

"I have no Mr Manors – or anyone close to being one."

Their legs touched for a second, a jolt of sexual electricity shot through Ritchie's body, making him shiver.

Indiana stood up. His eyes followed her as she slowly unzipped her dress, letting the smooth fabric slip down her inviting curves of her lean, athletic body. Gracefully, she stepped out of it, wearing nothing but her heels and her matching, black lace lingerie, leaving nothing to the imagination. Ritchie swallowed, his mouth feeling strangely dry. She sat down, crossing one lithe leg over the other, and reclaimed her glass.

The sexual tension was intoxicating. It had been fairly spicy, flirting with a colleague; it was the ultimate taboo, and the excitement it created aroused him immensely. His sex life had always been amazing with his wife, and still was, but the feeling he was experiencing was so intense he could barely contain himself.

He took Indiana's glass from her hand and put it, along with his, on the coffee table. As he leaned forward to steal a kiss, he lost his balance on legs shaky with desire, and fell over her, just catching his weight before he crushed her. Indiana laughed and responded by clasping Ritchie's shoulders, pushing him away just enough that they were face to face. Her lips met his in a succession of heated but tender kisses.

Ritchie groaned and traced the outline of her mouth with the tip of his tongue, and the hand not supporting his weight found its way down to her breast, caressing it with his palm in slow, lazy circles.

"Do you want this?" he asked, certain of the answer he would hear.

He pressed Indiana's hand on the zip of his jeans and she moaned softly, nodding her consent. Ritchie got to his feet, grabbing her hands to pull her up from the sofa.

The silence hung pleasantly between them as they stood face to face. Ritchie was mesmerised as he gazed at Indiana, waiting to see which of them would make the first move. When she reached out for him, he was relieved, certain he could not let the electricity sizzle between them for much longer without putting his hands on her.

Indiana unbuttoned his shirt, kissing his torso as she knelt down to undo the belt to his jeans. She tugged them over his hips and let them drop to his ankles. His boxers followed quickly and he braced his weight against her shoulders for a moment as he kicked them and his shoes off. Indiana moved closer, kissing his erect manhood for the briefest moment before parting her lips to take him into her warm mouth, letting him slide to the back of her throat.

Ritchie's legs shook as she let her mouth glide over him time and time again, changing the depth and the tempo constantly, leaving him utterly helpless. He felt himself grow harder and he could hear the ragged expletive and groan tumbling out of his mouth as she sucked on him. Encouraged, Indiana began to move faster and harder.

He was aware that he was quickly moving towards climax if she didn't stop soon. All too soon, she released him and got to her feet to press a passionate kiss against his mouth. He felt her teeth nipping at his lip, and the last of his self-control snapped. Ritchie stepped back just far enough to end the kiss and took her hands, pulling her towards the edge of the room. When he felt his back meet the wall, he grabbed her shoulders to spin her around, and push her up against it.

Frantic hands tore the lingerie from her body, revealing her pert bottom and breasts. Ritchie placed her hands on the wall above her head and tugged on her hips, encouraging her to brace her weight against the wall. He gently nudged at her ankles with one of his feet, urging her to part her legs.

Ritchie slid up behind her, his hands parting her thighs even more, allowing him access. He thrust into her, hard and fast, causing Indiana to cry out. He didn't leave her time to recover, plunging into her again and again, each stroke deeper and harder than the last.

Just as his breath started to catch in his throat and exhaustion began to drain the power from his legs and he was sure he could not keep up the pace for much longer, he felt Indiana's orgasm begin around him. His own discomfort was instantly forgotten and he began to thrust frantically as his own climax tore through him.

When the spasms drained away, leaving him shaken and spent and using the wall to support his weight on shaky arms, Indiana turned around. She wound her arms around his neck and pressed her face against his hot, flushed cheek before she ducked out of his embrace and grabbed him by the hand. She led the way to the bathroom and he watched as she turned on the shower, adjusted the temperature and pulled him into the cubicle with her. A cascade of warm water caressed his skin, reviving him almost instantly, and easing the exhaustion from his limbs.

It wasn't long before the warmth seeping into his skin left him energised, revived and turned on all over again. When his hands started to linger on Indiana's curves as he washed her, she smiled at him and led him out of the shower, back to the bedroom.

As she pushed him hard down onto the bed, Ritchie had no doubt that he wasn't the only one still hungry for more.

Ritchie slid into the bed beside her and turned Indiana into his arms, kissing her soundly. His hands worked over her flesh, as if trying to touch everything at once. One of his thighs nudged its way between her legs and he forced her to open them wider. He didn't wait to cup her breast and press the heel of his palm against her sensitive flesh with a firm yet gentle pressure, making her groan with pleasure. His tongue flicked in and out of her mouth, tracing the edges of her lips as his finger probed at her.

Indiana hissed appreciatively at the sensation and broke the kiss to bite at her own lip rather than his when he began to thrust deeper. Her face and chest grew hot as perspiration broke out on her skin and she tore the sheet away from them both, exposing her body to what was left of the cool air. Ritchie slid down the mattress and blazed a trail across her flesh with his hot, open mouth, sucking at her neck, her shoulder, her breast and then her hip as he made his way between her thighs.

He withdrew the finger he'd buried inside her and she opened her eyes to watch as he put his hands under her pert bottom and lowered his mouth to her groin. Her hips surged up from the bed at the first touch of his tongue against her ready flesh and she couldn't watch any longer as he sucked her into his mouth and swirled his tongue over her.

Her thighs trembled as he nibbled, sucked and licked her and Indiana grasped at the sheets as the exquisite torture went on and on, twisting the fabric in her fists. The sensations Ritchie was creating with his skilful mouth intensified. She arched her back, feeling herself growing hotter. She held her breath, her body tensing as the feeling became so acute she could barely stand it. She cried out as the first wave of her orgasm slammed through her in an explosive release that had her trembling and moaning as her insides convulsed in tight, powerful spasms.

Ritchie released her and she collapsed on to the mattress as if her bones had turned to jelly. For a moment, it went so quiet he thought she might have fallen asleep. Her breathing said otherwise, however, and he put himself firmly in the gap between her thighs.

She opened her eyes to meet his gaze when he got her attention by placing a gentle kiss on her abdomen. To his satisfaction, her eyes darkened with lust, so he balanced his weight on one arm, his eyes locked with hers as he entered her – tortuously slowly this time. Indiana grabbed at his shoulders when his weight pressed her down in to the mattress and she waited for him to slide in further. She opened her eyes again to find him watching her; he needed to see her react to his presence. He sensed it was taking every ounce of strength she had left to hold Ritchie's gaze as he slowly filled her.

When he could go no deeper and he was trembling almost as much as her from the gentle spasms of her insides clenching and unclenching around him, he placed a soft kiss against her open mouth and pulled out fast, only to plunge inside her again, this time without holding back.

Her body convulsed around him and he shut his eyes, unable to focus on anything but how tight she was and the way she felt as he thrust in and out of her.

Her body surrendered to his and when she heard him shout her name as his climax hit, the sweet sound of her name on his lips sent her crashing into her own, powerful orgasm.

*****

Ritchie woke wondering where he was, his mouth arid from the alcohol he'd consumed the previous evening. He looked at the clock on the bedside table; was it really only six hours since they had fallen asleep? He looked at Indiana, lying amongst her blood red sheets, almost comatose, naked, with her head under the pillow.

He broke into a sweat. What had he done?

He attempted to climb out the bed but a wave of nausea stopped him. Inhaling a long breath he attempted to climb out the bed once more, this time getting as far as a sitting position. He sat there for a few minutes before summoning the energy to reach his phone from the floor. Ten missed calls. Gemma, all the ten calls were from Gemma. How was he going to explain this one?

Possible stories ran around in his head. The best excuse he could come up with was to say he stayed at his mother's he could say she had felt unwell with one of her episodes, so he had put her to bed and couldn't leave her. His father wasn't around, so he had to stay, to make sure she was settled. The battery on his phone died and there was a power cut, so he couldn't even use the landline to get hold of her.

Was that good enough? Would she believe him? It would have to do.

Even with a pounding head from all his thinking, he was sure he could get out of this mess. It brought slight relief, but the guilt he felt from betraying his wife was beginning to magnify. How could he have got so intoxicated? Why was he attracted to Indiana? Why hadn't he stopped himself?

Questions were running amok like an army of ants marching home. He gathered just enough strength to get out of bed, his pounding head hurting even more, and decided that he needed water. His body was so dehydrated it was causing heart palpitations. He made his way into the dining room, briskly picking up his clothes from where they had fallen in the mad moment of lust. Modestly, he covered himself. A flashback of him pushing Indiana up against the wall came and went. A tear dropped onto his cheek. He felt nauseous again.

"No good feeling sorry about it now," Indiana said from the doorway. She had a white towel wrapped around her like a muse from a Grecian urn. "I'm not."

"It shouldn't have happened, but it did," he said heavily. "I am the one who has to live with that. I don't regret it, Indiana," he added, out of kindness. After all, he was supposed to be the older and wiser one. "I need to go."

"I'll call you a cab."

"No need, I'll walk, it will do me good. Goodbye Indiana." He kissed her on the cheek and left.

Indiana returned to her bed, the scent of Ritchie lingered in the air. She needed to grab a few more hours of sleep to be fresh for the important meeting she had to attend.

Dawn was breaking; Ritchie felt a faint sense of reassurance as his senses were slowly returning to normal. The small, twenty-four hour café had nearly put him right. Two mugs of black coffee and a bacon sandwich had done wonders. He'd managed to scoff them down while waiting for the taxi he'd booked. Now, he could see the outline of his mother's house as the taxi neared the driveway. The familiar stone lion heads erected on the wall beside the wrought iron gates gave an illusion of strength and bravery that he didn't feel.

Ritchie paid the driver and as the taxi drove off suddenly Ritchie was rooted to the spot. His car and Indiana's parked side by side. He couldn't drive yet. The squeak of the front door turned his focus to the house. His mother appeared in her dressing gown, hands on hips. She glowered at him until he walked past, not saying a word. He caught the look of elation spread across her face in the mirror and understood. She had arranged everything, intending Gemma to suffer.

Furious, Ritchie headed straight for the shower, hoping it would completely rid him of his throbbing head and ease his guilt. He needed his head to be in a better place before he returned home to Gemma. As he let the hot water cascade over him he began to feel better. He wouldn't hang around his mother and this house too long. Reminders of what happened yesterday were still raw in his mind.

Once he was dressed he retrieved his car keys from the fruit bowl on the console table in the hall.

"Goodbye, Mother," he called out, not waiting for a reply. He was out of the front door as quickly as his legs could take him. He didn't want an encounter with his mother right now; she would fire all sorts of questions at him, and the lingering suspicion that his encounter with Indiana had been a set up was still preying on his mind.

Parking the car in his own driveway, he was glad to see Gemma's car wasn't there, meaning she wasn't home and he would have more time to compose himself before he'd see her. He decided to cook a romantic meal as a sort of apology. Taking the steak out of the fridge, he glanced at the unopened bottle of wine. He poured himself a large glass and gulped it down, needing the alcohol to steady his resolve. Gemma could never know what had happened between him and Indiana. It would be too cruel – and she would leave him.

He busied himself laying the table before reaching for another glass of wine. With another sip, his nerves settled and he knew he could do it, put the affair with Indiana behind him. He felt devastated he'd undermined his relationship with Gemma with a silly one night stand. He had a genuine commitment to their relationship. He would never cheat on her again. Ever.

Chapter 12

Indiana pressed the red button on her mobile, glad the conversation she'd just had with Joan had ended. How on earth was she going to pull this one off? Being paid for her services by Joan Peacock was beginning to take its toll on her. True, the extra money she was getting enabled her to live an extravagant lifestyle, and rent a modern semi-detached house in a nice area but right now it didn't feel quite so appealing. Her feelings towards Ritchie were changing. What was intended to be just a flirtatious encounter had manifested into something much bigger – for her, at least. Her feelings had turned to love, not just lust anymore.

Joan had chosen Indiana to be the one to attempt to lure her son away from his wife. She wanted their marriage to disintegrate slowly, bit by bit, so that her detested daughter-in-law would suffer. She wanted to see the pain in Gemma's face when her husband decided to leave her.

By the time she had got in touch with Indiana, Joan had the plan already concocted in her head. She was so confident that it took no time at all to convince Indiana it would work. Ritchie would do anything she asked of him, like the dutiful son that he was. So, when Joan asked him to accompany her to Crete to view some properties, he automatically agreed. She told him it would be a financial agreement between them both: she would buy an apartment, but Ritchie would oversee the managerial side of things. She knew the extra money going into his account each month would be welcome. The only stipulation Joan made was that under no circumstances was Gemma ever to find out about their money-making scheme.

Naturally, she intended to send Indiana in her place, but he wasn't to know that.

At first, Ritchie had complained that lying about a financial arrangement was too much of a betrayal to Gemma, but Joan soon put him straight. She told him the extra income would be a bonus, especially when Gemma became pregnant.

Joan knew they were trying for a baby. She told Indiana she had found the used pregnancy test in the bin in their bathroom. She never usually visited Ritchie's home, because *that woman* didn't like her there, but this particular time she was happy that she had. The negative result was a positive for her, but she knew it wouldn't be long before Gemma became pregnant if they were trying for a baby. Joan hated the idea of Gemma bearing her a grandchild. Even Indiana was impressed by her irrational loathing.

That was where Indiana came in: she had been personally selected by Joan to replace her daughter-in-law. She would go with Ritchie to Crete, claiming Joan didn't feel up to it, giving her the opportunity to further seduce him and, if possible, become pregnant by him. If she managed this, Joan promised her she would be rich forever.

Indiana looked at herself in the mirror. What had she got herself into?

*****

Indiana met Ritchie at the airport. He looked disgruntled to see her rather than his mother. Indiana knew she'd have to alter that. If she was going to inherit big money from Joan she would have to make this work. Between them, she and Joan had managed to arrange the trip when Indiana was at her most fertile time in her monthly cycle. Indiana knew that after this, if she was only a day late with her period, it would result in a positive test, as she was as regular as clockwork each month.

"Hi, Ritchie," she said seductively.

"Hello, Indiana." Ritchie kissed her on both cheeks. The atmosphere between them was somewhat strained. After their last, highly charged, encounter they hadn't really seen much of each other. Just nodding in passing in the work place. Indiana suspected he had been avoiding her.

"We've about an hour until we board the plane. Do you fancy a drink?" Indiana smiled, which seemed to break the ice between them.

He was quiet as they walked to the bar; however it was clearly going to be more difficult than she had first thought to get him into bed again.

The airport was full of people bustling about. Walkways and seating areas were taken up by exuberant holidaymakers. They both welcomed the opportunity to sit down and have a drink.

Ritchie felt awful.

Not only was he lying to his wife again (he had told her this week was a recruitment seminar), he was also apparently spending it with the woman he had had a one night stand with. He'd beaten himself up about that betrayal ever since, swearing to himself he'd never let that happen again. He wouldn't be able to live with the guilt. Yet, here he was, alone with Indiana, and couldn't help revisiting their tryst together in his head. For a second his eyes remained on Indiana and she purposely looked away. Damn his mother and her money-making schemes!

The trip was going to be a little awkward, Ritchie sensed. He couldn't believe his mother would set him up like this. It had to be a set up. His mother had no intention of making this business trip with him. With the suspicion that she had engineered the one night stand, he had no illusions whatsoever that she had planned this whole thing. Still, he didn't want to let her down – and property they were looking at buying was a good one. He would be a fool to go home now. He was here to cement a business deal and once it was completed he would be on his way back home. He wasn't going to hang about for the whole week with Indiana as his only company.

They arrived at *Hotel Ramos*. Immediately Ritchie sensed a relaxed atmosphere. Ritchie read the brochure before entering the hotel:

Hotel Ramos is situated at close proximity to beautiful, organised beaches, making it ideal for those who want to relax on soft sands and swim in crystal-clear waters. Hotel Ramos is a cosy, hospitable hotel complex, built according to traditional Macedonian architecture, with comfortable rooms, stylish hotel facilities and first-rate services, guaranteeing guests a pleasant and comfortable stay.

Indiana was already at the reception desk, turning with one hand on her hip she looked at Ritchie.

"Come on, honey, we need to book in." She winked at Ritchie as she said it.

Ritchie was speechless.

The hotel receptionist introduced himself. "Welcome to sunny Crete, my friends. My name Stavros." He read the booking confirmation. "I have two rooms, if you want one, not a problem. You understand, my English not very good. Stavros stared at Ritchie and smiled.

"No. No, we are not together, we're colleagues nothing more. We would like the two rooms, please."

Ritchie looked at Indiana, daring her to disagree.

"Yes, the two rooms please." Indiana blushed.

Stavros studied her appreciatively; she stared back at him then looked away.

"Not a problem."

"I think I will retire to my room and freshen up," Ritchie said. Indiana nodded in agreement.

"Your rooms are 25a and 25b," Stavros told him. "Mrs Peacock insisted you have rooms close together."

Ritchie looked at Indiana, confused.

"Ah, that must be because we will be working together. I

suppose it makes sense for us to be close by." Ritchie grimaced, quickly dismissing any other connotations to his mother's request. "Shall we go?"

He couldn't wait to be alone in his apartment to contact his mother and find out what the hell she thought she was playing at. Not only had she organised things so he had to fly with Indiana, but she'd also booked adjoining rooms. And, having perused the brochure on the plane, it turned out the apartment his mother wanted to buy was part of a hotel that was already owned by a chain of hotels. He was beginning to think this trip was going to be a tremendous waste of time.

Ritchie's call went to voicemail. He didn't bother unpacking as he wasn't planning on staying that long. He fancied a swim so grabbed his towel and swimming shorts from his case and made his way down to the pool. There didn't seem to be anyone about. Even the pool loungers were empty, and the water was as still as glass. The only person around was a stunning, bikini clad young woman sitting on the edge of the pool. Her skin was soft, her body perfect.

His mouth fell open when he realised it was Indiana.

He couldn't take his eyes off her. It was as if she was magnetic to him. He considered whether to creep up on her and push her into the pool. He knew she was game for a laugh, but he wasn't sure how funny she would find it. Being pushed into cold water unexpectedly would not be anyone's idea of fun. He decided against it; instead he tiptoed up to her and put his hand over her eyes, forgetting that he was supposed to be married and not flirting with a colleague.

"Guess who?"

"Let me see," she said, playing along. "I think you could be the handsome muscular Adonis I noticed sunbathing earlier. On second thoughts, no – it must be you, Ritchie." Indiana laughed.

Ritchie removed his hands from her eyes and laughed along with her. Indiana held out her hands for Ritchie to help her stand up. Ritchie, the gentlemen that he was, took hold of them. The next thing he knew he was being pulled into the water with an enormous splash. He resurfaced, Indiana following behind. He looked at her, astonished.

"I can't believe you just did that."

Ritchie swam up to her; they were so close they were almost touching.

"Wasn't that what you were about to do to me?" Indiana said accusingly.

"No, I would never do that." Ritchie laughed. He put his hands on top of Indiana's head and pushed down hard until her head was submerged in the water. He held her head there for a few seconds then released his hand. Indiana jumped up, the smile on her face removed.

"Don't ever do that again!" she snapped, sputtering.

Indiana swam to the side of the pool starting to exit via the aluminium steps; Ritchie followed her like he was a participator in the Olympics. He grabbed Indiana's arm.

"Sorry, it was only a bit of fun," he apologised. "What's wrong?"

"My father used to do that to me," she explained angrily. "Hold my head under the water until I could barely breathe." Tears sprung into her eyes.

"I'm so sorry," he said, absolutely horrified.

"Ha-ha, got you!" Indiana laughed and jumped back into the water, swimming to the other side of the pool. She lifted herself out and sat on the edge, her legs dangling in the water.

Ritchie turned around and followed her. He couldn't believe she would joke about such a thing. He swam up to her and grabbed her legs, pulling them gently towards him. Her legs straddled around Ritchie's waist. She put her arms around his neck and kissed him softly on the lips. Ritchie pulled her off him and they both submerged into the water. Neither noticed Stavros watching them from the entrance to the bar.

Indiana clambered out of the water, a triumphant grin on her face.

"Bye for now, Ritchie," she declared. "I need some shut eye. Meet you later for dinner – eight thirty okay?"

"Yes, see you later," he said, enjoying the view as she walked gracefully away.

Ritchie was left alone in the pool. He pushed off from the side and started swimming on his back. He didn't know what was happening, but he knew that Indiana Manors excited him in a way he couldn't predict.

At eight o'clock sharp, Indiana knocked on the door of Ritchie's hotel room door. He answered it a few moments later, a pure white Egyptian towel wrapped around his waist, the rest of him still glistening from the shower.

His eyes travelled immediately to her breasts. Indiana grinned. The tight red dress with its plunging neckline had done half the work for her already.

I've got him, she said to Vonny.

Vonny giggled back. Although Indiana hadn't known her for long, every day their relationship was becoming stronger. She was beginning to love this facet of her imagination – the product of Joan's desire that she act as if she was bipolar. Initially sceptical that she could keep up the illusion, Indiana had truly begun to enjoy being a little eccentric and having a split personality. Really, the condition was so easy to impersonate she was beginning to wonder about her own sanity.

"Indiana, I thought you said to meet at eight thirty," said Ritchie, dragging his eyes away from her cleavage.

"Oh yes, I did," she said. "Just letting you know I will meet you in reception. Stavros has got us a welcome drink ready."

She looked him up and down appreciatively, remembering the muscled torso that had been laid on top of her, not so long ago. This was by far the most fun she'd ever had earning money.

"I'll just slip on something casual and meet you in ten minutes," he said.

"I'll be waiting."

Indiana walked off with a spring in her step.

Everything was going according to plan.

It was a warm humid night and Ritchie appreciated the slight breeze from the ceiling fan. He was glad of the cotton twill shorts he'd managed to secretly pack. Gemma had packed his case thinking she was packing for a spring week in the cold climate of Belgium.

Ritchie wondered if he was having a mid-life crisis early, with all the deceit he had been displaying of late. Next he would be buying a Porsche. He chuckled to himself. Maybe he would with all the extra money he'd be getting from his mother. It would serve her right for trying to set him up like this. Ritchie splashed the aftershave over his hands and patted his cheeks. He looked at his reflection in the mirror, his white Ralph Lauren polo shirt went well with the black shorts. The Nike sandals he'd bought at the airport were a pleasant relief too. He checked his wallet: one hundred Euros should be enough for dinner and drinks.

Ritchie headed downstairs. He scoured reception.

"Ms Manors is at bar," Stavros said, spotting him. "But first, have this Raki." Ritchie and Stavros clinked glasses and downed the shot in one. "Yamas."

"Yamas." Ritchie repeated. "Where is a good place to eat, Stavros?"

"I know place." Stavros wrote the name of a restaurant down on the back of a leaflet: Γατόψαρο μπιστρό.

Ritchie looked up, puzzled.

"*Catfish Bistro*, look for red sign like this," he said, tapping the name he had written in Greek with his finger. "It be light up, you enjoy."

Ritchie smiled and thanked him.

He found Indiana at the bar. The split in her dress was accentuated by the stool she was sitting on, revealing a tanned, toned leg. He walked towards her, choosing to stand rather than sit. He noticed how much Indiana had caught the sun in the short time they had been in Crete. Her nose had a hint of sunburn.

"A refill, Ms Manors?" he asked and kissed the top of her head.

"No thank you, I'm ravenous. Shall we go out to eat?" Indiana stood up, not waiting for an answer.

"Stavros has recommended a restaurant not far from here."

"Sounds good to me."

They left and as they walked through reception Stavros waved. Ritchie waved back, but Indiana ignored him, not even giving him a smile.

Stavros's advice turned out to be valuable. The food was stunning. The place was not too flash and not too expensive. It was a little gem, hidden away from the hustle and bustle of the main strip. If it hadn't been for Stavros they wouldn't have found it. They had Cuttlefish and chickpeas for starters. Indiana liked to sample different foods from different cultures, so she said, and

Ritchie didn't want to disappoint her, so he allowed her to persuade him to request the octopus for the main. It was delicious. Throughout the meal, red wine was flowing, removing the few remaining inhibitions he had.

Ritchie felt relaxed in Indiana's company. He hadn't realised how stressed he had been of late, what with work and the pressure his mother put on him. Tomorrow he would begin finding his mother an apartment – but tonight he was concentrating on Indiana. Gemma could not have been further from his mind.

The evening passed quickly; Ritchie and Indiana were enthralled in each other. Their continuous chatter and contagious laughter was the envy of all the other diners in the restaurant. It was nearly midnight when they left, strolling through the dark streets back to the hotel.

Indiana invited Ritchie back to her apartment for a nightcap. Both were already slightly tipsy from all the red wine they had consumed, but still mindful enough of their actions. Indiana poured Ritchie a gin and tonic, glad of the duty free she'd bought at the airport.

"Sorry, no ice," Indiana said as she passed the glass to Ritchie.

"That's not a problem."

Ritchie suddenly felt nervous. He really wanted to make a move on her, but he wasn't sure he was reading the right signs from Indiana. Should he chance it? No… he was sure there would be other occasions. He wasn't so bothered about rushing home to England now. In fact, he was enjoying himself so much he thought he might prolong the search for his mother's apartment.

He shrugged his shoulders, now wasn't the time to think about it.

Indiana was right in front of him, staring. "You okay, Ritchie? Only it seems you are preoccupied."

"Just thinking about work," he lied. "I think it's time I left. It's been a long day. A pleasurable one, though." Ritchie gulped his drink down, standing up sharply to make his exit.

"I've really enjoyed it," Indiana told him. "Perhaps we can do it again. Indiana kissed him on both cheeks. Goodnight, Ritchie."

She walked past him to open the door, swaying her hips provocatively.

"Goodnight, Indiana. I'm sure we can arrange something." He smiled as he left.

Fumbling in his shorts pocket he found his key card and opened his door glad he was next door to Indiana's apartment. He was shattered. He shut the door behind him, unaware Indiana was watching him.

What a missed opportunity, Indiana remarked to Vonny.

"You can't afford to miss any more opportunities like that," Vonny replied crossly.

Indiana frowned. When had she started to sound so real?

Chapter 13

Feeling refreshed from a goodnight's sleep, Ritchie went down to the hotel restaurant for breakfast. He served himself boiled eggs, toast, orange juice and coffee from the buffet, nodding to the fellow guests out of politeness, more than anything. There were only a handful of people grabbing their breakfast before time was called, ending self-service. He looked around – there was no sign of Indiana.

He planned to use the day for looking around the area for apartments for sale. Stavros had been helpful, giving him useful advice.

The phone call to his mother that morning had been a little strained. He started off the conversation to her arguing that she'd had other motives about this particular trip, which of course had made her break down, crying on the phone, asking how he could even think such a thing. Then came the long pause before saying she could feel one of her episodes about to begin. He had hung up then, imagining his father sighing and helping his hysterical wife to bed. Some days he couldn't help wondering if she did it to get her own way.

The next time he called he would explain the practicalities of having an apartment in a hotel complex where everything would be on hand. At her age, all the facilities would be ideal. However, he also intended to have a look around to see if anything else would be suitable. Finishing breakfast he went back to his apartment, changed, then set off on his exploration of the town. He felt really good today. The sun was shining in the blue cloudless sky. He thought about ringing Gemma, but decided to text her instead.

Hi babe, busy working, not much to do here apart from that. Hope you're okay. Love, me xx

No sooner had he put it down, his phone rings.

"Gemma," he answered, a smile already coming to his lips.

*****

From reception, Ritchie picked up a leaflet describing the Island and studied it carefully:

Hersonissos is 26km east of Heraklion - it has developed due to tourism and in just a few decades grown into the largest tourist resort in Crete. It has a population of 3,000 inhabitants, but this number increases each year due to the thousands of seasonal workers and the hundreds of thousands of tourists who come to this beautiful place on holiday.

"Looking very studious, Ritchie, what are you looking at?"

He looked up to see Indiana watching him. She removed her sunglasses, putting the end of the frame into her mouth.

"Just catching up on some light reading about this place," he told her. "Did you know it only has three thousand inhabitants, but due to tourism hundreds of thousands come here each summer?" he asked, pleased to be able to sound so knowledgeable.

"That sounds crazy. What are you up to today?"

"Looking for a suitable apartment for my mother, isn't that what we're both here for?" he asked, giving her a searching look.

Indiana didn't like his tone and it showed on her face. "I believe so," she said, with a shrug. "Why not view the show apartment here? They showcase it by appointments only. You could make a consultation for later this afternoon. I think it would be ideal, everything on hand for your mother."

"I did consider that," he admitted coolly. "But a look around the island will confirm whether it would be ideal or not. Catch you later."

Ritchie left Indiana standing there, open-mouthed.

Talking to Gemma had put things into perspective for Ritchie. She was missing him so much and she'd sounded so upset on the phone. Ritchie decided to forget the chemistry he had felt for Indiana. After all, it was probably nothing more than a fling – and where would that get him? He didn't like the way he was acting around Indiana and didn't understand why she had such power over him. What he did know was the way he had never stopped loving Gemma.

The quicker he got this business deal completed and got home, the better.

The streets were packed with holiday makers. Ritchie looked around. He had to admit, his mother was right. To buy an apartment in this popular tourist spot would be a money-maker. They could rent it out in the summer months and let family and friends use it in the winter, when everything shut down. Six months on, six months off.

Ritchie was beginning to feel excited about the venture. It would be nice to have a place to go to get some winter sun. Although not renowned for its warmth in the winter months, Crete would be better than the winter weather at home.

Tourists were attracted to high quality hotels, blue flag awarded beaches and amenities like water parks, golf courses, emergency medical centres, picturesque villages and historical monuments. Ritchie hadn't realised how much opportunity for tourism there was in Crete. It had it all. All he had to do was find the right apartment and they would be sitting pretty.

Later that afternoon he made his way back down to reception after drinking a beer on the balcony. He knew he'd been rude to Indiana and planned to put things right, so when he saw her standing out on the terrace, elegantly smoking a cigarette, he made his way over. He was slightly surprised to see her smoking; he hadn't realised that she did. He walked up to her and as soon as she saw him she stubbed the cigarette out.

"Smoking Ms Manors?" he said. "Tut tut."

"Only when I'm stressed," she replied tartly.

"What are you stressed about?"

"It doesn't matter," she said dismissively. "Where you off to?"

"Going to view an apartment." He couldn't help staring at her in her form fitting summer dress. She kept doing this to him, making him think of her as more than a work colleague. It was maddening.

"Shall I come with you, then?" Indiana asked.

"Guess you should, that's obviously what my mother wanted when she arranged this trip."

"If you'd rather go on your own, then go." Indiana obviously still didn't like his tone or mood. She turned to walk off, but Ritchie grabbed her arm.

"No, I'm sorry for being rude," he apologised. "Please come. I'd love your company – and your perspective."

"If you're sure." Indiana's face softened.

She obviously couldn't stay cross with him for long, he thought, trying to ignore the thrill he felt at that realisation.

"I'm sure, let's go. It's about a thirty minute walk to the Orion apartments, is that okay?"

"Fine by me. It will be a nice walk in the warm sunshine, I'll just get my sun hat, won't be long." Indiana strolled off.

Ritchie watched her walk away. He couldn't understand why he'd been so off with her. Yes, the phone call from Gemma had him feeling guilty, but it wasn't fair to take it out on her. She obviously couldn't be responsible for his mother's designs. He'd make it up to her, treat her to lunch. There had always been something between them, he felt, since day one. He remembered her first day at work, the long lasting look they'd given each other. They'd never talked about the sexual chemistry between them, just pushed it down when they were together, needing to remain professional.

Whilst he'd been daydreaming, he hadn't noticed Indiana return. Her white trilby was perched perfectly on her head and her wide brimmed sunglasses could make her pass as some sort of celebrity. Indiana linked arms with Ritchie. He felt like he had a supermodel on his arm; it made him feel good.

"Come on then, let's go."

They walked side by side on the narrow pavements, arms and hips bumping as they went. The roads in Crete didn't appear to be the safest. Several times it felt as though they were taking their life in their hands with the traffic so close to them. The number of mopeds, cyclists and cars was extraordinary.

Ritchie grabbed Indiana's arm, pulling her into the far side, away from the traffic. "Can't have you walking so close to the traffic," he said gallantly.

"Thank you. What a gentlemen." They both smiled at each other. Ritchie gave her a wink. "Wouldn't the roads be a little dangerous for your mother, Ritchie?" Indiana asked.

"I was just thinking that – great minds think alike. If she was to buy an apartment here, she wouldn't necessarily be out on the roads, though. I think she'd be a recluse in the apartment." He chortled. "I can't see my father enjoying this weather one bit. The moment the sun comes out back home he complains about it."

"Yes but even so there would be times, obviously, when she'd need to go out," Indiana argued. "Like shopping, for instance."

"True, I suppose."

Ritchie liked that Indiana had her business head on. After all, it was a big decision, picking which apartment he'd advise his mother to buy.

Arriving at the Orion apartments, first impressions were not great. The flaky paintwork was nothing less than shabby. There were smudges on the windows. A thick layer of dust had built up around the shelves in reception. The cigarette smell hit their nostrils and there was no escaping the black mould on the walls.

"I don't think we need to see any more of this place," Ritchie said, annoyed. "Let's go."

"That was a waste of time," Indiana remarked, as they left. "The *Ramos* is superior by far."

"You're right, Indiana. I think the apartment at the *Ramos* will probably be the one I'd like my mother to buy. I'll take some pictures when we get back later and e-mail them to her."

"We could still look at some others," Indiana suggested. "You don't want to rush things."

"Maybe, I'm hungry right now, though," he said. "What about you?"

Indiana smiled. "I think I could manage some lunch."

"Great, let's go."

They walked around for ten minutes before spotting a lovely Greek Taverna, its vibrant blue and white colour scheme and Greek Island atmosphere transporting them both to the heart of the Greek culture surrounding them. The ten mouth-watering dishes on offer cemented their decision to try it.

Taking a seat, they ordered courgette balls and octopus to start, followed by fish and calamari fresh from the Mediterranean and Aegean seas. They just about made room in their stomachs for the honey and Baklava for dessert. The traditional Raki and Tsipolino relaxed them both, any tension from earlier dissipating. It was so similar to the meal of the day before that it could almost have been déjà vu.

The ending, without doubt, wouldn't be. This was Indiana's second chance and this time she was going to seize it with both hands. The money was as good as hers. Relaxed and full of delicious food, they left to return to the *Ramos*, deciding on a post-dinner swim to bring them back to sobriety.

"Wait for me, then!" Indiana giggled as they hurried down the stairs.

"Come on slow coach, last one in gets to pay for dinner tonight," Ritchie teased.

Indiana sprinted past him and dived into the pool, shedding her towel as she went. "Looks like you're paying, then," Indiana shouted after resurfacing.

Ritchie followed her in as she revelled in the cold water hitting her body. He swam up to her and kissed her on the cheek. She kissed him back hard on the lips, then swam off. After a long swim she climbed up the steps, calling over her shoulder, "See you at eight in reception."

Ritchie saluted, which she took to mean that was good for him.

Indiana knew what she had to do. She had booked a hair and make-up appointment for six o'clock, giving her plenty of time to have a siesta. She needed to look her absolute best tonight to make her plan work. She would definitely get her man, there was no doubt about that.

Hotel Ramos' hairdressing salon adjoined a small selection of shops next to the foyer. Indiana took the image of a hairstyle she adored to the salon, managing to communicate what she wanted to the stylist in the small amount of Greek she knew. Fortunately, the young lady understood and, to Indiana's delight, when she looked in the mirror her hair looked identical to the picture. The loose braid it had been styled in looked almost bohemian. Her make-up was subtle, but sultry. Tripping back up to her suite, the long, black backless dress accentuated all her curves. She admired herself in the mirror. This was the longest she had ever taken to get ready for anything. Ritchie Peacock didn't stand a chance.

She smiled at the thought. Unexpectedly, she'd enjoyed the afternoon she'd spent with him. They'd had a good time – the kind of time a young couple might have on holiday. It was something she had never previously experienced, and she was rather enjoying it. She hoped Ritchie felt the same way. It would make her job simpler. Somehow, tonight she had to go one step further and entice him into another sexual tryst. Her body clock for ovulating was on schedule, so tonight would be an ideal time.

She decided to head downstairs a little early and order herself something from the bar. As she sat sipping her cocktail she smiled to herself. All the attention was on her, the men around her unable to take their eyes off her. Even women looked at her in awe.

Stavros spotted Ms Manors at the bar and thought she looked beautiful.

That Robert guy was a lucky man, he thought. He chuckled to himself, glad he wasn't on the dating scene – he was too old for that, now. He had a woman at home to keep him happy.

*****

Ritchie was looking forward to the evening. Having dinner with Indiana would be entertaining, at the very least. Lunch with her had been enjoyable and her company was making him jubilant.

His phone buzzed, announcing a text. It was from Gemma:

Hi babe, how's it going? Hope you're not working too hard. Miss you! Love, G x

He quickly texted back, as a dutiful husband would. But he wasn't as dutiful as he liked to think. His mind was already on the woman in the room next to him.

He looked at the clock: seven thirty. Half an hour to spare. He took a beer out the fridge and gulped it down, drinking it faster than he had expected. Suddenly feeling nervous, he had a shot of whisky, courtesy of the mini bar in his apartment. He checked his appearance in the wardrobe mirror.

Not bad...

His red, Ted Baker polo shirt went well with his black combats. He splashed aftershave onto his cheeks, feeling confident, and headed down to reception.

Indiana was already sitting at the bar, sipping on something fizzy.

Ritchie was taken aback by her beauty, but tried not to let it show. The vision in front of him was one of pure class. Her make-up was immaculate and the dress was a knockout. It fitted her like a second skin and seemed to go in and out in all the right places. He was aware that he was staring at her – and that he wasn't the only one. Everyone was staring at her. The bar was quite busy, particularly for the early hour. It was as if everybody had come out especially to see Indiana.

He walked slowly up to her. "I see you started before me." He nodded to the glass she had in her hand, her long, flaming red fingernails curled around it.

"My first, but not my last," she told him, elegantly finishing the white bubbly liquid. "Shall we go?"

Her lips were as red as her nails, he noted before looking up at her face. Indiana smiled, revealing a dimple on her left cheek Ritchie had never noticed before. There were many things he hadn't noticed before about Indiana Manors, but now he was noticing them all. Like the mole she had just above her right eyebrow. It was as if he were truly seeing her for the very first time.

Tonight, he would enjoy everything about her. Ever since they had checked into this hotel, he had been sexually attracted to this incredible woman. The night they'd slept together, months before had left him full of guilt, trying to erase it from his mind, but spending so much time with her in Crete had changed all that. He wanted her body and he intended to get it tonight. He could feel her boundless spirit and wanted to take a part of it for himself.

They returned to the restaurant where they had eaten earlier in the day. The waiters nodded at Ritchie in recognition. He knew what they were thinking. He was with the most beautiful woman they'd probably ever seen, and those nods were a form of congratulation. She looked fantastic and that made him – and the restaurant they had chosen to frequent – look good. Sex sells, after all. Ritchie was proud to have such a beautiful woman on his arm. They were offered a free bottle of house wine to start their meal. Ritchie looked around as they settled at their table, every man in the restaurant was sneaking hungry glances at the woman sitting with him.

Indiana was on great form, laughing, joking and even singing along with the music. She sang the first few lines of his favourite song. How she knew it, he didn't know. He took it as further proof that this was meant to be.

He hadn't taken his eyes off her since they'd met tonight, and he suspected that she knew it – and that she was enjoying it. The thought that she was in control of the situation and that she wanted him was a powerful aphrodisiac. Though they were both drinking, they were measuring themselves, wanting to maintain some control over themselves. The sexual chemistry between them was so intense they didn't want anyone or anything to get in their way.

Ritchie paid the bill, as per the bet he'd lost by the pool and together they strolled back to *Hotel Ramos* hand in hand, without stopping for a nightcap at the bar. They didn't need one. They were so intoxicated with one another they didn't need alcohol.

Indiana accepted his offer of coffee – a thinly veiled invitation to his bed – and followed him silently into his apartment, turning to face him as he closed the door behind them. Indiana wasted no time, pressing her body into his as she kissed him hard.

Ritchie grabbed her arms and swung her around to rest her back against the door. He lifted up her dress and ripped her panties off, making her gasp in surprise.

While he was occupied, Indiana reached up to undo her braid and let her hair cascade sensually around her shoulders. Ritchie dropped to his knees to begin trailing his tongue over her inner thighs. Her hands tangled in his hair at the erotic sensation and she pulled him closer, guiding him to where she wanted him. He willingly accepted, swirling his tongue around her thighs.

She began to pant and writhe, feeling like she was about to explode. Indiana pushed him away. She didn't want him to make her climax – not yet. She wanted to give him a night he would remember for the rest of his life.

He got to his feet, giving her the opportunity she'd been waiting for. Indiana quickly undressed him, yanking off his clothes so fast she almost tore them a couple of times. When they were both naked, she ducked out of his grasp when he tried to wrap her in his arms. Instead, she told him to lay down on the bed.

Ritchie did as he was told, grunting with pleasure when Indiana climbed over him and pressed her knees against his torso, resting her face on his chest. His erection lay between them, nestled in the gap between her breasts and the hard muscles of his abdomen.

Indiana began to slide her body up and down, grazing his manhood, making him jerk in response as she teased him with her careful, deliberate movements. He began to groan and she looked up at his face in time to see his perfect teeth biting down on his bottom lip. She smiled to herself, satisfied that she was driving him crazy – but she wasn't done with him yet, not by a long shot.

She wriggled down his legs, encouraging him to part his thighs so she could crawl into the gap between them. Her hand closed around his manhood and she let him see her lick her blood red lips before she lowered her head. Ritchie's cries grew louder as he began to moan in time with the tempo she was setting as she sucked on him. She felt his erection get even harder in her mouth. Indiana knew he wasn't going to be able to hold out much longer. Expertly, she flicked her tongue across his sensitive tip and he growled with desire.

Ritchie flipped Indiana onto her back beneath him, and slid down her body. Lovingly, he kissed the space between her breasts. Her skin carried the soft scent of the creamy lotion she used and she hoped the sweet, seductive scent of orchids would take him back to the first time they had made love.

He flicked his tongue over one of her nipples before taking it between his lips, letting his teeth skim against her skin. Indiana let out a shaky sigh and pushed her breast against his mouth, encouraging him to carry on. Ritchie lavished attention on one then moved to the other, his attention fixed on the way his wet mouth made her nipples glisten and her back arch towards him.

She squirmed beneath him, rolling her hips, grinding them against his torso. Ritchie didn't keep her waiting, sliding further down her body and trailing his tongue from her chest to the apex of her thighs. He slid a finger inside her. He gazed at her as she sucked air over her teeth, revelling at the feeling.

"Do you like that?" he asked softly.

Her body answered before she did. "Yes..."she purred.

"Do you want more?"

"Yes!"

Ritchie added another finger, pushing and pulling harder and faster. Indiana shuddered, feeling herself begin to throb around him again.

He sucked her into his mouth, holding her firmly as he added another finger and began to move his hand fast. Indiana's hips jerked from the bed as she started to shake and moan in response, expletives and broken syllables falling uncontrollably from her mouth.

That part of her which was still able to think doubted she was anywhere near as out of control as she'd made him earlier and she knew there was no way he'd leave her wanting this time. As if he'd read her mind, Ritchie increased the tempo, just the way she liked it, driving her to climax. Indiana let out a yell and clamped her fingers around his head, gripping him hard, as her orgasm took her. Her insides coiled tighter and tighter until the first wave crashed over and through her, sending her body into a chaotic series of jerks and shudders.

Looking very satisfied with himself, he crawled up to lay on top of her, not wanting to give her time to rest. Indiana purred at the hunger in his eyes. He couldn't keep his hands to himself. He pushed up her thighs, which she hooked around his hips, grinding her hips against his manhood to tell him how much she still wanted him. He got the message. He entered her in one, powerful motion, dragging his name from her throat; she sank her nails into him and dragged them all the way up his back to his shoulders.

He hissed in pain, arching his back to it and pushing even deeper inside her. She could tell from his expression that it had turned him on even more. He began to fuck her hard and fast, setting a punishing pace that quickly began to build tension in her abdomen again. She bucked her hips in time with him, wanting to enjoy every second of this. Ritchie bit his lip as he buried himself between her hips again and again with reckless abandon. Little electric shocks of pleasure rippled through her as she raced towards her release. His movements were becoming sloppy and she guessed that he, too was close to orgasm. Knowing that she had completely undone this strong, confident man sent her headlong into another, intense orgasm that jerked her hips and made her legs tremble with pleasure. The feel of her walls rippling around him as she screamed his name was too much for him and Ritchie exploded inside her.

They bucked against each other, riding the aftermath of their orgasms, until Ritchie collapsed onto the bed beside her, so exhausted he could barely keep his eyes open. With the last of his strength, he turned to look at Indiana, but she had already closed her eyes. She heard him sigh out of gratitude before he wrapped his arms around her and pulled her into his embrace. It wasn't long before both of them were sound asleep.

Ritchie woke to find his bed empty. Indiana had gone.

What he experienced last night was never going to happen again, he already knew that. He moved to get up, the pain in his back scorching like sunburn. He winced as he climbed out of bed. Looking in the wardrobe mirror over his left shoulder he started to tremble, three vicious fingernail marks were scored into his flesh, beginning from the back of his neck and reaching right down to his buttocks. Six deep, bloodied scratches. His mind went back to the night before, when he had been in ecstasy one moment then in pain the next. It had almost been sadistic – and he had enjoyed it.

Slowly, he made his way to the shower, the warm water soothing his pain. How was he going to hide the marks from Gemma?

"Gemma – my God, I'm sorry!" he exclaimed. "What have I done?"

Never before had he experienced sex like he had the night before. Indiana seemed insatiable. He remembered every detail of their love-making and knew he would never forget it – he never wanted to forget it. Somehow he'd have to push it to the back of his mind before returning home to Gemma. He was going to have to steer clear of Indiana for the next few days, or it would only happen again. He just couldn't help himself around her.

He would ring his mother later and get the business deal set up, he decided. He needed to return home and get back to normal, if he could. What had happened last night in his bed had been something he'd asked for – demanded, in fact. Hell, with a woman as attractive as Indiana, who wouldn't? He felt like he'd been deliberately seduced. She'd obviously wanted it to happen all along, and so had he, wife or no wife.

The soap and warm water rid him of the blood, but the deep scratches would remain for a while. He got dressed and decided to go for a walk, to get his head together before he rang his mother. Walking through reception he bumped into Stavros.

"Morning," Ritchie said, carrying on past.

"Morning, sorry to hear Ms Manors got to leave," said Stavros.

Ritchie turned on his heel, surprised. "Leave?"

"Yes, she check out," Stavros told him.

"Check out?" Ritchie was aware he was repeating Stavros's every word, but it was quite a shock.

"Emergency, she say. You not know?" Stavros looked at Ritchie, who must have looked as stunned as he felt.

"No, I didn't know," said Ritchie. "It's okay, I will ring her."

"You stay?"

"Yes, I will be staying until my business here is finished."

Ritchie walked off. He rang Indiana's number, but there was no reply. Ritchie carried on with his walk, thinking the fresh air might clear his banging head. Why Indiana had decided to leave in such a rush he didn't know; she was a complex person, that was for sure. She could be euphoric at times, then without warning, a dark mood would descend upon her. There was no mistaking that their lovemaking had been a euphoric moment. It reminded him of a feral animal.

The warm sun bearing down on his head worsened his headache. He decided to return to the *Ramos* and have a swim, hoping that would clear his head.

Almost immediately, the cool water soothed his throbbing head. He already felt better than he had when he first woke up that morning, so he decided to spend a little more time in the pool before calling his mother to get the business deal sorted. Hopefully, she would be happy with his decision. An apartment in the *Ramos* would be a great investment, particularly with Stavros watching over it. Ritchie would get the papers drawn up and prepared to sign, then he would be off home as soon as everything was sorted.

*****

Gazing out of the window of the aeroplane that was taking her back to London, Indiana knew what effect she'd had – and would likely still be having – on Ritchie Peacock. With any luck, her job was already done. He would never forget the night he had shared with her and if she was pregnant, his offspring would be her possession until it really mattered. Then, at the right time, she and Joan would use the baby to really hurt his wife.

It was a pity, really, that she hadn't been able to spend more time in Crete. Her early abandonment was all part of Joan Peacock's plan: ruin Ritchie and Gemma's marriage and then get out of there, leaving Ritchie to dwell on the night of passion they had shared. It would begin to poison his relationship with his wife, and that was exactly what Joan wanted.

Indiana frowned. She had never met anyone who hated someone quite so much as Joan hated her daughter-in-law. From what she could tell, Gemma's only transgression had been having Ritchie fall in love with her, and while she was used to undertaking work that wasn't what you might describe as fair, Indiana couldn't help feeling a little sorry for her. A mother-in-law who wanted her son's wife to disappear from their lives was nothing short of vindictive.

She would have to watch her, Indiana decided, in case she turned on her.

If Ritchie fathered a child with Indiana, Joan knew that would be the end of their marriage. Gemma would never forgive Ritchie's infidelity – Joan knew it. And she would have won.

Chapter 14

The day Indiana realised she was expecting Ritchie's baby was one of mixed emotions for her.

She'd been paid a large amount of money from Joan already to be in this position, and now if everything ran smoothly, that money would continue to be paid for a good number of years. This baby was her meal ticket. She should have been ecstatic, and yet...

She'd never had anyone in her life that relied on her before, but now she would and that was a little scary. She decided then and there she was going to do her best for this little life inside her, even if that meant going against Joan Peacock.

Indiana rubbed her hand over her stomach, though the life inside her was nothing but a bundle of cells, and whispered, "You will be loved so much, little one."

As soon as she became pregnant Indiana no longer thought of the baby as a money solution; now her focus was giving her baby the best possible life.

Indiana left Abacus recruitment agency without a word to anyone, not even Ritchie, besides handing in her resignation. A large part of her hated that she couldn't speak to him about the baby. He was such a kind, caring man and she imagined he would make a fantastic father. However, in order to keep the money she had to follow Joan's rules, and that was one of them: utter secrecy. As soon as she told her she was expecting, Joan took her to a three-bed flat away from prying eyes, about an hour's journey from her house. The rent on the flat and her house would be taken care of, courtesy of Joan, which was additional to the large sum she'd received when she'd provided proof of conception. For the duration of her pregnancy, a monthly allowance would be paid into her bank account for her to live comfortably. Nothing would be allowed to get in the way of her producing a happy, healthy child.

It was a lonely time for Indiana, with Joan as her only visitor, making the journey to check up on her once every fortnight. She also attended the ante-natal appointments with Indiana, pretending to be Indiana's mother. They were both elated when they discovered that the baby was a boy. Indiana had always dreamed about having a son, and she got the impression that Joan had only ever been used to dominating men in her lonely life. She was in no doubt that the woman thought she would be able to dominate her grandson, too. Indiana wasn't about to let her control him, however. He would grow up to be his own person.

*****

Five weeks before Indiana's due date, Joan could not be more excited. She couldn't remember feeling this level of delight since she had welcomed her beloved Ritchie into the world.

Joan had made all of the arrangements. She was going to spend the last week before Indiana's due date with her, giving her husband the excuse that she was going to stay at the apartment in Crete for a few weeks. He had seemed almost relieved when she told him, but she had ignored it. She was working towards a brighter future for her son – nothing could get in the way of that. David just didn't have the strength to do what needed to be done to remove that awful woman from Ritchie's life.

When she arrived at the flat Joan wasted no time before showing Indiana the secret contract she was required to sign. The future of her grandson was looking bright – she would see to that. He would never want for anything. The Peacock name he would inherit meant he would always have access to golden opportunities.

Reading the contract, Indiana's disappointment was obvious. "But why can't I live with him?" she asked.

"Because that's the way it has to be," said Joan sharply.

Indiana frowned at the document in her hands. "And you don't want Ritchie to know he has a son?"

"I don't want Ritchie to have anything to do with his son straight away," said Joan. "Or my plan won't work – and it has to work. It's my decision, Indiana, and you need to follow the rules. Don't forget, I can take all of this away from you." Joan wagged her finger at her.

*****

Ritchie had returned home from Crete to a warm welcome from Gemma. Almost too warm, considering what he'd done in Crete – but then, she didn't need to know that. He played along. She kissed him passionately, so he responded in the way she was expecting, taking her upstairs to tenderly make love to her. He kept his white Armani vest top on, hiding the scratches he still had on his back. Gemma questioned him about his slight suntan; he told her it was due to a few sunbed sessions. Gemma had laughed at him.

It had felt good to be back in her arms again; it felt like he'd never been away. The affair with Indiana was nearly erased from his mind – except for the night of passion they had shared together. He much preferred the normal passionate lovemaking with his wife. He knew that he needed to behave like a husband should, and if he did it wouldn't take long to get back to normal.

The only problem emerged a week after he had come home: his scars were not fading. In the end he resorted to some alternative remedies he had found online – anything was better than Gemma discovering his infidelity. To his relief, the cocoa butter he stole from his wife's bathroom cabinet seemed to do the trick, and finally the marks Indiana had left on him began to fade.

*****

Ritchie was in total shock as he read the letter his mother had sent him for the third time. His emotions ranged from anger to euphoria. He felt like screaming; he could barely contain himself.

How could his mother be so callous? He had a son. A son! And she had kept all knowledge of him secret for all these years! Not to mention that she had apparently engineered the situation so that he would choose his son – and Indiana – over Gemma. Well, whatever occurred, he wasn't going to let that happen. He would have to face up to the fact that he had betrayed his wife and admit his infidelity to her. As hard as that would be, it was just something he would have to do if he wanted little Oliver to be a part of his life – and he did. And if she chose not to stay with him, he would have to learn to live with it.

It was his indiscretion, not hers, and though he knew she would suffer because of it, he vowed he would at least be honest with her. He owed her that much.

He scowled at the letter. This was all his mother's fault.

If she hadn't interfered, none of this would have happened. Indiana wasn't to blame, that he knew. Yes, she'd played her part in the deception, but he was absolutely certain that his mother was behind it all.

His son had been well cared for, but he'd been denied a father's love – his love. And, from the look of things, the love of his mother. It must have been so hard for the little guy, only being able to see her once a week.

The letter contained a photograph and an invitation to meet little Oliver Peacock, and now he studied the picture, drinking in every detail. He was small and grinning brightly in a dinosaur t-shirt (probably his favourite, Ritchie imagined), holding an ice-cream. He had the same eyes, the same chin – even the same little quiff of blond hair. Something about him even brought to mind Ritchie's grandfather. It was extraordinary. There was really no doubt that he was his son.

He wondered what he was going to say to his son when he first set eyes on him. Would Oliver like him? Would he accept him, given that he'd never seen him before? He would love living at home with him and Gemma, Ritchie was sure of that. Organising a way of Indiana visiting regularly would be more difficult, especially when she found out about the affair.

He was getting ahead of himself though: first he had to meet him. Ritchie looked at his wristwatch and estimated the drive would take him an hour and a half if he went via the motorway – definitely the fastest route in this instance. He couldn't wait any longer to see his son – he had already missed so much. He was going to put that right, to start with.

The motorway was busy; Ritchie had taken it for granted the motorway would be clear at noon on a Friday. He hadn't calculated for this heavy traffic. It made him feel edgy. He didn't want to be late to see his son. That would not be a good way to start a relationship that should have begun years before. Cars were speeding past him in the outside lane, and he decided to follow their example. Pulling out, Ritchie took his eyes off the road for a split second to glance at the photograph on the passenger seat: his son, Oliver, making him smile.

That split-second was all it took.

He felt the jolt as the adrenaline kicked in, then everything seemed to go in slow motion. Ritchie watched in the rear view mirror as an articulated lorry rammed into the back of him. The car began to lift, and then it was spinning through the air. He couldn't move – he couldn't make a sound – all he could do was watch as the windscreen crumpled and smashed into a thousand pieces. The airbag deployed, forcing him back against the seat, but it was too late. The last thing he saw before his head hit the concrete was the photograph of his son, snatched away with the force of the impact.

Chapter 15

December 2016

Gemma got up from the sofa rather sluggishly and turned the television off.

Who on earth could be calling at this late hour? She was already ready for bed, where she would have been except her husband had yet to come home. Suspecting Ritchie had forgotten his keys again, she made her way to the front door.

"Okay love, I'm coming," she called.

When she reached the door, though, her face fell. The porch light revealed the outlines of two men, their clothes quickly resolving into the high-vis vests and tool belt of uniformed police officers.

Her first thought was that something must have happened in the street – but she quickly discarded it. Surely, she would have heard something, and anyway, didn't they only send two when they were carrying out a notification?

Gemma swallowed. Panic ran through her like lightning, making her heart pound in her chest. It was suddenly hard to breathe. She was rooted to the spot, afraid to open the door in case they were the bearers of bad news. The ring of the doorbell did nothing to bring her to her senses.

"Please – oh God. Please, not Ritchie," she breathed.

No, she told herself, *it can't be.*

Nothing had happened, she was being silly. They were probably just carrying out routine enquiries about crime in the area. Gemma opened the door.

"Evening officers," her voice cracked as she said it.

A third officer, a woman, had been hidden behind the two other officers. She stepped forward now, her soft, angular face arranged into a look of deep sympathy.

"Gemma Peacock?" she asked.

"Yes," said Gemma, dreading what was about to come.

"I'm sorry to disturb you so late, madam," said the officer. "May we come in?"

Gemma opened the door wider, holding it open until all three had made their way into the dining room.

"Have a seat, Mrs Peacock."

Gemma sank into the sofa. It didn't take them long to tell Gemma the news she'd been expecting. It had been a car accident, they said, on the motorway. She couldn't fathom why he would have been in that part of London at this time of day, but they assured her they had the right man. His wallet and ID had been recovered from the car.

The words 'pronounced dead at the scene' echoed around her

skull. She felt numb.

"You will have to make a formal identification tomorrow, but for now is there anyone we can ring for you, Mrs Peacock, so you're not alone tonight?"

"Gemma, you can call me Gemma," she said, wringing her hands. "And yes, my friend Maria, I would like her here too... Thank you."

Her ability to function lasted about as long as it took for Maria to arrive. As soon as she walked through the door, Gemma collapsed.

Chapter 16
Present day, 2017

Gemma looked at her phone. There was an incoming call from Mick. Suddenly, her face grew hot, her palms sweaty. She put the phone to her ear feeling nervous.

"Hello," she managed.

"Hi Gemma, it's good to hear your voice," said Mick. Was it her imagination, or did he sound oddly strained? "I'm returning to Australia next week, so I wondered if we could meet up one last time."

"Next week? That's sudden, isn't it?" Gemma couldn't hide the anxiety and disappointment she felt.

"There is nothing to keep me here now," he said blankly.

"Nothing?" Gemma echoed, feeling despondent.

"I came here for you, Gemma, now I'm leaving because of you," he said coldly. "Indiana filled me in on all the details – she explained why you don't care for me. I would still like to see you again before I leave, even so."

"Indiana – what do you mean Indiana?" she demanded. Gemma was dumbstruck. What was going on?

"Indiana rang me and told me to stay away from you," he said simply. "You are still grieving, which I understand. I would have given you the time you need to heal Gemma – I truly would have. Indiana said you didn't want me in your life, though, and although I found it difficult to accept after we'd grown so close, I will respect that."

"Stop right there, Mick!" Gemma interrupted. "I didn't say or feel any of those things! Indiana was lying. She had no right telling you I don't care for you. I don't know why she would even call you – or how she got your number! I thought I'd upset you after what happened between us. I wanted you to call, day after day. I suppose I'd given up thinking you still wanted me."

"I love you Gemma." The phone fell silent for a moment. "I will love you forever."

"Oh, Mick!" Gemma exclaimed. "Let's meet to talk things through. Please don't go back to Australia – I need you here – I want you here."

Gemma knew she was pleading and it was probably hopeless. Mick had already made up his mind to return to Australia and she wasn't going to be able to change that.

"Today?" Mick asked.

"Today? Yes! Yes – today."

They agreed to meet at seven o'clock that evening in Banstead, a residential village in Surrey that was about the same distance from them both.

Gemma was furious with Indiana. How dare she interfere with her personal life? It seemed like she had a vendetta against her, always trying to sabotage everything for her. This was the last time Indiana would attempt to destroy everything in Gemma's life. She didn't want Indiana in her life anymore. There was only one thing to do and Indiana wasn't going to like it.

Gemma caught the bus to Banstead, excited but nervous about meeting Mick. She knew she didn't want him to leave, but the only way to get him to stay would be engaging in some sort of commitment and she didn't know if she was ready.

A man on the other side of the bus was staring at her, his eyes not leaving her face. Gemma felt slightly uncomfortable; she hadn't wanted attention from anyone but Mick. She felt confident about the way she looked tonight, though. Her black dress with lace at the sides silhouetted her waistline and she had tied her short hair back into a neat ponytail, giving a natural, more relaxed look.

Her eyes wandered across to the man sat opposite her; he smiled, and Gemma looked away, glad her stop was next. She hoped Mick would be there ready to greet her – she didn't fancy standing alone at the bus station. Her face fell as she left the bus and couldn't see him anywhere. The man from the bus got out too, she could sense him behind her. She didn't dare look back, so she set off towards the inside of the bus station, where there were more people. The station was busy with people rushing in both directions, making her feel a little vulnerable. She walked faster. Gemma looked ahead, craning her neck as far as she could to see. Finally, she spotted the top of Mick's head, his six foot frame towering above everyone. As he neared her she waved and called out his name. The smile that spread across Mick's face melted her heart.

They embraced and Mick planted a kiss on Gemma's forehead. Gemma spied the man who was following her – he was still there, only a few feet behind her. He walked up to her and gave a cheeky wink; it was that moment where she realised who he was – Jonathan King, Indiana's counsellor.

"Hi, its Gemma, isn't it? Indiana's friend," he said. He held out his hand, Gemma shook it reluctantly.

"Yes, sorry I remember you now, Mr King. Her counsellor."

"Jonathan, please."

"Jonathan, this is Mick," Gemma said, deciding she shouldn't be rude.

"Hi Mick, nice to meet you." He shook Mick's hand.

"G'day," Mick said, in his strong Australian accent. Gemma sniggered, but covered it with a cough.

"A true Aussie, hey?"

"Yes, a true Aussie," said Mick, looking confused.

"How's Indiana now?" asked Gemma.

"I could ask you the same thing," said Mr King. "I haven't had an appointment with her for a while. Apparently she went to live with her son."

It seemed to Gemma that Jonathan was watching her, waiting for a reaction.

"Her son?" she asked, shocked. "I didn't know she had a son."

"Really, I thought you of all people would know that," he said unkindly. "However, Indiana has a talent for veiling the truth. I must go, I'm due at a meeting in ten minutes." King shook their hands and said his goodbye. He walked briskly off, leaving Gemma staring at Mick with her mouth open in surprise.

She shrugged her shoulders "She never ceases to astound me. Indiana having a child, how did she hide that from me?"

"Quite unbelievable." Mick shook his head. "Anyway, it's good to see you, Gemma. I've missed you."

"I've missed you too. You know – I did wait for your call." Gemma studied Mick's face, he was so handsome, and she felt the same attraction to him that had first sparked between them in Crete.

"Did you? That's not what Indiana told me." He rubbed the back of his neck. "It seems your Indiana is a compulsive liar, too." Mick took Gemma's hand and kissed the back of her palm. "Come on, let's go to the café over the road and sort out this mess."

The evening passed by quickly. Gemma and Mick had so much to talk about and catch up on. Gemma didn't want Mick to leave England and return to Australia. She wasn't about to tell him that, though, it wouldn't be fair. If he felt he wanted to stay and build a relationship with her, it had to be his decision.

When it came time for them to say goodbye, Mick grabbed her waist and pulled her gently close to him. He placed his hands at the side of her face, leaning in until their lips tenderly met. His lips were soft and she could smell his aftershave, making her go weak at the knees. She placed her arms around his neck, feeling his heart racing in his chest. He tasted of peppermint as she explored his mouth with her tongue. The flutter in her stomach told her she wanted all of him. She wanted Mick in her life forever.

*****

A few days later, Gemma left the house feeling optimistic. She had been looking forward to today. It was time she and Maria would have a long overdue catch up. The news about Indiana having a child would shock her, and she couldn't wait to tell her friend all about the feelings she had for Mick.

It was a beautiful Saturday and the sun was shining, the hazy blue of the morning sky warning Gemma it was going to be a hot one. She wondered why Maria wanted to meet in the park, then dismissed her confusion. It was obviously because of the mini heatwave the country was experiencing. It would be the ideal place to have a picnic, relaxing on a blanket in the sun.

Gemma chose to wear a flowered sundress; it would keep her nice and cool in the midday heat. She decided against driving as Maria was sure to have a bottle of wine packed in the picnic hamper, so instead she went for the ten o'clock bus. She began to sing to herself as she walked to the stop. Since she'd seen Mick the other night and the special kiss they'd shared she had a spring in her step, like she was walking on air. She didn't know what the outcome would be for the both of them, but she knew she wanted Mick in her life. He was a gentleman, witty, intelligent, polite and very sweet – and absolutely gorgeous, too, which didn't hurt. With those thoughts in her head she almost danced all the way to the bus stop.

The hour's journey passed by in no time and Gemma hopped off the bus and headed towards the park in high spirits, enjoying the ten minute walk in the summer sunshine. There already seemed to be a middling crowd gathering, with children playing excitedly on the soft play apparatus, mothers shouting to them to be careful, fathers reading the weekend news headlines, couples picnicking together on the benches. Gemma smiled at them, wondering why people still read newspapers when they could get all the latest news from their iPhone or Android instead.

A waving hand caught Gemma's eye, Maria was jumping up and down like a lunatic. Gemma waved back. She quickly walked over to the wooden bench where Maria was perched, ladylike. Her legs were crossed, her hand holding onto the wicker basket at her side. She looked radiant in a monochrome maxi dress, her hair hanging loosely around a white headband. Her skin was golden from this year's summer sun. Gemma kissed her on both cheeks.

"Hi babe, you look fantastic."

"You look stunning, Gemma. Glass of wine?" Maria reached into the basket removing two plastic champagne flutes and a bottle of fizzy wine. Gemma smiled to herself, she was right, Maria always thought of everything and a glass of wine would do nicely just now.

"What are you smiling about?" Maria cocked her head to one side, waiting for Gemma's reply.

"Just you – well... not just you."

"Tell me more." Maria patted the bench with her free hand for Gemma to sit down.

"Mick." Gemma said joyfully.

"Mick? Oh yes, what's been happening between you two?" Maria smiled as she passed a glass of wine to her friend and delivered a cheeky wink.

"We get on so well, Maria," Gemma told her excitedly. "It's like we've known each other all our lives. He's leaving though."

"Leaving – why?" Maria asked.

"To return to Australia," Gemma said quietly. She hoped if she said it quietly enough it wouldn't be true.

Maria gasped. "You need to stop him!"

"I can't make that decision for him," said Gemma sadly. "He needs to decide for himself."

"You're going to let him slip through your fingers, just like that," Maria clicked her fingers in protest.

"Maybe so, but Mick needs to make such an important decision on his own."

"Have you made it clear to him that you want him to stay?" Maria asked.

"Not in so many words, but my actions were pretty clear – I kissed him."

Maria clapped her hands happily. "You kissed him! You sexy minx. That's such a big step for you Gemma – but it's no good. You need to tell him how you feel." Maria shrugged her shoulders. "If he doesn't know how you feel, he's not going to stay."

"Can we change the subject?" Gemma asked sheepishly.

"Indiana has a son!" Maria blurted, as if she had been dying to say it for some time. She clapped her hands over her own mouth in shock.

"I know – but how do you know?" Gemma responded, surprised. "Jonathan King, Indiana's counsellor, told me when I bumped into him when I was with Mick."

"I saw her with her son in this park last Saturday," Maria said coyly.

"Last Saturday! And you didn't think to tell me?" Gemma snapped, irritated at Maria for not telling her sooner.

"This is why I arranged to meet you here," Maria explained. "Indiana looked like a doting mother and she looked happy. I thought perhaps she might be here again today, so you can see for yourself."

"So that's where she used to go every Saturday – to see her son," Gemma mused. "How strange, why doesn't she live with him, do you think?"

They chatted for a while, discussing Indiana and her bizarre life choices.

An hour passed and there was still no sign of Indiana and her son. It was a lovely warm summer's day just as it had been last Saturday and Maria felt sure Indiana would show up. Many families were attracted to this park because of its safety and beauty. It was surrounded by a six foot fence – no child could escape from their parents or carers, so they could run amok. A welcoming breeze softly flowed through the trees, the sun reflecting off the lake in shimmering ripples. It was a haven for ducks and noisy seagulls. Maria thought it was very picturesque. No wonder floods of families regularly engulfed the scene. A multitude of squealing and laughing youngsters were using the swings and roundabouts to their full extent. Trees, with their welcoming shade, had been planted in rows, their lush vegetation forming a gorgeous backdrop to the idyllic scene.

*****

Indiana sat her son down under the shade of the tree. They would picnic here – it was as good a spot as any. Indiana had lathered Oliver in sun cream before they left the house. His fair skin would easily burn in the midday sun. She enjoyed caring for her son. She had wondered, before he was born, whether she was cut out for motherhood, but as soon as Oliver had come along, she knew she would be the best she could be. He deserved nothing less. Somewhat to her own surprise, she'd taken to motherhood like it was the most natural thing in the world. How had her parents got it so wrong? She wondered. It was so easy!

The weekly visit to her son had now increased to twice a week, much to her delight. Joan still held the purse strings, so Indiana had no option but to obey her rules for now, but not for much longer. Soon, she would be beholden to no one; soon it would be just her and Oliver – full time. She couldn't wait for that day to come.

*****

Maria hoped that her gamble would pay off and that Indiana would bring her son to the park today. Gemma would easily recognise the boy as Ritchie's – just as she had done. Maria didn't want to be the one to break that news to Gemma. She wouldn't know where to start – and she wasn't sure Gemma would even believe her.

For the umpteenth time, Maria scanned the park. This time, she spotted Indiana and the small boy sat under the large oak tree, shielded from the hot sun. She studied them for a second. Indiana was showering love on the small boy, who was shrieking with delight at being tickled by his mother. Her unmistakeable red hair had fallen across her face as she blew raspberries on her son's stomach. They stopped to take a breath, both panting from laughing so much. Indiana poured orange juice into two glasses, handing one to her son. Hers, she downed in one.

"Maria? Maria, what are you looking at?" Gemma asked as she shook her arm, wondering why Maria was ignoring her.

"Look over there, Gemma." Maria pointed her index finger towards the oak tree at the centre of the green lawn to their right.

Gemma followed her gaze. Suddenly the blood drained from her face entirely. Indiana was sitting under the tree. There was no mistaking it was her, the flaming red hair hung loosely down her back. The small, handsome boy with her seemed to be laughing, his blond quiff of hair wavering slightly in the breeze. That's when it hit her, the striking resemblance was uncanny. There could be no question.

"Ritchie... Ritchie's a father?" Gemma stood up, feeling rather nauseous. She slowly brushed the dust from her dress. She began to take small steps down the embankment heading towards them both.

"Gemma, where are you going?" Maria asked, jumping off the bench.

"To speak to Indiana, of course."

"No! Leave it until you've had time to get over the shock," she urged.

"Get over the shock?" Gemma scoffed. "Indiana has a son fathered by my husband! I need to know if Ritchie knew. How much more has he kept from me?"

Gemma marched over towards the oak tree, furious.

Indiana's face was one of pure bewilderment. Gemma would have laughed if she hadn't been so angry. Indiana, sensing trouble, instinctively grabbed her son and placed him onto her crossed legs, pulling him close to her chest. She placed her finger upon her lip, pleading with Gemma to be quiet in front of her son. Gemma acknowledged this. What she had to say probably wasn't acceptable for a child's ears. She didn't want to upset him; none of this was his fault.

Gemma couldn't take her eyes off the little boy in Indiana's lap. It broke her heart just to look at him, but she couldn't tear her gaze away. He was identical to Ritchie in so many ways: the beautiful blue eyes, the blond hair with a little quiff at the front, even the same dimple in his cheeks. The boy gave her a warm smile.

"Hello, what's your name?" Gemma asked, almost in a whisper.

"My name is Oliver – you are not allowed to call me Olly," he told her importantly. "Some people do, but I don't like it." Oliver jumped up and down on Indiana's lap.

"Oliver stop now, sweetheart," said Indiana. "Let's go down to the play area where you can have a turn on a swing. It's not so busy now. Jump up, sweetie."

"Hooray!" he cheered. "Can you push me on the swings, Mummy? Make me go high!" He peered up at Gemma, charming in his innocence. Are you coming with us, lady?"

Gemma looked at Indiana. She nodded in agreement.

"My name is Gemma and I would love to see you on the swings. Thank you, Oliver."

"That's okay, come on then."

Indiana walked hand in hand with her son, a few paces ahead of Gemma. Gemma couldn't help but notice how much love there was between them. This new side to Indiana she was witnessing was unexpectedly heart-warming. Oddly, she reflected, she wasn't cross with Ritchie, though she probably should be. If she'd discovered the existence of Oliver earlier in the year – or even when he was alive – it might have been different, but at this present time she couldn't hate him, or his child. He was so adorable and Oliver was a part of her husband. Gemma realised she wanted to be a part of Oliver's life, if she was allowed. Ritchie would have made a fantastic father, there was no doubt about that.

Maria caught up with Gemma.

"This is why I asked you to meet me here," she whispered apologetically. "I spotted Indiana and her son here last Saturday. It's so obvious, Gemma, that he is Ritchie's son. I wanted to tell you, but – I just didn't know how. I'm sorry."

Maria hugged her. Gemma shed a few tears, which she hurriedly brushed away.

"It's okay," she said, grateful to have such a good friend. "It really isn't hurting as much as I thought it would. I knew about his betrayal and I'd already forgiven him, so the fact that his life goes on through his son is actually a comfort. I need to ask Indiana some questions, though, before we leave."

Gemma didn't want lies or half-truths anymore. She wanted it all, every single detail, and she would stay in the park with Indiana and Oliver until she got them. She was in a state of shock, but it was quickly wearing off. Now, she wanted clarity. She needed the whole story from Indiana to finally navigate her way through the last stages of grief and take the next steps to rebuilding her life without her husband.

Chapter 17

Five years earlier, 2012

Indiana's first visit to the integrated group therapy session had her feeling nervous.

It had been her decision to attend it. After years of suffering she wanted to put an end to her pain. It was time to face up to it and move on. The church hall was cosy and brightly lit, colourful tapestries hanging on the walls. It looked very inviting. She knew once she entered the white wooden door there would be no turning back. Cautiously, she opened the door. The sight that greeted her was a circle of wooden chairs in the middle of the hall. Beneath the tapestries, the white walls would usually make a place look clinical, but not here. It was quite pleasant.

Indiana noticed a middle-aged woman sitting alone, largely ignored by the others. She turned as Indiana's footsteps noisily clicked on the stone tiles, giving her the opportunity to take in her appearance. The woman had a presence that lit up the room. Her glamorous persona awed Indiana. Her hair was immaculately dressed, perfectly setting off her navy blue trouser suit. It was obviously a designer garment; it exuded affluence. A white silk blouse added a business-like flavour to the outfit.

"Young lady, take a seat," she instructed. She was obviously accustomed to giving orders.

Indiana sat down beside her.

"Joan Peacock, nice to meet you." Joan held out her hand, introducing herself.

"Indiana Manors, nice to meet you." They shook hands.

"Well, young lady, you've made the first step. It's always difficult taking the plunge," she said. "I'm a regular here. Have been for years."

"I thought I'd give it a go," Indiana said.

"That's what I like to hear," said Joan. "Now, you listen to me."

Joan talked and Indiana listened. Indiana wasn't used to someone talking at her. It was usually the other way around. Joan Peacock was of stern character. She'd had a troubled life, exactly like Indiana. She was a strong, respected member of the community, so she said, and Indiana believed her. Everyone looked up to her. She hid her illness to everyone except her husband and son. She insisted on teaching Indiana to do the same. Indiana liked the straight-talking Joan. She knew they'd get along well.

Joan observed Indiana. She would be the ideal woman to use in her plan. A beautiful, sensual woman who could act on her illness to get what she wanted. Joan couldn't believe her luck. She'd been looking for this very person for years, now she'd been delivered to her, she wasn't about to let her go.

Gemma's days were numbered.

Six more women joined the group. Indiana introduced herself and they all welcomed her with open arms. It was refreshing to be accepted so completely for something she had kept buried for so long. Indiana enjoyed being around women with the same problem. She didn't realise so many other women had suffered the same traumatic childhoods and negative behaviours. She now had a sense of belonging, something she had always lacked in her life.

The group leader encouraged the other members to introduce themselves to Indiana and tell her a little about their pasts, to explain how they had come to be at these meetings and help her understand her own motives a little better. This led to a discussion of their experiences and progress, which Indiana listened to, fascinated. She didn't want to talk this time, or take part in the activities, she just wanted to sit in and listen so she could decide whether this was the right form of therapy for her. There were a wide range of activities, and from what she could gather, they took up most of the sessions. They included skill development, problem solving and trust building exercises, among other things. Some of the women told her that these activities had changed the way they saw themselves, allowing them to examine their own personality and behaviours more clearly.

As she observed the workshop, Indiana knew she was going to benefit from these sessions and was feeling optimistic.

By the time the meeting was over, Indiana already looked up to Joan as if she was a mother figure for her. Her own mother had never been there for her, either when Freya was alive or when Freya was dead. Joan was going to look after her and she appreciated a stranger had taken to her so quickly and completely. They swapped numbers.

A few days later, Joan invited Indiana to her house to discuss how she was going to help change Indiana's life. Indiana felt intrigued as to what Joan might have planned for her. It was unusual for anyone to take this much of an interest in her welfare.

The very next morning, Indiana stood on Joan's doorstep, both curious and cautious about what the day would bring. She recognised an opportunity to enhance her dismal life when she saw it. Though she was very intelligent and had graduated with good qualifications from university, her negative behaviour had landed her in trouble and she'd found herself without a job, living in a dingy flat with very few people still willing to talk to her. She'd fallen on hard times, that was certain, but she couldn't help feeling that this meeting could change that.

"Good morning, Indiana," said Joan, opening the door.

"Morning, Joan," said Indiana. "I'm not too early, am I?"

"No, dear, you're right on time," Joan told her, ushering her inside. "I appreciate punctuality. Can I offer you a drink?"

"A coffee would be lovely, thank you," said Indiana politely.

"Just make yourself at home," said Joan, gesturing at the door to the living room.

Indiana looked around, impressed. The décor was modern and stylish, and wouldn't have looked out of place in a style magazine or a boutique hotel. It beat her little flat hands down. She looked up when Joan came back in, followed by an anonymous looking woman carrying a tray of coffee and biscotti.

She even has staff, Indiana thought, as the woman set the tray down and quietly left the room. *What luxury!*

"I could tell from the moment I met you that you are an intelligent, sophisticated woman," said Joan. "Just the person I need to help me out with a little project I've been working on. Biscotti?"

"Thank you," said Indiana, taking one. "What kind of project, may I ask?"

"A very delicate one," Joan replied. She walked to the sideboard and picked up a picture in a silver frame. "This is my wonderful son, Ritchie," she said, caressing the frame before passing it to Indiana, who smiled at it politely for a moment before handing it back. "My darling son is perfect in almost every way, but it pains me to say that he has made one mistake in his life, and that is in his choice of bride."

She put the picture down on the coffee table; Ritchie grinned out of it, blissfully unaware of the plot being formulated above him.

"He had the misfortune of being seduced by an appalling woman," Joan told her, with genuine venom. "A classless, ugly, jealous, greedy whore of a woman, who does everything she can to keep Ritchie and I apart." She dabbed dramatically at her eye with a tissue. "I had such a good relationship with my little boy, but Gemma has driven a wedge between us. That, Indiana, is where you come in."

"Me?" she asked, mystified.

What could she possibly do?

"You. You are beautiful, elegant and sophisticated – exactly the kind of woman my darling Ritchie should have married, if that awful creature hadn't got her talons into him first," said Joan. "I'm going to set you up with my son."

Indiana paused. She could see several problems with this plan already – not least the fact that 'darling Ritchie' probably loved his wife.

"You will be very well paid, of course," said Joan, and Indiana's ears pricked up. "I don't want to discuss a number outright, but let's just say, if you do this for me the way I've planned, you will never have to work a day in your life."

"I'm listening."

"First, we need to introduce the two of you, casually – at work, would be best," Joan told her. "Then you'll work on seducing him. Don't worry," she said, when Indiana made to object. "I'll help to put you in the right place at the right time. Next, we need him to get you pregnant."

Indiana felt her mouth fall open in surprise. "Pregnant?" she echoed.

"Yes, of course," said Joan, as if this was the most obvious thing in the world. "If *that woman* finds out that Ritchie has been unfaithful to her, and that the affair has resulted in a child, she won't be able to bear it. It will break her heart!" Joan crowed gleefully. "And then she will suffer as she deserves to! We," she said, with relish, "are going to drive that awful woman insane!"

Indiana listened intently to what Joan was offering. She thought about it long and hard before agreeing, but by the time they had finished their second cup of luxury coffee, she was nodding her head. Infiltrate her son's life and preying on him shouldn't be too hard. This job was a long-term one, but it would set her up for life, if Joan's plan came together.

First, she had to secure a job at Abacus Recruitment, where Ritchie worked. That would not present too much difficulty. She was good at selling herself.

There were no problems at all at the interview. The two male interviewers were impressed by Indiana's presentation on recruitment. She was offered the job there and then, with a good salary and an immediate start. Indiana let them stew for two days before she finally accepted the role.

Indiana was welcomed by all her new colleagues at Abacus Recruitment. Her first meeting went much better than expected. Not only had she made a good impression, but Ritchie Peacock had already introduced himself. She noticed the long, lingering look he sent her, but chose to shy away from it for now. She'd have her work cut out seducing him – from what her new colleagues said, he was deeply in love with his wife – but that look told her he would succumb in the end.

Joan thought it was too dangerous for Indiana to carry on meeting her at her house, so after a while they went out together after their therapy sessions in order to discuss their plans. Joan described in great depth how her plan was going to be put into action, going over and over the finer details so that nothing could go wrong.

When Indiana had been at Abacus Recruitment agency for nearly a year, it was time to move to the next phase of the plan in motion again. Joan was impatient to be rid of her daughter-in-law and it was obvious to Indiana that she hated that it was taking so long, but some things couldn't be rushed.

To speed things up, Joan invited Ritchie over to her house on his afternoon off from work, relying on Indiana to lure him into the first trap Joan had outlined. Indiana assured her she would act the part superbly. And what man would turn down Indiana? Not many! Ritchie wouldn't be able to resist, even though they both knew he was happily married and had never strayed once since he'd been with Gemma. There was always a first time for everything, which was what they were counting on. Before Ritchie arrived, Joan had laughed hysterically, over the moon that Gemma would soon be gone for good.

It couldn't have gone any smoother. Ritchie and Indiana were soon sipping cocktails, constantly smiling at each other. Joan relished every flirtatious look, making sure that she kept their glasses topped up. Soon, they were too tipsy to leave, just as she had planned. The idea she concocted about leaving their cars on the driveway worked like a charm, and as she watched Indiana and Ritchie leave together in a taxi, she hoped Indiana would succeed.

The next morning, Joan spied Ritchie getting out of the taxi, a little unsteady on his feet. She rushed to the front door hands on hips; her face looking disgusted. She never spoke a word to Ritchie as he passed her by, but it was hard to contain her delight until after Ritchie had left. Her plan was progressing in leaps and bounds. Indiana had already telephoned to inform her that the deed was done.

Joan's next priority was getting Indiana and Ritchie together again. This time it was down to Indiana to make it happen – all Joan could do was set the scene by persuading her son to accompany her to Crete and pulling out at the last minute. With any luck, a week-long business trip should be enough time for Indiana to seduce her son again and become pregnant.

Indiana soon got in touch to let her know the trip had been an out and out success. When she called again, a few weeks later, to tell Joan she was pregnant, Joan was over the moon. The news she had been waiting for, for more than a year was finally here. Indiana had done it and Joan would be eternally grateful. Her first grandchild would be well cared for. He or she would never abandon her; she'd make sure of that. When she found out she was expecting a boy, they were both ecstatic. Things were coming together. She dreamed of having a grandson, another male to dominate. It would be different this time, she vowed. She would ensure her grandson would grow to love her and devote himself to her, and she couldn't wait.

*****

The day little Oliver was born, she leaned over his cradle in the maternity suite, tears of joy in her eyes. He was so like Ritchie was when he was new born. She was sure his birth would put an end to her illness, along with Gemma's tyranny. She had never felt better. Joan decided that Indiana wouldn't tell Ritchie about his son yet. That day would come much, much later. For now, they would keep him to themselves. No one else was going to poison him against her.

When she had gleefully written Ritchie that letter, the last thing she had expected was that his wonderful life was about to end – and after all her hard work. It was all Gemma's fault!

Chapter 18

Present day, 2017

Indiana knew that the time had come to tell Gemma the truth. She owed her that much. Joan wouldn't like it, but she'd deal with her later. It was time to put things right.

"I know you have so many questions, Gemma, but this is not the right time or place," she said. "I don't want Oliver to hear what I've got to say. Can we meet later this evening, at the house?"

"Yes. Thank you, Indiana," said Gemma. "I need some answers from you."

"Come on, Mummy! Push me." Oliver climbed onto the swing, beaming angelically.

"Coming, darling," she called. "See you around eight, Gemma?"

Gemma nodded as she walked away; Indiana rushed to her son's side.

"Bye, lady!" Oliver shouted.

"Goodbye, Oliver. It was nice to meet you." Gemma waved to him. It wouldn't be the last time she saw him – she'd make sure of that.

Gemma and Maria finished their picnic together, neither one

enjoying it very much. Too much had happened. They both stayed silent. There wouldn't be anything to talk about until Gemma had visited Indiana and she had given her the truth.

Indiana was more than ready to confide to Gemma everything that had happened. It had been a long time coming, and she was tired of pretending. Defying Joan's wishes would certainly put her in jeopardy, but she had to do the right thing. The first thing she'd learnt about Joan was that crossing her would be a bad idea. She could be quite terrifying when she wanted to, and she had control over Oliver. Indiana steeled herself; this was the time to put things right. She wanted to be a normal, full-time mother to her son. She'd never liked the arrangement she'd had with Joan. Seeing Oliver only two times a week was torture.

Bridget, the live-in nanny, was clearly good at her job – and Oliver loved her – but Indiana wanted to be with her little boy. Bridget and Joan had access to her son every day and she wasn't sure about the influence they were having on him. Joan was not particularly balanced.

The knock at the door brought Indiana out of her thoughts and she rushed to the door, opening it wide – but it wasn't Gemma standing on her doorstep. It was Joan, looking particularly severe.

"Joan," said Indiana, surprised. She quickly covered it. "How nice to see you. Would you like a coffee?"

"No, I won't be staying that long," she said tartly, pushing past her. "This is going to be short and sweet. A little dickie bird told me Gemma is meeting you tonight. Now, I wonder why that is? Let me think; has it anything to do with me? I would hate to think what might happen if it was." She fixed Indiana with a penetrating stare. Indiana met her gaze, undaunted. "Remember, Indiana, I could take custody of Oliver at the click of my fingers. You cross me, and you will never see your child again."

Joan left without waiting for Indiana's reply. She slammed the door behind her and marched up the garden path. Bridget was sat in the driving seat of the car waiting for her; she could just see Oliver, asleep in the back of the car. Indiana shook her head. She should have known not to trust Bridget, she was clearly being paid to spy on her.

She paced around the living room. Joan's threats had struck a chord. The thought of losing Oliver scared the hell out of her. What had she got herself into? She glared at her own reflection in the mirror above the mantelpiece. Oliver was hers and hers to keep. Joan would have to kill her before she took her son away from her. And he deserved a mother who would do the right thing – better late than never. She would tell Gemma everything.

Maybe Gemma could help her, even get her out of this mess. Yes, despite all she had done to her, Indiana had grown to like Gemma; she had never given up on her, even though she probably should have. Ruining Gemma's life after the traumatic death of her husband had been merciless, but Indiana was not without guilt. Now Indiana just wanted the ordeal to end, to get on with her life, with her son – and allow Gemma to get on with hers.

Gemma arrived exactly at eight o'clock. Indiana smiled when she heard the bell ring. Indiana opened the door for the second time that evening. "Come on in, Gemma." Indiana gave her a genuine smile, which Gemma almost answered, despite the situation.

"Thank you." Gemma made her way into the dining room.

For the first time, the atmosphere was friendly. Gemma seemed to sense it – and that Indiana was on edge. Well, not on edge – absolutely terrified.

"Is everything okay, Indiana? Where's Oliver, in bed?" Gemma looked around as if she were half-expecting Oliver to show his face. "Where's Barney?"

"Oliver doesn't live here," Indiana explained. "And sadly I had to give Barney to a better home." Indiana gestured towards the chair signally for Gemma to sit down.

"Doesn't live here?" Gemma repeated, taking a seat. "Okay, where does he live?"

"He lives in a flat, an hour's journey from here." Indiana wasn't sure how she was going to tell Gemma everything, but she had to start somewhere.

For Oliver.

"Oh, so who's looking after him now?" Gemma looked puzzled.

"Bridget, she's the live-in nanny. I only have access to Oliver on Wednesdays and Saturdays. This might take a long time to explain, Gemma. Can you stay?"

"Of course, I'm ready to hear what you've got to say."

"Thank you," said Indiana, relieved. "I think we'll both need a drink, too. I'll put the kettle on."

It took nearly two hours to tell Gemma the story, and Indiana decided not to leave anything out. There were times when her voice broke with emotion and times when they both fell silent, needing a pause to process everything.

"Gemma, I am truly sorry," said Indiana and sat back, watching as resentment flowed across Gemma's features.

"I believe you," said Gemma, after a moment. "I'm beginning to think you're as caught up in this as Ritchie was." She shook her head, suddenly furious. "God, what have I ever done to Joan to deserve this?" she demanded.

Indiana didn't have an answer for her, so she stayed silent, simply grimacing with sympathy.

"Yes, our personalities clash, but that was due to Joan's awful behaviour," said Gemma, thinking aloud. "She's never liked me. I think she thought I wanted to steal Ritchie away from her, but I didn't at all! I just wanted a quiet life! I didn't realise she actually despised me."

Indiana shrugged helplessly. Joan had gone to great lengths to hurt Gemma and sabotage her life, even after Ritchie's death.

"I understand why you did what you did, Indiana," said Gemma, after a while. "I can't condone it, but I do understand. Joan is obvious a class A manipulator, and I can't say what I might do if I had fallen on such hard times. I forgive you."

Indiana burst into tears, surprising them both. "Th-thank you,

Gemma. Thank you."

*****

Gemma tapped loudly on the brass knocker, not caring whether the neighbours heard her. Too much had happened for her to care anymore. She deserved to be able to make a scene.

The last time she had been at this hell-hole of a house was the day of Ritchie's funeral. It had been an awful day and she had felt so vulnerable. Now, though, she had to push those thoughts aside. She needed to find strength to deal with Joan. She wasn't going to let this one go. It was time for this ridiculous farce to end.

Joan opened the door, looking perplexed when she caught sight of her daughter-in-law.

"What are you doing here?" she asked, distaste evident in her voice.

"Joan, can I come in?" Gemma asked in a confident voice.

"What do you want, Gemma?" Joan asked impatiently.

"To talk, if you could spare some of your precious time," said Gemma primly. "After all, you have been busy, lately. Particularly over the last five years."

"To talk about what?"

"Your grandson, Oliver, for one thing."

Joan's face was ashen. She was unable to disguise the shock on her face. Gemma presumed she'd never expected Indiana to tell her anything after she had threatened to take Oliver away from her. She opened the door wider, beckoning Gemma in and leading her into the study. Pictures of Ritchie were plastered all over the walls, including a hanging portrait which covered almost a whole wall. Trophies from when he was a child littered the shelves. It was like a shrine.

Gemma barely glanced around. She knew full well Joan had wanted to discompose her, and she wasn't going to let her. Not only was it time to stand up for herself, she also had people to protect, now: Indiana and her son.

"Do you know why I brought you in here, Gemma?" Joan asked vindictively.

"To upset me," said Gemma. "But I'm not the one who's upset, am I, Joan? It's you. You've been upset since the day Ritchie and I met. That was the day you lost your little boy." Gemma knew she had to try and pull some of Joan's emotional strings to enable her to end this preposterous vendetta.

"Lost my little boy?" Joan spat hysterically. "*You* stole my little boy! I tried to steal him back, but you wouldn't let him go would you, you horrible little bitch? When I lost Ritchie in that crash I knew Oliver would replace him. He won't desert me!"

"Joan, you need help – medical help," said Gemma, unswayed. "It's not right for you to ruin your grandson's life. You exploited Indiana's illness to manipulate her into doing something you couldn't. You used her to try to break Ritchie and me up, but what you didn't count on was your son doing the right thing. I didn't know about his betrayal until later, but I still found it in my heart to forgive him. I love him, Joan – that will never change." She gave Joan a look of pure disgust. "He was on his way to see his son for the first time when he died. *You* are responsible for your son's death. You and you alone. How could you do that, Joan? How could you kill your own son?"

"How dare you?" Joan screamed. "Get out! Get out! Get out!"

"It's not over yet, Joan, believe me it's not!" Gemma assured her. "*Leave Oliver alone!*"

Gemma barged past Joan and dodged around David, who had obviously heard the commotion and come to investigate, stalking out into the night. She hoped she'd done enough for Joan to see sense, she really did.

*****

The day Ritchie died, Joan was inconsolable.

The shock, pain and anger took over her whole life. It was like she was living through one of her psychotic episodes forever, instead of just the usual few weeks. She locked herself in her bedroom for days at a time, denying access to anyone – even David.

How could Gemma blame her for her own son's death? How dare *that woman* interfere?

"I will make her pay for that mistake!" Joan shrieked. "That little bitch, Indiana, too." She strode past her bewildered husband – clueless as always – and ran upstairs, slamming the bedroom door behind her.

"Oliver will be mine – always mine!"

Joan wiped furiously at her tear stained face. She had to pull herself together to prepare for what she was about to do next. She still controlled her grandson's whereabouts, and on Friday afternoon, Oliver would be at nursery for a couple of hours. That would give Joan enough time to pack a few essentials for him and whisk him away from everyone else. She'd have to worry about a long term plan later, but for the moment this would have to do.

She would make it work; no one was going to stop her.

*****

Joan didn't risk telling Bridget her plans, it would be too dangerous. She decided to wait to tell Oliver of her plans at the very last minute, so he wouldn't become too agitated. Telling him they were going to Disneyland would mute any awkward questions. Joan had already instilled in him the magic of Disneyland, in case she needed to take him away from Indiana at short notice. Gemma and Indiana were on her trail, so she had no choice. Gemma always ruined everything! Indiana wouldn't even know he was gone until Saturday morning.

Joan laughed cruelly. See how she'd cope with that!

Joan picked up Oliver from nursery like she usually did, acting as normal as possible so as not to raise any suspicion. She fastened up the seat belt of Oliver's car seat with trembling hands. What she was about to do needed nerves of steel. Now her life was centred on Oliver; Oliver would soon forget about his mother, she'd make sure of that. He would be happier with Joan, anyway.

"Granny, why are we going home in the car?" Oliver asked. "We walk home, don't we?" Oliver looked at Joan, his big blue eyes wide.

Joan hesitated knowing she had to make sure her answer wouldn't distress him. "Yes, we usually do, darling, but today I thought we'd go for a drive."

"Where to, Granny?"

"It's a surprise."

"I love surprises, Granny!" he exclaimed happily. "Is Mummy coming?" Oliver clapped his hands in excitement.

"No, Mummy's not coming," said Joan impatiently. "It isn't the day you see Mummy, is it?"

"No, but its Saturday tomorrow, that's when I see Mummy," he informed her with a note of disdain. "Can't we ring her to come?"

"No, Mummy's working sweetheart, she won't be seeing you tomorrow," Joan lied. "That's why I thought we could make this trip. See your bags there? I've packed lots of your favourite things." Joan pointed to the black holdall and Spiderman backpack on the seat beside him.

"Can I see?"

"Later, darling. Now we need to get going."

"Hooray! Hooray!" Oliver grinned at Joan as she shut the car door.

"Off we go."

Joan slowly pulled away in the car from the nursery car park, aware most of the parents had already departed, leaving her without an audience. Good. She hadn't realised how easy it would be – the first step had already been accomplished. In her mind, Joan calculated five more steps to get her and Oliver to their final destination. The ninety minute car journey to Dover would be step two. There would probably be breaks in the journey, due to the size of a four-year-old's bladder and need for food. Concentrating on the road for ninety minutes would likely prove a challenge; it had been quite some time since she had last driven so far. Even with good traffic, it would be several hours until she spied the white cliffs of Dover.

*****

Indiana walked up the path to the flat with a determined step. She had decided to visit Joan unannounced to tell her things were going to change. Gemma had already warned her off, so she was hoping Joan would be open to a new agreement. She wanted to see Oliver, too. Perhaps this would be the day she would take him home forever.

She would need to make some changes at the house, of course, like a nice garden for him to play in. She loved Oliver getting fresh air. She was sure Joan didn't spend enough time with him outdoors. She picked up the key from under the mat, glowering at the word `Welcome`. As if anyone was welcome here. She put the key in the lock, but only silence greeted her. She called out Oliver's name, but there was no answer. Bridget came hurrying out of the bedroom, duster in hand, looking vastly confused.

"What are you doing here?" she asked. "I thought you had gone with Joan and Oliver."

"Gone where? Where have Joan and Oliver gone?" Indiana's voice wavered. Surely, Joan wouldn't have abducted him – that was just too mad, even for her!

"I saw tickets for the ferry from Dover to Calais and passports," Bridget admitted. "They were half-hidden under the table mat this morning, now they've gone. I thought you must be going, too."

"Passports?" Indiana repeated, feeling breathless and panicked. "Oliver has a passport?"

She ran into Oliver's room. The wardrobe door was open and some of Oliver's clothes were strewn across the floor. Indiana looked in the small chest of drawers – it was empty. She ran into Joan's room and immediately saw that the blue suitcase that usually sat on top of the wardrobe had gone. She frantically checked Joan's wardrobe; items of clothing that she kept at the flat instead of at home had been removed from the hangers.

Indiana fell to her knees. "No, please God, no!"

Bridget rushed in, frightened. "Indiana! What's the matter?"

"She's taken Oliver! Joan's taken Oliver!"

"What?" Bridget asked.

Indiana told her, panicked, about Joan's threats.

"Oh my God!" Bridget gasped, horrified. "I'll call the police!"

"I need to call Gemma!" Indiana wailed. "I need to get her to drive to Dover. We need to catch Joan before she embarks onto the ferry with my son."

Frightened tears rolled down her face, she wiped them away with the back of her hand. She ran back into the dining room, searching in her bag for her phone. Oliver's face smiled back at her from her screen saver. She dialled Gemma's number with shaking hands.

"Gemma, its Indiana! Please, just listen! Joan has taken Oliver; they are on their way to Dover to catch the ferry to Calais. If we are quick, we might just catch them. Bridget thinks they left after Joan picked Oliver up from nursery. We are probably an hour behind them. Can we take your car to get to Dover?" she begged. "Please, Gemma – I don't know what else to do!"

"No, that can't be true," said Gemma, though Indiana thought she could already hear her grabbing her keys. "She wouldn't be so rash! I thought she'd listened to me."

"It's true, Gemma!" Indiana sobbed. "Please, we are wasting time! We need to hurry!"

"Okay, I'm leaving now – where are you?"

Indiana gave her the flat's address, feeling nauseous.

"Got it," said Gemma. "You need to call the police, Oliver could be –" She paused and Indiana's heart leapt into her mouth.

"Look, just call them."

"Bridget is. Oh, God, Gemma – if anything happens to him, I don't know what I might do."

"Indiana is on the phone to the police," said the woman Gemma presumed was Bridget when she arrived at the flat. She put her index finger to her lips, indicating that Gemma should be silent. Gemma nodded.

Indiana appeared calm talking on the phone, but Gemma imagined she was going through torture. Gemma found it difficult to comprehend what Joan had done. Abducting her grandson was a desperate, crazy thing to do. How far did Joan think she would get? Having a four year old in tow would be a burden for her, especially at her age and especially with her mental health issues. How would she look after him all by herself? From what Indiana had told her, Bridget helped her as much as possible when they were at the flat.

Gemma shook her head, appalled at her mother-in-law. She hoped Oliver was okay and not too upset by Joan's stupidity. Gemma deliberated as to whether she should contact David; at least she'd be doing something to help. She had a shrewd suspicion that he had no idea about Oliver. Her instinct told her not to, in case he called Joan to warn her that they knew. It might endanger Oliver even more.

Gemma went and sat next to Indiana, putting an arm around her shoulder and squeezing it gently. Indiana pressed the loud speaker button, so Gemma could hear the conversation. The police officer on the other end of the line was asking questions.

"Ms Manors, are their passports missing?"

"Yes," said Indiana, tearfully.

"Does Oliver have any medical conditions we should know about?"

"No – no, he's perfectly healthy."

"Are any of Oliver's belongings missing?"

"Yes – a lot of his clothes and some of his toys."

"Do you know what Oliver was wearing?"

"No, he was at nursery until four o'clock, like he usually is. Joan always picks him up."

"Can you give me a description of Oliver, Ms Manors?"

"Deep blue eyes, blond hair. He's about three foot ten inches tall and around three stone."

"Do you have a recent photograph?"

"Yes, I have a recent photograph here with me." Indiana began to weep.

"We'll send someone around with a liaison officer," said the officer. "Do not go anywhere, Ms Manors. We need you to stay put – but there are a few things you can do to help us. Make a list of all the items missing. Make sure you keep the phone lines free, in case Joan calls you. Don't touch a computer. Try to stay calm – I know this is an extraordinarily stressful situation, but the best thing you can do for Oliver is to look after yourself. Are you on your own?"

"My friend Gemma's here," she said, and Gemma gave her shoulders another squeeze.

"Good," said the officer. "We will be able to act quickly because of your quick thinking. If your child contacts you, it is important to remain calm and inquire gently as to where he is."

"He's only four years old, how is he going to contact me, for goodness' sake?" Indiana snapped. "We were going to drive down to Dover. I need to be there for my little boy."

"Ms Manors, I'm afraid you need to remain where you are. Joan Peacock may contact you – and young children have been known to use mobile phones. You never know – he might decide to call you himself. We will liaise with Canterbury and Dover Policing team. We *will* find your son."

Indiana looked at Gemma as she ended the call. Her body language told Gemma she was about to fall apart. Gemma hugged her. Gemma realised that the woman sitting next to her was nothing like the Indiana she'd first met. She was just a person who was hurting – afraid for her little boy. What had Joan done to her?

The wait was too much to bear for Indiana.

"I'll make some tea," Bridget suggested, but Indiana jumped to her feet.

"No, I will," she said. She met Bridget's eyes, wringing her hands. "I'm sorry – I just – I have to keep busy."

Bridget nodded and stepped back to allow her out of the room. When she had gone she looked at Gemma with genuine horror.

"I knew Joan was a little controlling," she said, "but I never thought she would do something like this!"

Gemma nodded, understanding. Neither had she. "That's not all she's done," she found herself saying.

Making tea for everyone took Indiana's mind off things for a few, brief minutes. At least it enabled her to breathe more easily. By the time the tea was brewed, the liaison officer had arrived, along with a greying, middle-aged man in a suit who introduced himself as Detective Inspector Ian Parker. He seemed confident and capable to Gemma, and the family liaison officer – whose name she immediately forgot – was a calming influence even on Indiana, who was just on the edge of frantic.

DI Parker, having spoken in a gentle, reassuring voice to them all and declined a cup of tea from Bridget, accessed Joan's computer. He found what he was looking for in her browser history.

"Looks like Mrs Peacock bought two tickets for a ferry from Dover to Calais three days ago, one adult and one child," he hit a few keys. "The ferry leaves this evening."

He got up from the computer chair as Indiana burst into tears.

"Don't worry, Ms Manors, I'll make some calls and liaise with the Kent Constabulary," he said, as reassuringly as he could. "They'll be waiting for Mrs Peacock when she gets to Dover. You've given us her car registration, so I'll also notify the interceptor teams in the counties between here and the port to be on the lookout for them. You're doing everything right, staying here and staying as calm as you can."

"Okay," said Indiana, tearfully. "I just want my son back."

"I understand, Ms Manors. I'm going to go make some phone calls – is there a room where I can do that in private?"

"Um, yes," said Indiana, rising from the sofa, but Bridget interrupted. "I'll show him," she said kindly. "You stay put."

Indiana sank back, trembling slightly, and Gemma put her arm around her again. To her surprise, Indiana turned and sobbed into her shoulder. Gemma rubbed her back, feeling helpless.

"It's going to be okay, Indiana."

*****

Oliver had fallen asleep, the long journey proving too much for him. Joan looked at him fondly in the rear view mirror.

"Oh, Ritchie, you are so beautiful," she said softly to herself. "I'm going to look after you now. You will be safe with me. Nothing will happen to you, I promise."

Joan glanced down at her hands on the steering wheel; they were trembling again. She realised she hadn't taken her tablets for over a week now. Though she knew with absolute certainty that she didn't really need them – of course she didn't, she was perfectly rational – she couldn't quite quiet that tiny part of her mind that felt a modicum of panic about it. Her hands were trembling every day now. She had tried her hardest not to let Oliver see, but when they had pulled over earlier for a break, he asked what was wrong.

"Why are your hands shaking, Granny? You are spilling my drink on the floor."

"The cup just slipped a little, that's all sweetheart," she told him, ruffling his fair hair. "Granny is fine."

Oliver didn't appear to be worried by it, but he certainly didn't feel sure about her answer. She had caught him watching her hands more and more as they continued south. Ritchie was wise for his years, just like his daddy. No, not Ritchie – Oliver. Joan shook herself and looked into the mirror again. It wasn't Ritchie sitting back there, though he looked so much like him.

More and more these days she was having visions of Ritchie. They would come and go, and she got confused. Ever since the day he died she'd seen him, always as a small boy – the boy she had loved more than the whole world, and who had loved her. The boy she saw now smothered her with love. He looked just like the little boy sleeping in the car seat.

Soon, Ritchie would be hers again and no one would take him away from her – no one.

Joan glanced at the time; she was making progress, another forty minutes and they would be in Dover. An hour's wait for the ferry should give them enough time for her and Ritchie to grab something to eat. She hoped they'd have fish fingers, Ritchie's favourite. She usually saved them for special occasions, and this was certainly one of those times.

She smiled, imagining how happy he would be to have his favourite food. He would ask for tomato sauce in a sachet, which he would struggle to open. Frustrated, he would bite it with his teeth and the red liquid would explode all over his mouth. She laughed aloud and the little boy in the back of the car woke with a start.

"Ha ha, Ritchie, I love you," Joan called back to him.

"My name is Oliver, Granny, not Ritchie." Oliver put his hand to his mouth stifling a yawn.

"So it is, baby, I sometimes get confused," she smiled and he smiled back.

He looked out of the window, rubbing his eyes. "Are we nearly there yet? It's nearly dark Granny."

"Not long now, darling," she replied. "Are you hungry?"

"A little, but I need to go to the toilet." With this realisation, an expression of urgency came over his face. Oliver jerked up and down in the car seat.

"Okay, I'll stop in a minute," she told him. "I could do with stretching my legs."

"Granny-old-legs!" Oliver laughed.

Joan stopped the car in a little picnic area off the hard shoulder, which was as a good a place as any to pause for a while. Oliver hurtled out the car, looking for an acceptable spot he could go to the toilet. He looked at Joan for approval, pointing to a small grass verge that was almost hidden from eyesight. Not a second after Joan nodded her consent, Oliver sped off, not wanting to wait any longer. Joan watched him like a hawk as he attempted to hide himself among the green foliage. She smiled to herself, remembering the toilet breaks of Ritchie's youth when the Peacocks had travelled to the coast for their regular seaside holiday. She had been a young woman then, with a small son, whom she adored.

Oliver came rushing back; he looked scared.

"What's the matter, poppet?" Joan asked.

"I was being brave Granny, there was a big spider right by me!" he told her. "I stood on it with my foot. When I looked at it all its legs had come off."

"Oh sweetie, you were so brave." Joan ruffled the top of his hair and gave him a big hug.

"But Mummy said I shouldn't hurt anything littler than me," Oliver said sadly, peering up into Joan's eyes.

"No you shouldn't, but sometimes you have to, so don't worry. Mummy won't mind."

"You won't tell her, will you?" he asked, sounding desperate.

"No, there's no need, it will be our secret."

"When are we going to see Mummy? I miss her."

Joan forced a smiled. "Soon, darling, very soon. Now, jump back into the car, we haven't got far to go now."

"But Granny, where are we going to sleep?"

"We can sleep on the ferry, then when we wake up there will be a big surprise."

"What surprise, Granny? Tell me!" Oliver jumped up and down with excitement.

"Tomorrow you will see," she promised, laughing. "It might be best if you try and get some more sleep. It's going to be a big day!"

"Okay, Granny I will try," she told him. "Can I speak to Mummy to tell her I'm having a surprise?"

"You can tell Mummy when we get to the ferry, darling, I promise." Oliver looked satisfied with that, giving her a half-smile.

He hopped back into the car, content to be getting nearer to his surprise. It wasn't long before he fell asleep again. Joan relaxed, knowing he'd probably be asleep for the rest of the journey. She couldn't wait to be at the hotel and take him to Disneyland. Oliver was going to love it. It felt wonderful to know that Oliver didn't seem to mind just being in her company. He was probably used to it by now. She had made every effort to be at the flat with him as often as she could. David never asked questions about where she went; he chose to ignore her, as he always had. Seeing his fancy woman was far more interesting than what was going on in his wife's life.

Sometimes she wondered why she had married such a dull bore – and how he had managed to produce such a handsome, bright son and grandson.

At long last, the white cliffs of Dover were in Joan's range of vision. As she neared the port, a glimpse of flashing blue lights from stationary cars made her panic. They were ranged around the slipway that led towards the port. She calmed herself, thinking there must have been some sort of accident. Surely, the police wouldn't be looking for her, would they? With a small degree of paranoia she veered off the route into the port. What was she to do now? She stopped driving to think, pulling over into a layby. Her phone vibrated loudly in her bag and she checked it, feeling anxious. David. What did he want? Something inside her head told her to answer it.

"David, is everything okay?"

"Joan, listen to me, what you are doing is wrong. The police are here. They know everything. Joan, you need to hand over Oliver to them. They are waiting for you at Dover. You can't put Oliver through this. He loves Indiana and he loves you, too, darling – but you've got to do the right thing!"

The urgency in his voice made Joan end the call. That conversation constituted the most words her husband had spoken to her for a while, and it rattled her. Her hands shook as she turned the key in the ignition. She turned to look at Oliver. He was still asleep.

She sped off and headed for the cliffs that were beckoning her. No one was going to take her Ritchie away from her; she needed to be with him forever. She'd replayed those words so many times in her head, it must be true. Why couldn't they understand that? If she couldn't be with Ritchie in this life then it would be in another.

As they raced towards the coast, blue flashing lights appeared in her rear view mirror and the sound of sirens broke the silence.

Oliver woke up with fright and began to cry. Joan parked up, scrambled out the car and ran round to the passenger door. She undid Oliver's seat belt then lifted him out of the car.

"Don't be scared, Ritchie. Everything is going to be alright. You believe Granny, don't you?"

"I'm Oliver, Granny."

Oliver squeezed his hands tighter around Joan's neck, wondering what was going on. Apart from the flashing of blue lights it was so dark. He could make out the sea beyond the cliffs, but it seemed a long way below him. Granny was carrying him, but she was struggling to hold onto him. She seemed like she was in an awful hurry. She placed him down on the grass, which suddenly ended in front of him. It looked like he could step off the edge of the earth. Frightened, he looked behind him. Police cars lined the road behind his granny's car, and police men and women were getting out of their cars. One of them, a man, was talking funny into a thing in his hand; it was loud – very loud.

He held tightly onto his granny's hand. He could sense something bad was happening. He really wanted his mummy, but she wasn't here and she always told him when something bad was happening he needed to think of her. So he did.

"Put the boy down, Joan! He will be safe with us."

The line of police officers slowly advanced towards them. Joan's heart hammered in her chest.

"No! Ritchie is safe with me! We will always be together."

Joan walked closer to the edge of the cliff, taking Oliver with her.

"It's Oliver, Joan, your grandson."

"No it's not, its Ritchie... its Ritchie! Do you hear me?" shouted Joan.

"Okay, Joan, its Ritchie," the man with the megaphone said. "You need to let Ritchie go, you are upsetting him. You don't want to do that, Joan – do you? Ritchie is scared. Sam is going to walk up to you, Joan. Is that okay? She just wants to talk to you."

Samantha Featherstone was an experienced negotiator. At thirty nine years of age she'd talked down five similar cases. Sam was a tall, slim brunette with dark brown eyes. Having studied psychology and human behaviour for years, she had a variety of techniques at her fingertips. She turned to Sergeant Brookes, who lowered the megaphone and nodded his assent. Samantha walked slowly up to Joan so she could get in earshot without startling her. When she saw her, Joan stared at her coldly.

Sam smiled, and instantly she gained a reaction from Joan: the corners of her mouth were turning up; Sam knew this could mean either a grimace of disgust or a smile of pleasure. Sam had to act fast if she was going to be able to seize Oliver from her.

"Joan, how old is Ritchie?" Sam winked at Oliver, trying to relax him a little. She didn't want him to say anything just yet, in case it made things worse.

"Ritchie is four, nearly five." Joan ruffled Oliver's hair with her free hand.

"Where are you taking Ritchie, Joan?"

"To Disneyland."

"To Disneyland, Granny? Is that my surprise?" Delighted, Oliver pulled his hand away from Joan's and put both arms around her waist instead. "I love you, Granny."

"I love you too, sweetheart. Now let go and hold my hand." Joan edged one step backwards towards the edge, tugging Oliver with her.

"Joan, wait," Sam said, thinking quickly. "Why don't you bring Ritchie closer to me? He might like a ride in a police car before he goes to Disneyland." Sam knew she didn't have much more time to play with. Two more steps and Joan would be over the cliff. "Would you like that, Ritchie?"

"I'm Oliver." He tugged Joan's hand, trying to get out of her tight grasp. "Can I, Granny? Can I? I can tell Zach that I went in a real police car!"

Sam winced, hoping Oliver hadn't put himself into jeopardy. She had to act.

"Joan," she began gently. "That's Oliver, your grandson. Ritchie died nearly two years ago… remember? Oliver needs to be with his mother. Joan, please bring Oliver to me."

Sam held her breath, watching the other woman's face. She was on the edge – in more ways than one. Finally, she nodded, and Sam let out a small sigh of relief.

Joan's tears fell as she released Oliver's hand. "Goodbye sweetie, Granny loves you. The police lady will take you to Mummy."

"What about you, Granny?" he asked, looking up at her.

"I will be fine, I'll come along later."

That simple statement set off warning bells in Sam's head, but it was too late – her priority was the boy, and she couldn't get him to safety and stop the woman going over. There wouldn't be time. Sam held out her hand for Oliver, who ran to her. She held him tightly, making sure his face was turned away from his grandmother as she took a final step forward and vanished from the edge of the cliff.

She closed her eyes. Oliver was safe, but she couldn't help but feel it was only half a victory; this time, she'd failed.

*****

Indiana paced the room.

Waiting was agony. The hours since she had realised Oliver and Joan were missing had been torture. It was tearing her apart. She couldn't imagine life without Oliver; her life had only really begun the day he was born. She didn't want the loneliness and regret she had lived with through her childhood for Oliver. In the two days a week she was allowed to be with him she made every second count, doing her best to ensure Oliver was loved.

He was going to have good childhood memories to relive, she would make sure of it.

DI Parker strode in, making her jump. She glanced at Gemma, who got up from the sofa, hopefully.

"Indiana, we have someone on the phone for you," he said, grinning widely. Indiana's heart leapt.

"It's Oliver." Ian passed her the phone with a huge smile on his face. "Try to keep calm, Indiana, Oliver just needs his mummy and he'll expect you to be the same as you normally are," Ian whispered.

Indiana nodded in agreement, trying to calm her breathing. "Hello, baby. Are you okay, darling?"

"Hello, Mummy!" Oliver said, as soon as he heard her voice. "I'm having a ride in a police car with a proper policeman!"

Indiana closed her eyes, relief flooding through her.

"Are you? How fantastic is that?" she managed, deliriously happy to hear his voice.

"Mummy, I was going to Disneyland!" he told her, a little breathlessly. "It was a surprise! Granny was going to take me."

"I know, baby, but you are coming home now to Mummy," she said, sounding remarkably calm. "I will take you there one day, I promise." Indiana began to cry. She had come so close to never seeing him again.

"Mummy, are you crying?"

"No – no, darling, I'm not crying," she said. "I'm so happy that you're coming home."

"Me too!" said Oliver, reassured. "The policeman is going to put the flashing lights on now, Mummy."

"Wow, that is exciting!" Indiana told him. "I need to put the phone down now, darling. I will see you soon. Mummy loves you."

"Love you too! Bye Mummy."

The phone went dead. Indiana collapsed to the floor, sobbing uncontrollably. She felt Gemma kneel on one side of her and Bridget on the other, and she clung to them as DI Parker made uncomfortable sounds at the family liaison to make another cup of strong, sweet tea.

It took some time, but when Indiana had calmed down, DI Parker related the details of what had happened.

By the time he had finished, Indiana, Gemma and Bridget were all sitting in stunned silence on the sofa, hands pressed to their mouths.

It was nearly midnight and Gemma was making sandwiches.

It seemed silly, to do such an ordinary activity on an evening as extraordinary as this, but after the tension had finally left them and Indiana had talked and sobbed all of the stress at nearly losing her son away, the feeling had stolen over Gemma that people could not exist on tea and horror alone, so she had slunk off to the kitchen.

As she worked, she marvelled at the lengths Joan had taken to destroy her and Ritchie's marriage. If Ritchie hadn't died prematurely she wondered what might have happened. She liked to think they would have been able to conquer any obstacles in their lives, but after everything that Joan had made happen she wasn't so sure. It wasn't worth dwelling on, however, as now she would never know.

They had just finished their sandwiches when a soft knock on the front door of the flat made Indiana leap out of her seat and wrench it open.

"Oliver!" she cried, and swept the small, tired boy into her arms.

Watching Indiana being reunited with her son was touching. It was tearful, but also joyful and oddly cathartic for Gemma, as a spectator.

She knew Indiana hadn't deliberately set out to destroy her — at least, not while she was in her right mind. Her circumstances and her battle with mental health had allowed Joan to maliciously control her life.

It was time, Gemma decided, to take control.

She would befriend Indiana, who had begun to take charge of her own condition. She felt a good deal closer to her than she had expected to, after all the things she had done, and it seemed the right thing to do. Joan might have pushed the two of them together, but it was up to them how they behaved and how they chose to move forward. Also, Indiana would always have a link to Ritchie because of Oliver, and Gemma wanted to be part of that link too.

Once Oliver was tucked up in bed, Gemma sensed it was time to leave.

Indiana, quite naturally, had only had eyes for Oliver from the moment he had come home. She was now free to be a wonderful mother to Oliver and Gemma had a shrewd suspicion she was going to do an excellent job.

Luckily, Oliver didn't seem affected by the day's events, but he had asked about his granny. Indiana had told him she'd gone away for a while and he appeared to be happy with that answer for the moment. It wasn't the right time to tell him the truth. Indiana murmured to Gemma, when Oliver was in the bath, that she was going to seek a counsellor's advice on the best way to approach dealing with this kind of traumatic bereavement. She didn't want to be honest and open with Oliver just yet, but she answered any questions he asked as best as she could.

Gemma popped her head around Oliver's bedroom door. He was fast asleep now, all tucked up in his Batman duvet. A tear rolled down Gemma's cheek; she wiped it away and blew a kiss, closing the door behind her.

Indiana watched Gemma closely as she crept out of her son's room and recognised she was hurting over so many things, from her husband's unfaithfulness to her mother-in-law's dreadful vendetta. Indiana felt so indebted to Gemma for accepting her apology on her appalling behaviour. She hadn't thought she would be able to forgive her – Indiana certainly wasn't prepared to forgive herself, just yet – but she had. And more, besides: Gemma had been her rock while they'd been awaiting news on Oliver. Indiana didn't know how she would have got through the night without her, even with Bridget (who had been unexpectedly kind, given that she had once been a spy for Joan).

Before Gemma stepped out of the front door the two women – friends now, through circumstance and choice – hugged each other, both sensing it would be a while before they'd see each other again, but both certain that they would.

Chapter 19

Mick decided to give it one last shot.

Gemma was the woman he wanted to share the rest of his life with. Anxiously, he patted the pocket of his shirt where two tickets to Australia were hiding. He was taking quite a gamble, but sometimes life was a gamble. His nerves grew as he neared her house – he wasn't quite sure how Gemma was going to react to his visit, nor his request. Inhaling deeply he marched up to the front door, outwardly displaying a confidence he did not feel.

Here goes, Mick said to himself. He tapped lightly on the door and waited, his heart racing and his stomach churning.

Gemma ran down the stairs two at a time, wondering who could be at her door. Both Maria and Indiana would have knocked first. It had been two days since she arrived home from Indiana's and she'd been enjoying the silence that surrounded her. She hadn't realised before just how much she liked her own company. Perhaps it was down to all the emotional strain she'd been under since Ritchie's passing.

She opened the door, standing still for a second as her brain processed Mick's unexpected appearance.

"Hello, Gemma, hope I'm not disturbing you."

"Not at all, come in Mick," she said.

As Mick walked through the door he gave Gemma a peck on the cheek, making her smile. She closed the door, slowly turning her back to it and leaning against it. "This is a surprise, Mick."

"I know, but I had to see you one last time before I leave." Mick took her hand, kissing it lovingly.

"Before you leave!" Gemma gasped.

"I'm booked on a flight to Australia, on Friday," he told her.

"Friday!" Gemma exclaimed. "But that's in three days' time."

"I know." He gave her a look of deep sincerity. "Come with me, Gemma. I love you, I think I fell for you the first time I met you." Gemma went to interrupt, but he put his finger to her lips. "You don't have to answer me now, but will you think about it? Please, just think about it. He pulled the tickets out of his shirt pocket, fanning them in the air. Your ticket is here with mine."

"Oh Mick, I can't just up and leave! My whole life is here." Gemma held his hand in hers, leading him to the dining room sofa. They both sat down, but neither one spoke for a while. It was Gemma who broke the silence. "Mick, what I've been through these last few months – no, this last year, has caused me to revaluate my life. The person I married was not the person I thought he was. I loved him – still do love him, I think I always will."

"I know that, Gemma, but I know we could have something special," said Mick desperately. "I know it. I love you and I think you love me. It's different to the way you loved Ritchie, but I can accept that."

"But what if you can't? What if I can't love you like you deserve to be loved?" Gemma asked, voicing her fears. "I do love you, but not in the same way I loved my husband."

"You can learn to love again, Gemma – perhaps you're not letting yourself right now."

Mick inched closer to her, cupping his hands around Gemma's face and pulling her towards him. He placed his lips softly onto hers, kissing her passionately, letting his tongue explore her mouth. Gemma responded by kissing him passionately back, gently biting his lower lip. When they both finally parted, gasping for air, Gemma giggled.

"What's so funny, Ms Peacock?" asked Mick.

"I don't know," she laughed. "You, me – you coming here to whisk me off to Australia – that kiss."

"What about it??

"I love you, Mick Delaney. I love you." Gemma put her arms around Mick's neck – he lifted her up and swung her around.

"You do? You do? Are you sure?" he asked giddily. "I love you so much Gemma."

"This is crazy – me jetting off to Australia with a man I hardly know." She giggled. "Well, this last year has been crazy, so what have I got to lose?"

"Nothing, sweetheart. You are not going to lose anything."

"Where do we start? What about this house? Where will we live?" Gemma had so many questions running amok in her head she felt dizzy.

"Slow down, everything will sort itself out, darling," Mick assured her. "I can't believe you are coming with me. You won't change your mind, will you?"

"Nothing will change my mind, nothing in the whole wide world."

*****

Indiana found it strange to be back in Jonathan King's consulting room. It was such a different experience this time. He had willingly offered to help Indiana with Oliver without any hesitation, though her phone call had come out of the blue.

She could tell, though she was nervous for her son, that he hadn't expected to see her again – and that he liked this new, friendlier, warmer version of her. The real her.

He handed over the information leaflets to her, pointing out that the 'Grief Encounters' book would be a good place to start, as a workbook designed to encourage conversations with children about death and help them explore their feelings through activities. Indiana asked Jonathan openly about the best way to help Oliver deal with the sad news of his granny's death. She desperately wanted to do the right thing and support him as best she could.

"That looks good, an activity book we can work on together."
Indiana gave Jonathan a grateful smile.

"I know many parents that have used this book successfully," he
said.

"Oliver didn't cry when I told him, is that normal?" asked
Indiana.

"Very normal, try not to worry I'm sure Oliver will be fine. You
know you are a good mother Indiana, remember that."

"I try to be, but you know what my childhood was like, and I
want to make sure Oliver has a happy one."

Jonathan smiled. "Well, you're doing a good job." He paused.
"You look well, Indiana. Have you had any episodes recently?"

"Not one," she said happily. "My life is complete, now. I only
need Oliver to keep me happy."

"You are a changed person since I saw you last," he remarked.

"I was in a bad place back then – doing bad things."

"Were you and me a bad thing?" he couldn't help but ask.

"No – we weren't a bad thing." Indiana raised her eyebrows and
laughed.

"It's good to see you smile Indiana."

"I feel good, the best I ever have. Joan left all of her estate to
Oliver, you know. He will be loved and taken care of and have a
good life. I really couldn't be happier."

"Couldn't I make you even happier?"

"How do you mean?" she asked, though she knew very well what he meant.

"Have dinner with me tonight."

She grinned, pleased. "Counsellors seeing their patients isn't allowed is it?" Indiana pretended to be coy; she loved the fact that Jonathan was thinking of her in a new light.

"Technically, no, but although you are on the books as a patient I haven't actually seen you for months," he said. Indiana raised an eyebrow. He hadn't seemed all that bothered when she *had* been on the books. What's your answer going to be?"

"I would very much like to have dinner with you tonight, Jonathan," she said, making up her mind.

He shot her a hungry look, which made her laugh again. Indiana stood up, put her coat over her arm and walked over to Jonathan. She kissed him on the lips. "Shall we say, eight o'clock?"

"Eight will be good, I'll pick you up," he offered.

"You know where I live?" she asked.

"I certainly do. It's in your patient file."

Jonathan gave her another wink which made Indiana's stomach flutter. For the first time in her life she wasn't playing games, this was for real. "See you then. Oh – and thank you for today, it's helped me so much."

"Today isn't over yet." He picked up the leaflets and placed them into Indiana's hands, holding onto her hands longer than he should.

"See you later." Indiana took the leaflets, beaming to herself. Her future was turning out happier than ever she could have expected. Perhaps Jonathan King was going to be her knight in shining armour.

*****

Indiana sensed there was something different about Gemma. She'd called her unexpectedly, asking if she could visit. She had a glow about her, enhancing her beauty, but she sat there nervously picking at her fingernails. Something was definitely up.

"Is everything okay, Gemma?" Indiana asked.

"Yes, why do you ask?"

"You look nervous – as if you're on edge." For a moment she was afraid that Gemma was here to tell her that they couldn't be friends after all, but she quickly dismissed the idea as the other woman spoke.

"I'm leaving for Australia tomorrow, with Mick," Gemma blurted, almost mumbling.

"What?" Indiana gasped, delighted. "Oh, Gemma how exciting! How did that come about?! Indiana gave Gemma a big hug. "I'm so happy for you."

"It happened so quickly – I'm in a whirlwind," said Gemma excitedly. "He came to see me and asked me there and then. I wasn't sure at first, but I'm sure now. I love him."

"So something good has come out of this, after all," Indiana said. "If it wasn't for me you wouldn't have met him." Indiana nudged Gemma in the ribs.

"Well, I suppose so, but let's not go there." Gemma smiled to show there was no harm done.

"You do know how sorry I am, don't you, Gemma?" Indiana asked. "I never wanted to hurt you."

"We've been through this a dozen times, yes I know." She changed the subject. "How's Oliver doing? Where is he? I'd liked to see him before I leave."

"He's doing fine. He's round Zach's at the moment, but he's due home soon." It was Indiana's turn to grin. "Jonathan has supported me so much; I don't know what I would have done without him."

"Jonathan? Not Jonathan King – your counsellor?" Gemma asked, surprised.

"Ex-counsellor," said Indiana shyly.

Gemma laughed. "You're blushing! Come on, spill the beans." Gemma sat up straight like she was in a doctor's waiting room.

"We had dinner and now we are officially dating," said Indiana, amused. "There you go."

"Really? That's fantastic news," Gemma said happily. "I guess we both have moved on."

"I'm going to miss you, Gemma."

"I'm going to miss you, too."

Oliver called through the letterbox, "Mummy open the door!"

Indiana got up and ran to open it, letting her son bound into the room, his blond quiff slightly flattened and his knees dirty.

"Hello Gemma," he said cheerfully. "I've been playing football with Zach. I'm not very good, so I stay in goal." He ran and gave Gemma a hug, much to her obvious delight.

"Hi, Oliver! I bet you are good, you just don't realise it yet." She ruffled the top of his hair, brushing her fingers through his fringe.

Gemma knew he would always remind her of Ritchie and she was determined not to lose contact with him.

"I've got something to tell you Oliver," she said. "I'm going on a big plane way up in the sky, all the way to a place called Australia."

"Where kangaroos live?" Oliver asked, wide-eyed.

"Yes, where kangaroos live." Gemma laughed. "I will be leaving tomorrow. I will send you postcards and you can get Mummy to help you write letters to me. Would you like that?"

"Yes, but I can nearly write all by myself," he told her proudly. Oliver gave Gemma another hug this time it was like he didn't want to let go.

It did Indiana's heart good to see it.

"Wow! You're such a clever boy," Gemma declared. "I'm going to miss you, little man."

"Can we come and visit? I want to go on a plane way up in the sky." Oliver ran around the room impersonating a plane, his arms outstretched and making a 'zoom' noise.

"Of course you can – I'd love that," Gemma said. "Come here and give me a hug, I need to say goodbye. I've got lots to do before I leave tomorrow."

Oliver ran and jumped onto Gemma's lap; she hugged and kissed him. Indiana wondered if she would ever see him again.

"Be good for your mum, Oliver."

He jumped off her lap and ran to his room. Both women watched him go, fondly.

"Well, Indiana, I guess this is goodbye." Gemma pulled out a watch from her bag and placed it carefully in Indiana's hands. "This was Ritchie's. I'd like Oliver to have it when you think he's old enough to understand what happened to his father."

"Oh, Gemma," Indiana cried, her heart swelling with emotion. "That's lovely, thank you. We will come and visit one day, I promise."

"You'd better," Gemma warned. "Take care, Indiana."

"You too."

As Gemma was about to leave Indiana grabbed her arm. "Ritchie really loved you, you know."

"I know." Gemma kissed Indiana on the cheek. There wasn't anything else to say. Both had watery eyes and both tried hard to hide it.

*****

Gemma carried the bunch of vibrant sunflowers with a heavy heart. There was one thing left she wanted to do before she left for her new life with Mick. The glaring sun illuminated the black marble headstone where her husband was buried, picking his name out in sparkling gold. She rubbed her fingers along the etching.

There was only her in the graveyard; she liked it that way. It meant she would be able to say her final goodbye to the man she loved without anyone else intruding. Leaving him behind for good had played deeply with her emotions. There would always be a place for Ritchie in her heart – always. His betrayal wouldn't be forgotten, but Gemma had decided not to let it continually mar what they'd shared together. She knew Ritchie must have suffered, carrying around his secret. He would have felt totally miserable letting her down.

She'd gone over and over her memories in her mind and she couldn't remember one instance when he'd acted differently towards her. Maybe back then she had been the one who had been complacent in their marriage.

Forgiving Ritchie was going to allow her to heal more quickly. Since she had made her decision she was spending less and less time feeling hurt and angry. Sometimes she dwelled on the fact she'd thought Ritchie was perfect, but she realised now no one was. She certainly wasn't.

She placed all the sunflowers except one into the vase – kissing each one individually.

"Goodbye, Ritchie. I love you," she said softly.

Gemma carried the last remaining sunflower to another headstone close by. The soil here was freshly turned and covered with flowers from the recent, well-attended funeral. The headstone was almost identical to Ritchie's, which she supposed was no accident. She laid the last sunflower amongst a bed of red roses.

"Goodbye Joan."

*****

Checking in at the airport, Gemma felt both elated and optimistic. The frantic arrangements that had preoccupied her for the last few days now seemed a blur. She looked at the man beside her, a little awed at how lucky she was. His signature ponytail and muscular frame had him standing out from the crowd, as usual. It felt surreal waiting in the airport departure lounge for their flight to Australia. She had to pinch herself to believe it.

"Any regrets, Gemma?" asked Mick

She smiled ecstatically. "None whatsoever. You?"

"Of course not," he responded. "This is what I wanted since the day I first saw you. You are one special lady, Gemma. I love you." Mick kissed Gemma tenderly.

"You are special, too, Mick. You really are. Thank you."

"Thank you for what," he asked, confused.

"For letting me start my life over again."

I know you hear this a lot, but reviews are so massively important to authors. If you enjoyed Befriended and could spare a few minutes to write a short review to say so, I would so appreciate that. For Amazon purchases, please add your review on Amazon. For other online purchases, please add your review to their site. Alternatively, I am happy to receive reviews directly through my email address: ruthoneill63@yahoo.co.uk

Best Wishes
Ruth x